PRAISE FOR
THE NOVELS OF STEVE PERRY . . .

The Forever Drug

"A hard science fiction story with an attractive and believable hero . . . a substantially satisfying read."   —*Ft. Lauderdale Sun-Sentinel*

"A hard-boiled thriller with an sf setting . . . good entertainment."   —*Booklist*

Spindoc

"Fast-paced . . . His future world seems very real. *Spindoc* is a fun read."   —*Analog*

"A lively tale of intrigue, murder, and sabotage."   —*Booklist*

The *Matador* series

"Perry excels at hard-boiled writing, flashing dialogue, and stripped-down action."   —*The Oregonian*

"Effective and logical . . . recommended highly for all who enjoy intelligent, thoughtful outer-space adventure!"   —*Science Fiction Review*

"Noteworthy!"   —*Fantasy and Science Fiction*

"Perry writes thrilling, action-packed, compelling science fiction. His *Matador* series has become a classic . . . Pick up one of Perry's novels. You won't be disappointed."   —*VOYA*

Ace Books by Steve Perry

THE MAN WHO NEVER MISSED
MATADORA
THE MACHIAVELLI INTERFACE
THE OMEGA CAGE*
THE 97TH STEP
THE ALBINO KNIFE
BLACK STEEL
BROTHER DEATH
SPINDOC
THE FOREVER DRUG
THE TRINITY VECTOR

And from Berkley Books

HELLSTAR*
DOME*

(*written with Michael Reaves)

THE TRINITY VECTOR

STEVE PERRY

ACE BOOKS, NEW YORK

This book is an Ace original edition,
and has never been previously published.

THE TRINITY VECTOR

An Ace Book / published by arrangement with
the author

PRINTING HISTORY
Ace edition / July 1996

The Putnam Berkley World Wide Web site address is
http://www.berkley.com

ISBN: 0-441-00350-8

ACE®
Ace Books are published by The Berkley Publishing Group,
200 Madison Avenue, New York, New York 10016.
ACE and the "A" design are trademarks
belonging to Charter Communications, Inc.

PRINTED IN THE UNITED STATES OF AMERICA

10 9 8 7 6 5 4 3 2 1

For Dianne

Acknowledgments

Thanks go to the usual cast and crew, and they know who they are. Add to them John DeCamp and Vince Kohler for their useful input. I'd also like to take this space to pay a small tribute to Cary Grant and Harrison Ford, who both deserve more respect: Grant for what he did, Ford for what he still does, both of them better at it than anybody else in the biz. Because it is funny or active does not mean that it is easy. Some of us can see that. Thanks for the inspiration, guys.

—SP

THE
TRINITY
VECTOR

Part One

Before Time began there was only the God and the Goddess, and between them the Void. Attracted again as they had been before, the God and the Goddess went to each other and in the going, compressed between them the Void until it became no more than a ball of white fire.

And when the God and Goddess embraced, so powerful was their joining that it compressed the Void into an infinitesimal point.

And when the God and Goddess reached the peak of their pleasure together and were One, the Void burst and passed through them and became the Universe.

—*First Book of the Void*, C1, v. 1–3

Languid from their lovemaking, the God and Goddess sought to amuse themselves. They created Time and the stars and great clouds and filled the heavens with strings and bubbles, and when it had cooled sufficiently, added to that planets and moons.

And they brought forth that which could bring forth more of itself and named it Life.

And the God and Goddess were greatly amused indeed.

—*The Book of Life*, C1, v. 1–3

The Way of the Samurai is found in Death.

—Yamamoto Tsunetomo, *Hagakure*

1

THERE WERE TWO of them, and if it had been summer they probably would have gotten him. But early January in Oregon gave Long advantages—first was the fog and second was his old leather jacket.

The night in the Portland alley was cold, just below freezing, and the mist was dense enough to shroud the building lamps and dim the fuzzy-edged cones of damp light they cast. The cold, gray murk kept them from getting a good look at him. The heavy air also revealed the needle-thick red beam of the first one's laser sight as it flicked on and showed its source.

Long used to wonder why the fog didn't turn to ice and just fall from the air when the temp dropped below thirty, but somewhere he'd heard about crystallization and moving currents, and that had finally explained it. Kind of like running water.

Because he wore his leather jacket, he was able to get to his weapon faster. In the summer, when you were wearing shorts or jeans and a T-shirt in the heat, there wasn't any place to hide a good-sized handgun. When it was body temp outside, a jacket was a giveaway and real uncomfortable besides. So he wore a belly pouch. When the weather got cold enough, he switched the gun from his pouch into a paddle holster that rode over his right hip. The paddle slipped inside his jeans and a little notch snagged under his waistline. Pull the gun up hard and it came out, but the holster stayed in place. Put a little twist on it, push forward, and the holster and piece came out together. It saved having to thread your belt through it all the time, and if you wanted to take the jacket off in public, you could sneak the holster off with it and nobody would know you were hardwared—

The second shooter's laser sight lit.

Long stopped thinking.

The closer one was four meters away, the farther one a meter past that. Long dropped into a crouch and snatched his revolver. He whipped it out, caught his right hand in his left, lined the three glowing green tritium dots on his sights up on the bright red spot. Pulled the trigger, once, twice—

Swung the gun to his right a hair. The muzzle flashes left a purple afterimage and the other shooter was a blur, but he point-indexed him by feel and—

Shot him twice, too.

Time: Half a second after he made them, a second and a half since he went for his gun. Four shots, two seconds in all, though it felt like hours. . . .

He came up from the crouch, his ears ringing. He didn't really remember hearing the shots, but he knew it must have sounded as if four bombs had gone off in the confines of the alley. And even with the low-flash powder in the shells, the short-barreled S&W .357 had belched and spat like a dragon, shattered the darkness with yellow-orange tongues of fire. The clammy, cold air was now tainted with the chemical stink of burned gunpowder.

He kept the gun pointed in front of him and quick-stepped to where the first shooter lay. The guy wasn't moving; his gun lay on the dirty concrete, half a meter from his hand. He was pale, blond, maybe twenty-three. He had a tattoo of something on his forehead but Long couldn't make it out in the dark.

He scooted over to check the second shooter. This one was making small bubbling noises in his throat, but he was also out of it. Long kicked away the pistol the shooter still clutched, watched it bounce against a wall. This one must have gotten at least one shot off—smoke curled up from the pistol's muzzle—but Long didn't know where the bullet had gone, hadn't been aware the man had fired. The guy had two holes in his chest, a few centimeters apart, blood welling from them even through the Kevlar vest he wore. He was light-skinned but had Negroid features, and the whites of his eyes showed. About as old as the other one.

''Should have bought the good spidersilk softweave, boys.'' Long patted his jacket; the leather was lined with the more expensive armor, though he hadn't needed it. ''Sorry.''

Long stood and looked both ways down the alley. Somebody had surely heard the cannon roars his .357 made, but nobody was brave enough to stick his nose out and risk looking yet. Aside from the two dying shooters, he was alone.

Time to leave.

He holstered the S&W and took off for the street. The cops would find the bodies soon enough. The thieves had been well equipped. Both had carried Glocks with integral laser sights, suppressors, and compensators; the guns were caseless nines or forties. Both wore spookeyes, probably 4- or 5gen military surplus, both wore Kevlar vests that would have stopped most legal civilian handgun rounds. Fairly high tech for a couple of freelance thieves. Maybe they were yak; more likely, Mama's Boys, this was their turf. *Mors tua, vita mea*: You die so I can live.

Sorry.

He shook his head. It was the high-tech stuff that fucked them up. That and luck. If they'd been mouth-breathing arm breakers with bats or irons and they'd waited until he passed and busted his skull, they'd have done better. But the fog had given him their lasers; his muzzle flashes had probably kicked in their spookeyes' blast shields, effectively blinding them; and the Smith's pencil-point armor-piercing steel-and-Teflon-clad bullets had punched through the Kevlar weave like it was wet paper. That was where the luck came in. Pistol AP wasn't very good as a man stopper, it didn't expand. The .357 had some velocity, so there was a shock-wave effect, but mush-nose lead hollow-point was better. Even so, they were down and he was up. High tech was fine—when it worked and when you knew what you were doing—but low tech had some advantages. A knife didn't run out of ammo, a rock didn't give away your position. Revolvers had been old seventy-five years before his father had bought the one Long carried, and while the Smith wasn't an antique—it was about the same age as he was at forty—it would still kill a man as dead as any freshly minted plasma gun the bright new .year, A.D. 2030, had to offer.

There were a few pedestrians out on the cold walks; a dozen electric cars, a bus, and a few gas-alkie burners rolled past as he crossed Burnside and walked toward his own car two blocks away. He strolled as casually as he could so as not to attract any undue attention. At the car, he disarmed the circuit kick-out with the little transmitter. He tapped his code into the keypad and unlocked the door, slid in behind the wheel. The car was a twelve-year-old Saab-Volvo—a Salvo—station wagon, rusty, dirty, and beat up enough so it wouldn't interest a serious car thief. The plastic seat covers were torn, the radio was visibly bead-welded to an extruded frame tie, and not worth the trouble to pry loose; there wasn't a grid computer or a holoproj on board. He tapped in his ignition code, switched on the control-panel lights, saw he had half a charge left in the main battery.

Plenty enough to pass by his place and still get to the Hillsboro Airport in time for his 4 A.M. flight to Seattle. He could plug it into the charger at the port and it would be full by the time he got back tomorrow.

He lit the running lamps, pulled out of the parking slot, and circled through Old Town toward the 405 freeway on-ramp. It was past midnight, traffic was light, he should be able to make it home in half an hour.

It wasn't until he'd pulled onto the freeway and headed west on the Sunset Highway that the reaction finally overcame his defenses and he started to shake. His breathing grew ragged, shuddered into something that neared sobs, and despite the car's heater, he went cold. It had been a while since he'd had to shoot anywhere but the practice range.

Somebody had tried to kill him and he had killed them instead.

It wasn't the first time. Might not be the last, either.

If he'd been a little slower, if it hadn't been foggy, if he'd been wearing the belly pouch, it could be him dead in an alley instead of the two thieves who'd thought to steal his package. At the thought, he reached down and patted the small keeper on his belt, almost an automatic action. It was there, next to his personal comp, locked securely onto his thick belt. He didn't know what was in the sealed keeper, didn't care. Probably diamonds, given his client, but it didn't really matter. Could be computer chips or high-test designer drugs. He didn't see it go in, he wouldn't see it come out. As far as he was concerned, the keeper was a solid block. That was how he'd been taught to think about it.

Once again, he wasn't dead. He had gone up against the would-be assassins and here he was, driving away. There were no witnesses, no way the cops could connect him to it, and it had been self-defense anyway. He could have stayed and legaled it out but it wasn't good business for a courier to spend time in the public eye. He'd get off, eventually, but the shooters might have friends or associates who wouldn't be happy with Long. Dead was dead, and if nobody knew he'd done it, that was fine with him.

All reasonable ways of looking at it, but that didn't help the shakes. He wanted to go home, crawl under the bed covers, and sleep until spring.

Before he left for the run to Seattle, he would go home, but not to sleep, only to fix his gun. He'd change the barrel so nobody could get a ballistics match on the fired bullets. Dump the rest of that box of AP, plus what was in the Smith, and there went the metallurgical-lot comparison. Over the years, he'd bought and stocked up a dozen spare barrels for the revolver. You didn't need a license to get that particular part, and he'd used phony names and IDs in four states to make the buys. A different barrel, bore-sighted with a plug-in laser—not perfect but would have to do until he could shoot again—ammo from another lot, and the old Smith became a new gun, a virgin only distantly related to the killing machine it had been. He had bought twelve of the barrels. He had eight of them left. As a civilian, he had shot six men and none of them were around to tell tales. It had been them or him, and so far, it had been them. Two of the fights had been witnessed and the cops had run him through the procedures, but they'd been righteous shootings and he'd been cut loose. Unlikely they could tie him to the two in the alley. It was a common enough caliber, .357, and H. A. Long was a bonded courier, licensed in Washington, Oregon, California, and Idaho, with an application pending in Nevada. A marine veteran of the Castroito conflict in Cuba in the winter of '11, honorably discharged with a Purple Heart and the Silver Star. A hero to his grateful country two decades ago, a taxpaying, credit card–carrying citizen. The cops probably wouldn't come looking for him, and his employer on this run wouldn't have anything to gain by stepping forward. He was in the clear. Maybe someday the bad guys would be faster or smarter and that would be the end of him, but not this time. Once again, he had looked into Death's yellow eyes, smelled his carrion breath, and lived to be amazed that he had.

Well. What the hell. He'd been living on borrowed time for the last twenty years. It was all gravy anyhow.

His exit was just ahead. He put his blinker on like a good cit, left the slow lane at Murray Boulevard, and headed home.

Blackest of shadows, darkest of nights, deepest of pits, none can withstand the pure light of the Goddess.

—Sun Po, *The Book of Heaven*

2

MIRANDA MOON BOWED before the statuettes, her hands pressed together in *namaste*. There were half a dozen of the Manifestations on the mantel above the crackling fireplace: Kali, Nu Kwa, the Morrigan, Songi, Pelé, Changing Woman. Throughout the temple were many others, not so much as icons of worship as reminders that the Goddess could wrap Herself in any form she chose, that the Goddess was Essence and not merely shape.

As Moon came out of her bow, divine in saluting the divine of the Goddess, a voice from the next room shrilled loudly, "Yeah, well, *fuck* that and fuck you!"

Moon sighed. So much for bliss and harmony. Such language from the sweet mouth of a twelve-year-old.

The temple was a Victorian two-story house in northwest Portland, almost all the way out to the warehouse district, and it had seen better decades; in truth, it had seen better centuries. The wooden floorboards creaked as Moon walked down the short hall from the front room to the room across from it. There, below the red-and-blue-and-yellow tie-dyed parachute silk draped from the ceiling in artful billows by one of Moon's students, stood Dawn and Alyssa. They were two meters apart, glaring at each other. Alyssa, fifteen, had her hands on her slim hips, feet wide. Dawn stood with her arms knotted across her chest. Both wore tight jeans, dark zip-lock sport shoes and colorful cotton sweaters with three-quarter sleeves and stiff collars that stood up like something from an old Dracula movie. Dawn's sweater was blue, Alyssa's purple. Anybody with one working eye could pick them out of a crowd as sisters. They had their father's ash blond hair, his pale blue eyes, his determined chin, his dimples. Moon could never look at her girls without seeing Martin. Despite her attempts at being open-hearted and loving. Martin was her treasured wound and, given her current feelings, the rest of her life wouldn't be enough to heal him. Forgiving Martin was the biggest obstacle she had yet to overcome. She could do it in theory; after all, he had helped make her daughters. That was the theory. Practice was something else.

"What's the problem, girls?"

"Alyssa is the *problem*! She's calling me names again."

Moon looked at her older daughter. "Alyssa?"

"I didn't say anything that wasn't true."

"Mom, she called me 'titless'!"

Moon rolled her eyes and looked at her fifteen-year-old. "Well, flatso, if the bra fits. Or doesn't fit . . .'"

"Yeah, well, you're a *cunt*, too—"

"That'll be enough."

"She was listening on the extension while I was having a private conversation," Alyssa said.

"Yeah, playing sugar lips with Django the whango—"

"Shut up, you little twat!"

"Enough, I said." Moon shook her head. "Come here, both of you."

It was hard for Moon to keep a straight face then. They knew what was coming.

"Ah, jeez, Mom, don't—"

"Right here." She tried to put as much love over the steel as she could but the core was there. She wasn't asking.

Her daughters shuffled toward her. When they were in arm's reach, she put a hand on each girl's shoulder and turned them to face each other. She looked into Alyssa's eyes, then Dawn's. "This is your only sister," she said to them both. "You will never have another. I want you to hug each other."

"Jesus, Mom—" Alyssa began.

"Do it. When you grow up and move out on your own you can do what you want, but while I'm responsible, I get to do this. Hug each other."

Now the girls were of like mind, both pissed off at their mother. Fine. As long as they were in accord about something. They embraced, stiff, wooden, as if each were forced to wrap her arms around a giant snake or a freshly dug-up zombie.

"Now. You don't call your little sister names, all right?"

"Mm."

"And you don't listen in on private conversations."

"It was an accident, I heard it ring—"

"Dawn."

"Okay, okay."

"Fine. Are you going to be at evening service?"

"I've got a date," Alyssa said quickly.

"School night."

"I'll be home by ten."

"Dawn?"

"Yeah, I'll be there."

"All right, then. Go on about your business."

She watched the two girls as they left. Beautiful and bright and convinced they were adults, they made her want to smile and cry at the same time. Her babies, only they weren't babies anymore.

She went to the main room and began to set up for the evening service. The temple meeting hall was the largest of the downstairs rooms—made from two bedrooms with the dividing wall taken out—and could seat twenty people, if they didn't mind togetherness. She lit a chunk of sandalwood incense and set it into the burner. It would send fragrant smoke into the air for a few minutes and be out long before the scheduled service, but the scent would remain in the background. She filled the water pitchers with ice and lemon slices, checked the cranky thermostat to make sure the room wouldn't be an oven or a freezer, and was pretty much done. On a good night in the winter, she got eighteen or twenty at the evening service, half that many at the sunrise gathering. It was better during the late spring and early summer, when the weather was good. She'd hold the service outdoors in the high-fenced backyard, and the attendees could shuck most of their clothes in the warmth and shade and lie on beach towels or blankets. The Goddess wasn't ashamed of Her bodies and neither should Her devotees be. On a nice summer evening with the sun still up until almost ten P.M., she'd get fifty or sixty people in the yard. Even a few men, some of whom came for the free nudity, some of whom seemed really interested.

Not what you'd call a major congregation. No more than a hundred in all of Oregon, but some of them were fairly well off, and they always had enough to keep the rent paid and food on the table. "Maja will provide," her teachers had told her, and so far, She always had, though Maja surely had a great sense of humor, given some of the provisions and their timing.

Moon smiled. Well. Nobody had ever promised her that being a priestess of the Goddess would be easy, nor the paths paved with gold. In a lot of ways, it was worse than being a part-time secretary at a fat clinic, the last real job she'd had. Service had its compensations but high living wasn't one of them.

As long as you stayed in the front part of the house, you could almost pretend that the first third of the twenty-first century lay well in the future and not the past. But in the

..n, the surf of time had slopped onshore: the micro-
.ve oven and ceramic-element stove, the ultrasonic dish-
washer and teapot, the holoprojic computer console that
controlled the house systems. . . . Well, the Victorian build-
ers would have been hard pressed to understand those.
Touch a button and you could talk to and see anybody on
the planet who had access to a com unit—assuming they
wanted to answer your call. Another button would allow
you to order and have delivered to your doorstep virtually
anything for sale that you could pay for, from food to the
truck it came in. Had you enough money, you would never
have to leave home and you could not only survive, you
could be on the cutting edge of everything except live entertainment. If you didn't feel like pushing the buttons, you
could talk to the computer, tell it what to do, and it would
thank you afterward in just about any voice you decided it
ought to use.

It was addictive, the technology. There was no prohibi-
tion against such things, though the teachings warned
against becoming ensnared in the superficial aspects of life.
Too many toys could become very distracting to one who
wished to walk with the Goddess. It might bring up the
question, Why walk when you can ride . . . ?

Moon grinned as she told the computer to fix a pot of
tea. She could, she supposed, draw the water, filter it, heat
it, drop the tea lozenge into it, strain the particulate, add
the sweet and creamer, and pour it into her favorite old
china cup, the white one with the dragons on it. A Zen tea
ceremony had much to recommend it, didn't it? The im-
mediacy of *doing* it. But while the computer was directing
her tea maker to produce what was very nearly a perfect
cup of Earl Grey—given that it was a lozenge and not
leaves—she could be about something else more useful to
the Goddess. Setting up appointments with corporate spon-
sors for fund-raising. The Goddess was perfection and she
didn't think this temple would ever be rich, but money

helped spread the word, Maja notwithstanding. If she could snare a couple more CEOs, somebody with leanings toward the Goddess, it would go a long way toward net time, the biggest of any temple's expenses. You had to reach them to teach them, and there wasn't a lot of foot traffic out here next to the aluminum plate–and-bar warehouse.

The ceiling vibrated with a deep thrum, a bass note that she felt in her back teeth and chest. Dawn had her 'proj cranked up again, listening to those old voodoo rock recordings her grandfather had sent her over the wire. It was primal stuff, full circle from the African beat through rock and rap and twanga and back again. And it was too loud, but Moon tried to tune it out. Let Dawn show her rebellion by playing her music too loud for a few minutes. There were a lot worse ways she could choose to protest the indignity of being a pre-teenager. She could be derming psychedelic drugs or playing conjugal games, something her older sister had learned all too early. Moon liked the latest boy wonder well enough—Django was sixteen, only a child himself and much preferable to the forty-six-year-old cop Alyssa had run with three months ago. But were it up to her, she would have had the Goddess direct her daughter into other paths until she was a few years farther along. Even with the hormone implants to keep any babies from happening, sex had its entanglements. Alyssa didn't believe it, she was above it all, so she said, but sharing that close a karma with somebody left psychic stains that didn't wash out easily. Alyssa was going to learn the hard way that lying in bed with a man in intimate contact had a cost. Unfortunately, the Goddess didn't seem to care much for a mother's opinion on this particular matter, priestess or not. Well. When you are in the swollen river, you either go along with the current or get real tired trying to fight it and wind up losing anyway. Such was the way, and once you accepted that, it saved you a lot of sore muscles and exhaustion. Some days were easier than others, however, and the monkey brain with its theories and the spirit with its reality meshed only now and then. Great when it happened, a struggle to be worked at when it didn't.

Such, the Goddess would say, was the Way. . . .

The greatest danger with mercenaries lies in their cowardice and reluctance to fight, but with auxiliaries the danger lies in their courage.

—Niccolò Machiavelli, *The Prince*

3

GOD SAVE ME from stupid men, Ford Wentworth thought.

He stood on the corner of Constitution and Tenth, outside the old Justice Department building and across from the Natural History Museum. He was with Representative Marc Bennett, a fairly young and fairly stupid fifth-term Republican congressman from Colorado. Slushy snow lay on the ground, piled into dirty waves on the edges of the walks and streets, with more fat, wet flakes beginning to drift down. The two men waited to cross Tenth with a clot of other cold-congealed pedestrians idly watching the workers doing the umpteenth face-lift—perhaps "butt-lift" might be more appropriate from this angle—on the museum. One of the new Dtrans electrics splashed through the slop toward the intersection, and Wentworth briefly considered shoving Bennett off the curb in front of the bus. He could have gotten away with it without being noticed, and if he could be sure Bennett would be killed immediately . . .

He smiled. Well, no, that wasn't his style, was it? As

director of the National Security Agency's PSS—President's Special Section—he didn't need to get his hands quite that directly dirty. He had a few boys and girls on the payroll who could delete Bennett without raising their heart rates and who wouldn't ask why, only when and how he wanted it to look. But it wouldn't happen that way. Politics was a much better weapon than the SIG .40s his agents carried, or even the custom-made Coonan Cadet riding his own shoulder holster. He hadn't spent twelve years running the section without learning where mounds of bodies were buried. The trick to threatening a man was to do it in such a way that he could rationalize that giving in to the threat was the right thing. A ham-handed fool would slap Bennett on the shoulder and say, ''Well, Marc, old son, you either vote my way or that recording of you pronging those two hookers all night long in that vibrating-gel-bed motel in Weed will find its way to General T. P. 'Bull' Wilson's desk at the Special Forces enclave in Nevada. Probably at about the same time your wife gets her copy. Then you can explain to Bull what his pencil-necked geek of a son-in-law was doing porking two whores while his favorite little girl Mary Lea was home sick with the flu. She's the apple of her daddy's eye, so they say, and after he beats the shit out of you, he'll probably call every right-wing money man in the country and you can kiss your reelection good-bye. Bull never liked you anyway, remember?''

No, that blunt approach would work, but where was the skill? Wentworth was never one to use a maul when a scalpel would do. Bennett liked to dip his wick in honey pots other than his wife's; that made him a bad husband, but not in itself a bad politician. Wentworth had the stick and Bennett, while hardheaded and stubborn about some things, knew it. There was no need to use it. What they were doing here was allowing the man to save face by pretending something else was going on.

The light changed, the signs blinked the walk sign, and the computer chipvox speaker droned the word over and over, first in English, then in Spanish, French, and Japanese for any blind folk who might have left their dogs at home. As the small knot of people slogged through the icy mush across the street and past the bombed-out Internal Revenue Service complex, Wentworth offered the honorable choice. He said, "You know, Marc, according to my ear in the Pentagon, that big base closure deal is about ready to go public. They say Eisenhower is on the block."

Bennett nodded and looked grim. "Yeah. I heard."

"I'm not without influence in those circles."

Bennett looked at him. Raised one eyebrow in question. Christ, the guy had been on the Hill almost ten years, you think he would have learned something.

"If I didn't have to dick around so much on this emergency appropriations thing, I could maybe spend more time on the links with Admiral Stowe."

"Ah."

Well, he knew that much, at least. Business got done on the D.C. golf courses, same as everywhere else. Stowe, head of the Joint Chiefs, was a gambler and a so-so golfer, usually shot in the low eighties. They played two or three times a month. Wentworth could manage par on just about any course in town, but he didn't think Stowe knew that. About half of their games, he'd let the old salt stay within a few strokes until the last five or six holes, then allow him to catch up and move past by a stroke or two. Losing was easy; making it look like he was trying to win while doing it was a little harder, but not much. So Stowe would win a hundred noodle—New Dollars—nothing money for either of them, but he loved a victory. Beating a forty-four-year-old ex–FBI jock pleased the old man to no end—he practically crowed when it happened. Maybe it brought back his glory days, when he'd steamed across the Gulf of Mexico into Havana on his missile cruiser at the head of the fleet that helped squash the shit-for-brains Castroitos. Wentworth thought Stowe had been born a couple hundred years too late and on the wrong side of the Atlantic. He'd have

been right at home during the apex of the British raj, sitting
on a Calcutta veranda in whites while a bevy of wogs
brought him rum drinks and fanned him with palm leaves.
Hunting tiger on the weekends with the local maharaja, an
officer and a gentleman who knew the ways of the empire
and thus the world. Rule Brittania . . .

Maybe not. What mattered was, Wentworth could get the
old bastard to swap bases, to close one in Florida or Texas
or somewhere and leave the one in Bennett's district be, at
least for a couple of years. He was a lousy golfer but he
knew D.C. politics, and he'd know Wentworth would give
him something for it. NSA had ears where even the Joint
Chiefs were deaf, and Stowe always liked knowing more
than those who would be chairman in his place. He'd go
for it, especially since it didn't cost him anything important.
A base here instead of there? Who gave a rat's ass?

All Bennett had to do was wait for the closure announce-
ment to come out, let his constituents stew and worry for
a few days, then give a press conference in which he girded
his loins and went forth to slay the dragons. When the military changed its mind publicly, Bennett would look like
Saint George and his sixth term would be a shoo-in.

"Closing Eisenhower would hurt a lot of my constituents," Bennett said.

"I know that, Marc. I'd hate to see it happen. If I could
count on you to make sure the committee doesn't logjam
me on this piddly little money thing, I could speak to Stowe
about maybe killing that base down in Texas, you know,
the one in Flores's district? instead of Eisenhower."

The grin lit Bennett's face awfully quick. Caesar Flores,
a liberal Democrat from just outside San Antonio, was a
perpetual thorn in Bennett's side. If Bennett got up on the
House floor to say it got dark at night, Flores would leap
up and deny it on general principles.

Wentworth continued: "And it's not as if we are talking
about any real money here, just an emergency thirty million. Peanuts."

"Yes, I can see that," Bennett said. "Tell you what, Ford, why don't you just set your mind at ease about this little matter. I'll take care of it."

Wentworth slapped Bennett on the shoulder, dislodging some of the wet snow on his leather overcoat. "I knew I could count on you, Marc."

"What are friends for?"

"Soon as it stops snowing, I'll invite the admiral out for a quick nine holes. Of course, he'll probably have to announce that Eisenhower is gone anyway, might be a few days or a week before they can shuffle things around." He kept his face serious, a grin might give away too much contempt.

Bennett nodded. Even a stupid man could feel which way *that* wind blew. Time enough to put on his shiniest armor, pick up the dull show sword and pose for the holographers. *They mean to close our base? Never! I will ride forth and stop the the evil scum*!

"Yeah. Well. That would give me some time to, you know, talk to a few people, put the proper spin on things."

"Of course."

He left Bennett at the next corner and turned, headed back toward his office. NSA had space in the government building next to the old Bureau of Engraving on Fourteenth near Maine. It was not the shiniest jewel in the federal crown; he could have pulled in favors and gotten a high-rent, high-rez space, but there was no point to that. The place was sufficient for his needs. With an extra thirty million to lube the motor here and there, his department would run smoother for the next year and there was no point in rubbing anybody's nose in it by perking himself a chauffeured Mercedes or putting in eighty-noodle-a-meter carpet. The frills weren't important. It was the job that counted. He was the President's personal watchdog, he had a great deal of power and clout and he knew where the bodies were buried. Including some put there by the Presidents themselves, all three of the ones he'd served

under. His loyalty was to the office, not the man, and whoever sat on the chair got the best he could give, all things
considered. He wasn't ready to do a Secret Service and
jump in front of an incoming bullet for the man in the
Oval Office, certainly not the current Democrat, though he
might have for Ben Morris when he sat on the hot seat.
Morris had been a family friend, he and Wentworth's father had been roommates at Harvard. Hell, Morris had
probably spent as much time at their Boston home as his
own father had when Wentworth had been a boy. Morris
had been a Connecticut Republican, old money, a hard-
nosed businessman and a straight shooter. Wentworth had
wept at the funeral.

The give-away-the-store liberal in charge now was not
cut from the same cloth. He was smart, but it was as much
cunning as real intelligence, and he would have abolished
Wentworth's department in a New York second if he could
have, probably the second thing on his list after taking the
oath. Thing was, Richard "R. J." Allen had a rather messy
private life. Drugs, women, shady deals, kickbacks while
governor of New Jersey, more women sneaking in and out
of the White House while his wife slept the sleep of the
dead in a *ménage à trois* with Mr. Nembutal and Mr. Elavil.
According to one report that circulated to amuse the Secret
Service, President Allen had once made it with a twenty-
five-year-old cheerleader for the Virginia Planters pro basketball team on the same bed where Mrs. Allen slept,
blissfully unaware she had company.

Wentworth had a file half a meter thick on Allen, including pornographic holos, notarized eyewitness accounts,
hotel receipts, bank records, IOUs to mobsters, and assorted
medical stats. Enough to dig a pitfall halfway to the Earth's
molten core into which the President of the United States
would fall, screaming his innocence all the way.

Which was not to say he was all that bad a President,
especially for a Democrat. They understood each other. If

Allen left him alone, Wentworth would keep his mouth shut and the files locked safely away. Simple politics. Allen hadn't liked it, but a relatively recent picture of him with his wife's secretary, both of them naked in a Maryland motel owned by Samuel "Big Dog" Giordana, was enough to convince the President-elect he didn't really want to abolish the PSS when he took office. In fact, Wentworth went on to explain, having him on the President's team could be very useful.

Allen had tried a bluff. What, he'd said, if I called Big Dog and let it be known you were bothering me?

Wentworth had smiled. Well, I *could* have the IRS shove its nose so far up Giordana's ass he'd see it when he brushed his teeth. Or the FBI *could* take a sudden interest in him and RICO him to distraction. Or if he sends his goons to shoot at me, I could have some of my people delete them, Giordana, and half the state of New Jersey. I have people who can shoot the eyetooth out of your smile from fifty meters, that on a bad day using a pistol with a bent barrel. People who make the mob's hitmen look like children playing cops and robbers. You know there is one freelance guy we use, an ex-Marine sniper in Cuba, who can drop a man at almost two kilometers? That far away, guy he shoots is dead and the lawyers are reading his will to the family before the sound of the bullet even gets there.

Allen wasn't a coward but he was smart enough to have been elected President. He could see the writing on the wall. He nodded. They had a deal.

Wentworth smiled at the memory. One did what one had to do to get the job done. It wasn't a question of morality or ethics or law, it was a matter of pragmatics. He did good work, every President he'd served under would agree with that, even if a couple of them didn't like how he'd made them let him keep his job. The end did justify the means, if the end was good enough and the means not too bad.

That was how he figured it, and so far, he hadn't seen anything to convince him otherwise.

Take care of business, that was the thing. He planned to keep on doing it as long as he could.

> Ye cannot drink the cup of the Lord, and the cup of
> devils: ye cannot be partakers of the Lord's table, and
> of the table of devils.
>
> —Paul the Apostle, *First Corinthians*, 10:5–6

4

THERE WERE TIMES when the Reverend Walter Martin
Luther Abraham Green wished he could call on the Lord
for a few bolts of carefully aimed lightning. He could use
a little help from the Old Testament Jehovah, He who thun-
dered and smote and rained brimstone and fire upon the
wicked. Of course, that thought was in and of itself wicked
and did him no good to be thinking it; still, sometimes the
New Testament turn-the-other-cheek business got down-
right tiring. He was no Gandhi, he knew that. Merely a
backwoods black Baptist preacher who'd risen far beyond
his or anybody else's expectations, to heights he'd not
known even existed when he'd first entered the service of
the Lord.

Green straightened his long legs under the table,
stretched his back. He was a big man: six four, weighing
220 pounds. Oops. There he went again, using the old mea-
surements. What was that in centimeters and kilograms—
190 and 100? Yeah, that was right. Whatever it was, he
was getting a numb butt and stiff back out of this session,

and right now that seemed to be about it. He'd come far in his fifty-nine years. From a child in Tallahassee, Florida, to an assistant preacher at the First Baptist Congregational Church, in Tuscaloosa, Alabama, to the chairmanship of the United World Council of Churches, in Los Angeles. It was a long road indeed, and there were times when he wished he knew why he'd been chosen to make the trip.

Like now.

Lord, I know I cannot fathom Your mind, but a sign now and then would be appreciated, Amen.

Green sat at the big round conference table in the UWCC building in Santa Monica, looking at the other nine elected council members. Three Christians, counting the Catholic, two Moslems, a Hindu, a Shintoist, a Buddhist, and a New Ager. Hardly all of the world's religions and not, in Green's opinion, the best representatives of those faiths that were here, but it was what he had to work with. Fostering the idea of united anything with this bunch was akin to passing the camel through the eye of a needle. Sideways.

"With all due respect to my colleague from India, I must say that the idea is absurd." That from the Jehovah's Witness. "He knows when monsoon season is, I hope."

And the Hindu was quick to respond in his singsong lilt of a voice: "Certainly I know this. I also know that to be baked into dust upon your Arizona desert in the summer is much less appealing."

"We have air conditioning in our country!"

"And we have buildings with roofs to keep out the rain, idiot!"

"Gentlemen," the Catholic began, "surely we can get past this without *ad hominem* attacks—"

"Don't fling your Latin at us again, Father," said the New Ager. "This is the twenty-first century, not the sixteenth—"

Green repressed a sigh. For just a moment, he allowed the wrangling to continue while he drifted off into a pleasant fantasy of his own. Loretta Mae and Sunday dinner, with Bradley and his wife and the grandchildren, a nice fire in the fireplace. It had been too long—

"Don't patronize *me*, Sunni. My father was an ayatollah, as was his father, as was his father, as was *his*—there is nothing *you* can teach me about the will of Allah, blessings on his holy name—"

"Gentlemen, please," Green said. As usual, he kept his voice low, so low it was almost inaudible. The others at the table had to lean forward and be silent to hear him, exactly as he wished. "If we can't agree on something as simple as a location for the meeting, how are we going to present a message that all of our flocks can live with?"

"You have a suggestion, Reverend Green?" That from the Methodist.

"I have. We've talked it into a coma. It's time to stop arguing and decide. Each of you log your first, second, and third choice into the table's computer. We'll use the New Zealand tally: whichever spot totals the most points is the site. Does this seem fair?"

He saw the calculating looks around the table. There were three serious sites in the running for the First International Conference of the UWCC, an event that might draw as many as fifty thousand of the top religious leaders on the planet. The sites were in India, the United States, and Egypt. There had also been some mention of a European locale but nobody really took that one seriously. With nine men voting, the total number of points to be divided was 108. Firsts were worth six; seconds worth four; thirds worth two. That made things tricky. If, say, one site got all nine firsts and another got all the seconds and thirds, it would be a tie. You could probably assume that each of the voters would pick his own favorite first. With the nine members more or less equally divided on their choices, the firsts would pretty much cancel each other out. It was possible to win under these rules with only one first-place vote, and generally the second-place votes would decide the issue. That made it harder to rig the elections, and if it didn't make everybody ecstatically happy, it tended to keep peace—better you should get your second choice than your last. If for some reason the choice still ended in a tie, Green could cast the deciding vote as chairman, and he would sell it dearly if it came to that. The Lord works in mysterious ways.

"Any objections?"

"Ah, Reverend, I wonder if we might take a short break before we vote? I, ah, need to use the facilities," the Catholic said.

"Certainly," Green said. He kept his smile in place. Not only a Catholic, but trained as a Jesuit before he'd gone mainstream, the man had a mind sharp as a boxcar full of razors. Green would bet all the sugar in Cuba Father Sims would be lobbying for second-place votes all the way to and from the urinals.

Ah, well. That didn't matter. What mattered was that it got decided, not who won. Green didn't think that God's ears and eyes were any worse in India or Egypt than they'd be in Phoenix. Of course, the American flocks would have to spring for more expensive tickets to travel abroad, but faith needed to be tested fairly regularly to make sure it was intact, now didn't it? The idea was to get the deed done. This was important—nearly all of the world's organized religions were losing members. It wasn't so much that people had forsaken God, in whichever aspect they chose to worship Him, but that they were deserting the churches and temples and mosques and zendos. That was bad for everybody's business and surely the Lord must be frowning upon all His empty houses. . . .

When the other men had filed out of the room, Green pulled his com from his belt and told it to call home.

Loretta Mae answered. "Hi, honey." The tang of Alabama was thick and syrupy in her voice. It made him instantly homesick.

"Hello, sweetie. How's everything?"

"We all just fine here. You going to be home for Sunday?"

"I hope so. We're still at the stage of deciding what shape the tables are going to be for the delegates. Amazing how stubborn people can be."

"Especially when they're wrong?"

"I didn't say that."

"We been married going on thirty-seven years, Walter. You reckon I don't know what you thinkin' by now?" When she wanted it so, Loretta's diction was as crisp as a fresh New Dollar bill—she *had* been a speech teacher—but when they were alone, sometimes they both let a little more corn pone out than usual. They had cold mouths out here in California, no soul in their voices.

He grinned into the com, pleased to be talking to her. She was a good woman. When Kyle was killed with Green's mother in '98, it was Loretta kept them going; his faith had been insufficient to the task. Later, when he was older and stronger, he could have borne it alone, but not then; then she had been the rock.

"Listen, I plan on being home Saturday night. Y'all take care, and I'll call you when I get back to the hotel later this evening."

"Okay, 'bye, I love you."

"I love you, too, Lorrie May."

He folded the phone away and felt better. He stood, stretched again, bent, and touched his toes. He'd never been real athletic. Well, he'd played basketball in school and he liked to hike and take long walks when he could, but he wasn't in too bad a shape for a man his age. Still breathing the air, still doing the Lord's work. If he could get this group to pull together on this thing, it could be a significant piece of business, praise God. This might be enough to turn the tide, to bring them back into the churches. And if the various religions of the world could actually learn to work together, why, that would be a miracle in itself. There was a river of juice to be squeezed from that fruit. Were they united, truly united in spirit as well as in name, there wouldn't be much they couldn't manage. They'd be a powerful force for good in the world, powerful. Dogma and doctrine were problems, always had been, always would be, but if they could just get past their interpretations . . .

He grinned as the others began to file back into the conference room. Loretta was right. He wasn't as hard-shell as his father had been when he preached for the Southern Baptists. The church had gotten a little more liberal since then, but they still dunked instead of sprinkled, and in his heart, Green believed his way was the right way. Intellectually he could understand how a man in Lebanon or Iwo Jima or Pakistan could see it another way, that's what he grew up with, that's what he was exposed to, that's what he would believe. But in his soul, Green knew they were misguided. He used to believe that ten men like his father could convert the whole Middle East, get them to Jesus, but that was a long time ago. His experiences in religious politics had taught him nothing was ever that simple. Aside from the vast historical and cultural differences, some people just seem to glory in being wrong, there was no way around it.

He smiled at the others. "Okay, gentlemen, are we ready to vote?"

The Catholic smiled at him, and at that moment, Green would have bet all that Cuban sugarcane, plus all the tea in China *and* all the truffles in France, that the duly elected representatives of the UWCC were about to decide that its First International Conference was going to be held next year in Phoenix, Arizona. That's what the Jesuit wanted, and it looked like he had the numbers.

It had only taken three days to get that little bit of business finished and it was the easiest part but it looked like it was about done. Thank you, Jesus.

It was going to be a long year.

In combat whether you will be victorious or not is greatly decided prior to engagement with an enemy. A long, heavy sword is not good for use in combat. It is patent that no truly excellent practical blade can be found among heavy and very long-pointed swords.

—Risuke Otake, *Katori Shinto Ryu: The Deity and the Sword*

5

LONG CAME ASHORE with his unit just west of the mouth of the Guantánamo River, a few klicks west of the destroyed U.S. naval station. The Castroitos had gotten their hands on an antique Pakistani nuke and delivered it via a suicide pilot in an old Cessna STOL used for smuggling tobacco after the stuff was made pretty much illegal in the States. The Navy and Marines at the base had shot the little jet to pieces but the bomb had been plated and it survived and landed close enough to the base HQ to flatten it. The nuke was fairly clean and, outside of a few tacticals, supposedly the only one the bad guys had. Small consolation for the troops who got cooked.

The thirty men and women of the special combat assault team boiled out of the amphib high and dry, and less than a hundred meters from the landing craft found themselves crossing a six-lane highway into a patch of scrubby bushes and trees. The sky was overcast and thick with dark clouds. Going to rain soon. There was some lightning off in the distance—unless that was the Navy shelling the poor cocksuckers elsewhere on the island.

Welcome to Cuba, Marines.

"Awright, you turds, let's move it, asses and elbows, by the goddamned numbers!"

The sarge's voice over Long's bonefone didn't sound any different than it did in a drill, but he knew better. This was enemy territory and they weren't going to be shooting back with light-taggers that made your SIPEsuit's computer ping and tell you you were hit, to lay down. They were going to be using real bullets. The suit was supposed to stop most of the small-arms stuff and it fucking should, it weighed almost twenty kilos, most of that spidersilk and carbon-ceramic armor, but guys who could get their hands on a nuke to take out a base could probably get AP rifle ammo, too. Long didn't feel much like Superman.

"Lopez, Marvin, Bodie, fan the point! Long and Smith, back 'em up. Marino and Jessup, you all got the tail. Everybody else give me open-field dispersal. Go, people, go!" The sarge affected a hillbilly accent but Long happened to know he'd graduated with honors from MIT and turned down officer training because he wanted to stay on the ground. Which showed how smart he really was.

Long hurried forward to his position. The heads-up display in front of his goggles was lit and if it was working right, there weren't any tanks, personnel carriers, or trucks around. The only blips were human heat sigs, and they were code-blue friendlies from the Marines on point and on Long's perimeter. The GPS gave him a location grid and compass heading, the wolf ears didn't hear any machines other than the departing amphib. So far, so good.

He glanced down at his weapon. The M-17's diodes were all green, thermal sights on-line. He had thirty rounds of antipersonnel hardball in the magazine, high-velocity caseless .300 Whispers, using the big .125-grain Nosler ballistic tip. And five more mags just like it, plus one of AP, just in case.

Describe your rifle, Marine!

Sir, my rifle is a five-point-one-kilogram, fully automatic, seven-hundred-and-fifty-RPM-cyclic-rate-four-position-gas-operated-shoulder-weapon, sir!

Yes, sir, and it would damn well punch right through his SIPEsuit's own armor, so some cane cutter's surplus Kevlar or scavenged steel-belted radial tire vest wouldn't do jack shit to slow it down. Somebody flashed a red heat sig or he eyeballed them visual, and Long was going to plink them like a practice run in a Hogan's Alley combatsit. Blam! and *adiós*, Paco. Sorry, but if it's you or me, then better it's you. He had the selector on single fire, too. He wasn't going to run dry hosing the real estate and then have nothing to shine at them but his smile. One at a time, unless a real big horde came out of the woods.

"Sarge, we got heat up ahead. Five hundred meters, NNW, about twenty blips." That from Bodie.

"Lock it down," the sarge said. "Light, you get that?"

"Copy," the lieutenant said. "Proceed apace." The light was in a copter four klicks offshore, watching it all on the vidcams in the units' helmets. Some of the guys thought that was shit-easy duty, riding and directing traffic, but Long didn't think so. If the bean eaters had nukes, they damn sure had Stingers and HS Lances, and a copter all by itself in the middle of nowhere could turn into a falling fireball in a big hurry. Ol' Paco straps on a rebreather and swims a ways out, floats up to the surface and *whoosh!*— no more command post, we gonna need us a new officer. No, thanks. He'd take his chances down here on the ground with the sarge. At least he could see the enemy coming.

There was a boom that he thought was enemy fire for a second until the sarge comcast: "Thunder, people. Don't nobody get itchy fingers on them triggers just yet. We got a lock on them blips, Bodie?"

"Not yet, Sarge," Lopez said. "Can't see 'em good for the trees and shit, don't look like any motorized armor, but they seem kinda funny for humans."

"There's an old school up ahead," the sarge said.

Long had already toggled his LORAN maps and zoomed his heads-up in to look at the school. According to the computer, the place was a Catholic girls' academy. Secondary ed, fifteen-, sixteen-year-olds.

"Pussy!" somebody said.

"I am going to pretend I didn't hear that," the light said from his copter. "Otherwise some would-be child molester is going to have to spend the next three months cleaning toilets with a toothbrush."

It started to rain. But here, rain was a mild term. It poured. All of a sudden, it was like standing under a shower at full blast. Jesus!

His goggles were coated with repellent and everything was supposed to be absolutely waterproof, but within seconds they were wading through ankle-deep puddles. Christ, what a mess.

"Stay calm, people. It's just a little tropical thunderstorm."

"Our blips ain't running for cover," Bodie said. "Kind of makes you wonder if that's the girls out for phys ed, don't it?"

Lightning struck a tree fifty meters to his left then, and the heads-up display on Long's visor went black.

"Shit!"

He looked around. Radio was out, too, he couldn't hear anybody chattering. Repellent or not, the visor was streamed with water. He lifted it. The rain was still coming down like the first day of the Deluge and Long tried to spot the sarge. There he was, using hand signals. Long recognized the jive: Everybody hold your position.

He could do that.

After a minute the sarge came by. "Status report."

Long had been checking his gear. The rifle was okay but the SIPE computer was down. No GPS, no LORAN, no compass, no video, no heat-sig readings. Thing was a big paperweight.

"Damn," the sarge said. "We lost twelve systems from

that bolt, plus Stanton's helmet leaked and shorted his out.
I guess we're going to have to ask for our money back.''

Lightning hit another tree a hundred meters ahead of
them. The flash and boom seemed almost one, and a splin-
ter the size of his arm flew past and stuck up in the ground
a meter or two behind the sarge.

''Fuck!'' Long dropped into a crouch, then came up
when he saw what it was. The wet wood was stripped of
bark, a bright yellow in the rain.

The sarge came out of his own crouch and looked back
at Long.

''What do we do now, Sarge?''

''Maybe the shock is temporary. Maybe they'll come
back on-line. Meanwhile, watch my hand signals. We'll do
this the old-fashioned way.''

''Jesus, Sarge—''

''Hey, we're no worse off than the locals. You still got
your armor and your rifle, that's all a United States Marine
needs.''

Semper fi, Long thought.

''Watch me for the move.''

The sarge finished his rounds, then signaled.

The rain had slackened a little, but not much. It came
down in windy sheets, blowing waves that gave a little
space to see between them, and not a whole lot of that.

Even though his electronics were screwed, there wasn't
anything wrong with his ears. Lopez, on point, laughed.
''It's fucking *sheep*, man. Check it out.''

Long was ten meters back and he scuttled toward where
Lopez lay sprawled in the mud. Long stretched out next to
her. They had the same birthday, he and Lopez—14
March—and were the same age, twenty-two.

''No wonder the heat sig looks so funny. Sheep. Baaa!''

The sheep didn't look any happier than Long felt; they
were huddled in a soggy mass under what looked like a big
oak tree sixty meters ahead. Good way to get hit by light-

ning, though the last couple of strikes had been well behind
the advancing Marines.

"So now we can get up and walk and stop crawling
through the damned mud," Lopez said. "School is still a
few hundred meters ahead, other side of that clump of
trees." She pointed her weapon.

Long looked at the sheep again. They were all butt-out,
heads in together. *Must be bitching about the weather.* He
counted asses. As best he could tell, there were twelve or
fourteen of them.

The sarge arrived and went prone in the muck next to
Long. He shook his head. "Little industry for the girls'
school. Maybe they make sweaters."

"Yeah, that'd come in handy here, all right," Lopez
said. "Thick, heavy sweaters to keep this snow out."

The sarge waved his upraised hand and pointed across
the field. Bodie and Lopez went out, Marvin with them.
Long started to rise, but the sarge waved him down. "Your
gear is fucked, I want people who can see up front. Stay
here until Marino and Jessup bring up the rear and stick
between them, they're still SIPE functional."

"Got it."

The points went out, the rest of the unit started after
them. Long wiped his eyes, the damned goggles were useless in this kind of rain, even if the computer had been
working. About two-thirds of the Marines were in the field
and advancing when Long realized something was wrong.
If his heat-sig gear had been on-line, maybe he would have
gotten it quicker. Bodie had said there were twenty blips.
And there were only a dozen sheep, fifteen at the most.
Bodie could have been wrong, but assuming his gear had
been operational, the number would have been flashing big
as hell right there in the display alongside the blips.

He looked at the sheep again. One of them bleated and
turned.

Or tried to turn. He saw that there was something
clamped to its neck in the front, looked like a ring or clip,

and a short piece of dark wire or rope ran from it, keeping the sheep from moving. A tether.

Long jumped up and screamed.

"Down, everybody down! It's an ambush!"

He swung his rifle around.

A sheet of what appeared to be brown plywood suddenly appeared and fell on the sheep to one side. The startled animals bleated loudly.

Behind the plywood, three of the sheep stood up.

That's what it looked like. He knew it was men in camo, probably real sheepskins. They must have been under the ground, some kind of pit covered with a board, the sheep standing around it for cover.

It was surreal. The rain pouring down, the three sheep started shooting.

Some of the unit had hit the deck when they heard Long yell, maybe half of them, but the others were in the open and exposed. The three ambushers were using submachine guns; the roar of the weapons was a continuous rumble. Empty plastic shell casings flew from the weapons in shallow arcs.

Marines started to fall, hit. Long saw Lopez's vest fly away from her body in the rear as she spun, realized she'd been punched by an AP round that went through the front of her armor and her body and had enough left to move the back plates. Fuck!

He couldn't remember doing it but somehow he flicked the selector from single fire to full auto. He started running toward the sheep and the snipers. He didn't wait for the thermal sights. He waved the gun back and forth, hosing them just like he said he would never do. What he hit was sheep, the real sheep. He saw two of the animals go down, chopped by the fat bullets. Two sheep, and then his high-tech, super-efficient, state-of-the-art shoulder weapon jammed, the bolt frozen halfway open.

The three snipers had company in that hole in the ground. Two more of them popped up like targets at the range and one of them was pointing a beat-up and ancient AK-47 at Long—Long, whose rifle was now a useless piece of shit. He didn't have time to disassemble the fucking thing and find out what caused the stoppage. He threw the rifle aside, kept running, and dug for his sidearm.

It was non-regulation, the handgun. A snub-nosed .357 S&W his father had given him on the day Long joined the Corps. SCAT troops were supposed to carry H&K Tacticals, polymer-framed pistols that held sixteen rounds of potent 10mm, and had integral laser sights and compensators. His father, a state trooper captain in Louisiana, had sneered and called the H&K a ''Tupperware gun.'' Had ten things that could go wrong with it, he'd said. With a revolver, if you used good ammo, it was simple. Point it, pull the trigger. If it didn't go *bang!* then you pulled the trigger again until it did go bang.

Later, when Long saw the computer-enhanced tapes cut together from the helmet cams, he'd been amazed. He didn't remember much of it.

The guy in the sheep suit facing him started shooting.

Long just kept running full out, water and mud splashing. He came up with the stainless steel revolver and pointed it at the shooter one-handed. By this time he was only ten meters away from the ambushers. He pulled the trigger as fast as he could. The snub-nose spat long tongues of flame in the rain, six of them. Three of the men went down, including the one facing him. The fourth man spun, the sheepskin billowing.

Long was three meters away. There was no sound—

Somebody smashed his right thigh with a baseball bat. The leg went dead but he was pushing off on his left and he was right on top of the shooters now. He slammed into them, knocked the two still standing down. He still held the revolver, empty, but he used it as a club, drove the butt of it into the nearer man's face, felt the bone give over the nose, but he kept hammering. The wooden grips split on one side, shattered, a piece of it stuck in the Cuban's mushy forehead, and he hit it with the gun butt and his hand, driving it in like a roofing nail. Some of the blood on his hand was his; the piece of wood was sharp and it sliced right through the muscle.

The other Cuban screamed something in Spanish. Long didn't understand it, but as he tried to bring his SMG around, Long gave him a whack with the back of his hand. The bones under his ring and little fingers broke from the force, backed by the weight of the revolver, and the second Cuban fell back into the big hole that Long had just noticed, splashed into a chocolate-and-gray puddle that had to be twenty centimeters deep. Long went back to pulping the first one's head—

"Hey, Long, hey, okay, okay!" somebody yelled into his ear. "At ease, at ease!"

Long woke up, his head leaning against the jet's window. He looked around. It was the late flight from Seattle to Portland and half the passengers were sleeping. He took a deep breath, let it out slowly. Almost twenty years and the dream was still as vivid each time he had it. It didn't happen as often as it once had, three or four times a year now, usually after something dangerous. A reminder that he should have been chopped to pieces in the Cuban rain a long time ago.

He shifted in the seat, moved the S&W on his belt around a little. Some years back, the only way you could carry a weapon on a commercial airliner was if you were an active-duty federal or local cop, and even then, it was usually up to the particular pilot. When things had gotten crazy in the early teens, with every other flight leaving anywhere being hijacked, the airlines decided that armed off-duty cops would be helpful if they happened to be flying the unfriendly skies. So the policy was changed. When they passed the law that licensed all handguns and required testing and a stiff background check, the airlines decided that upstanding citizens could declare and carry, too. It was a risk, but after a couple of hijackings were thwarted by security or bodyguards on vacation, somebody uplevels had made a decision. No airliner had ever been 'jacked by somebody legally carrying, something the pro-gun people pointed out endlessly.

Long looked out through the window into the darkness. He had the two seats to himself and was glad of the room. He hadn't slept on the way to Seattle, but now that the package was delivered, it was okay. The nap hadn't helped much, though. He had a little money put away. Maybe he would take a few weeks off and take it easy. Work out, get in shape, recharge his batteries. A tired man was dangerous, to himself and others. He was apt to make stupid mistakes. After the shooting in the alley, Long realized he'd gone too long without a break. If he'd been at full sharpness, he would have spotted those two shooters before he ever left the building. Yeah. A few days at the hot springs at Kanee-tah, maybe. Drop a few bucks in the casino there. Or on the coast in a rented cabin, watching it rain, watching the surf roll in, walking on the long, sandy beaches. Yeah. Maybe he'd do that.

And even the premeditated murder of one brother by another is not as serious an offense as disobeying authority by eating from the tree of knowledge. For it is not Cain's killing of his own brother Abel that condemns humanity to live forever in sorrow; it is, rather, Eve's unauthorized or independent "taste" of what is evil or good.

—Riane Eisler, *The Chalice and the Blade*

6

IT HAD BEEN a pretty good service this evening, Moon thought. Twenty-three people, not counting Dawn and herself. She had opened by reading from Mayli Wu's translation of the *Tao Teh Ching*, the fifty-second verse, the Mother of the World. Fem Wu's translation was not gender-neuter, like some of the later revisions, but even so, it was a kinder rendition than most of the earlier versions.

After a short prayer, they had chanted the mama-nam, taken testimony and affirmations from those willing to share them, listened to Katerina's trio play and sing a lovely madrigal. The voice of Sister Kat's guitar was smooth, mellow, a balm for the spirit. There was a twenty-minute silent candle meditation, another chant, then temple social hour. A few of the sisters stayed to help clean up. After the last one had hugged her and left, Moon made a final pass through the meeting room before she reached for the lights. It was then she saw the silver brick.

Well, no, on second look it wasn't a brick, it was more the size of a paperback book but it shined like mercury under the cranky overhead fluoros. The silver rectangle lay on the table next to the wooden bowl containing the night's offering, sixty or eighty New Dollars in small bills and coin.

Odd, she hadn't seen it before and she'd passed right by the bowl while cleaning up. Someone has left a . . . ?

What *was* this thing? It looked almost alive, gleaming that way.

Moon went to the table and picked the silver object up. It was much lighter than it looked, as if made from mylar or spuncarb. Light but solid, no give to it. No markings. Huh.

"And what have we here, hmm? What are you, little shiny brick?"

Some amount of time passed, she could not have said exactly how much.

More than a few minutes and less than an eon.

Moon very carefully put the silver block back on the table and stared at it. Had it turned into a werewolf and started howling at her, she could not have been more surprised. Surprised and stunned. Offhand, three possibilities occurred to her: the thing was a miracle; the thing was a curse—or she had lost her mind. She didn't feel crazy, however *that* felt, so for the moment, she considered the other two choices.

Why would her temple be so blessed—or cursed? How had it come to be in here? What did it mean?

What *could* it mean?

She stared at the shiny rectangular object.

She reached for it again.

Wentworth leaned back in his chair and rubbed his eyes. The chair hummed and vibrated under him, trying to soothe his stiff muscles. It was one of his few luxuries, the chair, nine hundred NDs' worth of cloned horsehide and machinery from TST's catalog, with built-in massage and electrostim, a music player and speakers, biogel climate-controlled shapeshifter padding. A button or voxcom would cause it to stretch out into a bed, another control or a couple of words would play a recording of the surf at Big Sur, to lull him into sleep. He'd spent many nights on the chair when he'd been too tired to go home.

Not tonight. Even though it was almost midnight and the third snowfall of the season was still coming down in a thick flurry, he wasn't done yet. It had been three or four weeks since the last storm, the day he'd worked the deal with that moron Bennett. Lot of water under a lot of bridges since then. He had his money, biz was running smoothly. February looked like it was going to be a good month.

He had an appointment with Gray in a few minutes and he would have to put on his coat and go out into that crap if he were going to make it in time.

Gray was a crafty son of a bitch. He was the best in the business, even though he was a freelance, better than anybody the Israelis had, better than anybody the CIA had, better than anybody *any*body had. His network of ears and eyes heard and saw everything worth hearing. If it happened and it had any bearing on national security, sooner or later one of Gray's people got it, usually sooner, and almost always sooner than anybody else's field ops. Gray was a cotton-top of sixty, he looked like your father, but he could still do fifteen chins and fifty push-ups, run two klicks in under twelve minutes and outshoot half the best pistoleers in the PSS; more, he could outthink the average genius. The real beauty about Gray was that, save for a dozen or so very savvy people, nobody in official Washington even knew he *existed. That* was power. That was smart. If you wanted something, if it could be gotten and if Gray were willing to work for you, you could put a check mark by it and forget it. Gray always delivered.

So it was that when Gray came to town and wanted to meet in a bowling alley or a sleazy bar or a performance of the Washington Symphony or wherever, Wentworth met him there. In the eight years Gray had been jobbing for the section, he had never been to Wentworth's office. At least not to Wentworth's knowledge. The man was like the Shadow; he ghosted in and out of places and maybe he had spent a few nights on this very chair for all Wentworth knew. Or cared. As long as he got the job done. And when he'd called earlier, he said he had something the section ought to know. That was good enough for Wentworth.

He stood, stretched his back. Reached into his desk drawer and removed the Coonan and its shoulder rig, slipped the harness on, adjusted the extra magazines on the right to counterbalance the pistol on his left. He pulled the gun out, ejected the magazine and the round in the chamber, to be exchanged with the spare magazine in the carrier. A little superstition of his, to always go into the field with changed ammo in his pistol. He reloaded the single round and tucked the magazine into the carrier. There. All ready.

He went to collect his coat.

Three A.M. and Walter Green sat propped up in the hotel room's bed on three pillows, reading the Bible by the glow of the lamp on the nightstand. He couldn't sleep, that seemed to happen more and more as he grew older. He'd wake up in the middle of the night, his mind buzzing, thinking of the things he had get done, and he couldn't drop back off until he occupied his thoughts with something other than work.

As it happened, when he picked up the leather-bound King James his grandfather had given him on his sixth birthday—the Fourth of July, 1976, also the two hundredth birthday of the United States—it opened to Ezekiel, chapter 13:

"And the word of the LORD came unto me, saying,
2 Son of man, prophesy against the prophets of Israel that prophesy, and say thou unto them that prophesy out of their own hearts, Hear ye the word of the LORD;
3 Thus saith the Lord GOD; Woe unto the foolish prophets

that follow their own spirit, and have seen nothing!
4   O Israel, thy prophets are like the foxes in the desert.
5   Ye have not gone up into the gaps, neither made up the
hedges for the house of Israel to stand in the battle in the
day of the LORD.
6   They have seen vanity and lying divination, saying, The
LORD saith: and the LORD hath not sent them: and they have
made *others* to hope that they would confirm the word.''

Green shook his head. Even the Good Book was putting
it in his face tonight. The Lord was death on false prophets
and he would lay flat the walls of untempered mortar with
hailstorms and stormy winds.

Green shut the Book and closed his eyes. As he often
did when he was alone, he offered his thoughts aloud: ''I
know they aren't following the true path, Lord, most of
them aren't even Christians and those that are seem to be
just about as far off the track as those that aren't. But I'm
trying to look down the road here, Father. There are three
hundred million people in these United States, billions more
in the rest of the world, and while the population keeps
going up, the numbers in Your churches keep going down.
If all the people my age were to die tomorrow, there would
only be a relative handful left to carry the word. We aren't
pulling in the young ones. The New Ager has got almost
as many people watching his kind's offering as all those
who attend services among the Baptists, Methodists, Catholics and Presbyterians put together. The women are going
back to the Goddess. The heathen abound everywhere.
That's not right. Somebody has got to round those souls
up, somebody has got to keep the wolves from slaughtering
the flock. We need us a few good shepherds, Lord.''

God did not see fit to respond to this in a way Green
could understand, so he added the prayer he spoke every
night of his life before retiring: ''Not my will, Lord, but
thine. Amen.''

He wouldn't mind a little more direction from on high,

but that would be too easy, he supposed. It wasn't God's job to provide Walter Green a path strewn with rose petals. If he had to walk barefoot on thorns, well, that was how it was and part of His plan. He'd just have to live with it.

Praise God and Amen.

. . . the soul walks upon all paths.

—Kahlil Gibran, "On Self Knowledge," *The Prophet*

7

WENTWORTH LEANED BACK and looked at the naked woman standing behind Gray. Her eyes were closed in ecstasy or a good imitation of it as she rubbed herself with her fingers, swaying back and forth to some internal beat. Unlike the other dancers who had preceded her, this one looked as if she really were having a good time. She was young, probably fifteen years younger than Wentworth; that would put her just over thirty. Her body was lean, her breasts were small, but natural. You could see the ridge of implants in the dancer who'd been out just before this one, also a thin woman, and Wentworth thought that fairly stupid. What was the point of big tits if they were so obviously fake? This one had black hair, it hung past her shoulders, and her pubic thatch was trimmed, but thick even so. Her vaginal lips pouted, swollen by her self-stimulation. Even though he didn't frequent such places, he found himself getting hard watching the woman.

She knew it, too. When she opened her eyes, she was looking right at him through the haze of illegal tobacco

smoke, playing to him of all the patrons in the private club.
The music throbbed with a primal rhythm and if he didn't
match the dancer's, damned if he didn't throb some himself.

Gray said, "What do you want to do?"

Do? He wanted to get up, take this dancer by the hand,
lead her to a flat spot and fall on her. But that wasn't what
Gray was talking about.

She turned around, bent over, and did that trick with her
pussy again, that clench and release. Yes. He was going to
have her.

To Gray, he said, "I'll send some people to take care of
it. You say there's no security?"

"House alarm system, a ten-year-old could bypass it."

"Fine. I appreciate your efforts here." He stared at the
pulsating vagina.

Gray laughed. "I can see that." He stood, finished his
champagne, and nodded down at the still-seated man.
"Later." He turned and walked away.

The dancer moved closer toward him. If she knew shit
about D.C., she probably knew who he was. Just because
she pranced around naked didn't mean she was a dummy.
Some of the smartest women he'd ever met had been
whores, dancers, models. Pretty did not automatically
equate with stupid. Neither did it mean smart; it just meant
pretty.

Wentworth unfolded a couple of twenties from his
money clip and straightened them, folded them lengthwise,
and laid them on the table.

The dancer moved closer, bent, and put her right nipple
next to his lips. Her perfume was something musky. She
looked at the bills. "That for me?"

"Yes. You do any private dances?"

"What did you have in mind?"

"You, me, a bed. This and that."

She smiled. "Three hundred for this, five hundred for
that. My last set is in half an hour."

He nodded. "I'll have a car pick you up. Driver's name is Nguyen."

She smiled again, picked up the twenties, then twirled away.

Wentworth sipped his drink, then, when it was not embarrassing, stood and left.

Long took the antique watch from the pocket of his jeans and looked at it. Straight-up twelve. The little ring connected to the chain was kind of loose so he put the watch away very carefully. The other end of the chain was attached to a World War I Victory Medal, a brass disk almost as big around as the gold, art deco Waltham pocket watch itself. "The Great War for Civilization," the medal said. It and the watch had belonged to Long's great-grandfather. The watch gained a couple of minutes a day, had to be wound morning and night or it would stop, and was fairly fragile. He could have worn a wrist chrono tuned to the Naval Observatory, a device that told him the time, day, date, current weather forecast, and the Dow Jones if he wanted it, as well as his location anywhere on the planet. Or he could have had his com cheep and announce any or all of those things. But he liked the idea of having to dig time out of his pocket and actually look at it.

He'd made one pass around the block in his car and checked the neighborhood. Mostly industrial, a few old houses like this one. Now he was finishing the circuit on foot. In his business, it paid to know the ins and outs of a place before you committed yourself to it. Especially given his close call in the alley not so long ago.

The place had a high, wooden fence in back but the fence wasn't wired for alarms or shock. A man in a hurry could shoot out the back door and vault the barrier easily enough. If he had enough reason to do so.

There was a small sign on the front door that said "Embrace of the Goddess."

An east wind had come out of the Gorge and finally

blown the persistent fog away this morning, but the temperature had dropped. It was clear and achingly cold, close to freezing, and the chill factor from the wind was probably ten degrees lower than that. He wore his leather jacket and a thermal cap, and thin leather baseball batting gloves. The last offered little protection from the cold but they were flexible enough so he could use his hands in a hurry, if need be.

Long started across the street toward the entrance. He'd run the place through the credit net and public records and come up with not much. A feminist religion based in San Francisco, this branch was run by a woman calling herself Miranda Moon. No trouble with the law, no problems with their credit, though they didn't have much of that, either. What would they want with a courier?

He climbed the short flight of steps and crossed the porch to the door. Well, he'd find out in a minute.

He knocked on the door.

"It's open!"

Long opened the door and stepped inside. He found himself in a hallway. The place smelled faintly of spice. From his left, the woman said, "In here."

He pulled his cap off and stuck it in his jacket pocket. Began removing his gloves.

She was about thirty-five, had long black hair and blue eyes, might tip the scales at fifty-seven or -eight kilos, to judge from her face—he couldn't really see her body, she wore a white kaftan-style robe that went all the way to her ankles. Her feet were bare. She was maybe fifteen centimeters shorter than Long. Not classically pretty, but a striking woman, what his mother would call "handsome." She was dusting a table with something that looked like a fuzzy red powder puff.

"M. Moon?"

"Yes. You're M. Long?"

"Yes."

She dropped the duster on the table and wiped her hands

on her robe, moved to where he stood. Pressed her hands together and bowed slightly. "Namaste," she said.

He gave her an inclined head in return.

"Would you like to take your jacket off?"

Long thought about it for a second. He was wearing his gun in the paddle holster. He could probably slip it off and wrap it in the jacket without her seeing it, but she obviously intended to take the jacket from him and hang it somewhere. He didn't know what the protocol for bringing a weapon into a temple was. Then he mentally shrugged. If she wanted to hire him, she might as well know he walked around armed.

He said, "Okay." and took his jacket off.

She saw the gun right away, but didn't say anything until after she came back from hanging his jacket. When she did speak, it surprised him.

"Thirty-eight?"

"Three fifty-seven."

"Are those ivory grips?"

Long felt a slight grin begin. The gun obviously didn't fluster her.

"Yes."

"I thought ivory was illegal."

"Only if it was taken after the law was passed. If you can prove it was collected before then, it's still legal."

Long had a sudden memory surge. Lying in bed in the VA hospital in Miami, recovering from the shattered thigh they'd rebuilt with stainless steel and Kevlar and titanium. The sarge coming in with the box, a gift from the survivors of the squad. He'd opened the small package and seen the china white stocks for his Smith. "To replace the ones you busted saving our asses," the sarge'd said. "Everybody chipped in."

Now the grips on his revolver were almost twenty years old, and time had turned them from white to a buttery pale yellow, somewhere between heavy cream and fresh straw.

He said, "You know something about guns?"

She shrugged. "I was born in Montana. I had an uncle who was a deputy sheriff in Butte."

"My father was a state trooper in Louisiana. This was a gift from him when I joined the Marines."

She nodded.

"How did you come by my name?" he asked.

"Sister Throwbridge—that's Louise Throwbridge—said you did some work for her husband."

He nodded. Mel Throwbridge was a chip programmer who fed his stuff mostly to Intel. He'd sent a couple of items to Silicon Valley firms, presumably computer circuits or embedded-light programs.

"She said her husband thought you were dependable."

"I am. What can I do for you?"

"I have something I need to have delivered to San Francisco. To the Embrace of the Goddess, the main temple."

He waited.

"It—this object is of great value. It has to reach there safely."

"My fees are fairly high," he said.

"It doesn't matter, whatever the cost."

"How large an item?"

"About the size of a handheld reader."

He nodded again. "No problem. When would you need it delivered?"

"As soon as possible."

"All right. I'll bring you a carrier. A case. You put the item into it and seal it. Give the address and the name of the person to whom it needs to go. I'll need a holo or photo of them, a thumbprint or retinal scan, plus a password."

"All right. When can you go?"

"I have a carrier in my car. I'll go get it, you can arrange for the ID while I'm gone, I can leave this afternoon."

She looked vastly relieved. "Thank you, M. Long." There was a short pause. "Do you have a first name?"

"People call me Hal. My initials."

She looked at him quizzically. As if she knew he was

holding something back. He shook his head. "My father had a weird sense of humor. He named me Huey."

"Huey Long?" She chuckled. "Oh, I'm sorry."

"Don't be. I've gotten used to it."

"Hal, then. I appreciate your help. This . . . object, it, well, it's—"

He raised a hand. "Don't tell me what it is. I don't need to know. I deliver sealed packages, that protects me and my clients." True, that might not save him from a smuggling charge if he were caught with illegal drugs or stolen property, but his lawyer could try to argue *Fallon* v. *United States*, the delivery workers' protection decision, if it ever came to that. The don't-ask-don't-tell policy had held up before. He'd be willing to undergo a mind drug scan to prove he had no knowledge of his cargo. So far, it hadn't been necessary.

"Well, I guess I'll get your coat, then."

A young woman came to the door behind them. Long saw the family resemblance easily enough. She looked just like a blonde version of her mother. He figured her at fourteen, sixteen. She wore black jeans tucked into black patent leather riding boots, a black T-shirt with the neck cut out and held together with safety pins. She was an attractive teenager. She'd be a spectacularly attractive woman in a few years.

"Mom, I'm going to the concert at OMSI, I'm meeting Django there—" She stopped suddenly.

Saw the gun, he figured.

"Is . . . is everything okay in here, Mom?"

Long grinned. Yep. Definitely saw the gun.

Moon said, "Everything is fine. M. Long here is going to deliver that . . . thing we found to the main temple."

"Oh. He's not a cop?"

"Why would you think that?"

"Well, the gun and all. I thought maybe something might have happened to Terry."

"Wishful thinking," Moon said, and obviously regretted

saying it immediately. "Sorry, I didn't mean that. And even if something had, why would they come tell us? Wouldn't his *wife* be the one to inform?"

Long felt the old energy around whatever they were talking about and it was powerful. And cold and ugly, too.

"M. Long, this is my daughter, Alyssa. M. Long is a courier."

"Oh. That explains the gun."

Long saw the girl give him a once-over look, and while he kept his face neutral, it surprised him. He had seen that gleam in women's eyes before and it usually indicated a sexual interest. *Christ, with her mother standing right there and me old enough to be her father.*

"I gotta go. Nice to meet you, M. Long." She smiled at him, then left.

After she was gone, Moon said, "Terry was a policeman my daughter used to spend some time with. He was ten years older than I am. Thirty years older than Alyssa."

And if a tone of voice could kill, old Terry would be a smoking spot on the floor, too.

He let it pass. It was none of his business.

"I'll get your jacket."

The softest of all things
Overrides the hardest of all things

—Lao-tzu, Verse 43, *Tao Teh Ching*

8

MOON CAME BACK to where Long stood, carrying his jacket. The black leather was old and a little faded across the shoulders and there were brush burns and scratches all over it; still, it was in pretty good shape—supple, at least. It had a mild scent to it, musky. Maybe he treated the jacket with mink oil or something.

He stood there, staring into nothingness, the ivory-handled gun on his hip a focus for her. She didn't like any of this, having to hire a man who carried a weapon, but she also knew she had to do it. Once she got the *thing* to the high priestess, it would be somebody else's problem, and not Moon's. The thing was invaluable, if it wasn't some kind of elaborate hoax, and she did not want responsibility for it, no way.

Long looked as if he were capable enough.

"You let your daughter travel in the city alone?"

She handed him the jacket. "As long as she's on pub-trans, yes. She's fifteen going on thirty. If I forbade it, she'd just sneak around and do it anyway. This way, I know where to start looking if she doesn't come home. The rule is pretty much that she can go and do what she wants, as long as she tells me about it.''

Long shook his head.

''You disapprove?''

''She's your child, it's not my place to say.''

Moon didn't want to let it go that easy, even though what he said was true. ''But you do disapprove.''

He shrugged. ''The city is a dangerous place. We're not D.C. or L.A. or Detroit, but even Portland has its gangs and sickos. I wouldn't let my daughter run around alone without some means of protecting herself.''

''Such as what? A gun?''

''She's not old enough to carry one legally. There are other ways. Pepper spray, electrical stunners, strobe wands. At the very least, some kind of martial arts training.''

''A man's answer,'' she said.

He slipped into his jacket. ''And what is a woman's answer?''

''To carry peace in one's heart, to radiate it at those around you. To be secure in purity.''

''In a perfect world, yeah. We live in this world. An icehead with a knife might not pick up on the message.''

''Change doesn't come cheap or easy, M. Long.''

''Would you pay for it with your daughter's life?''

He had her there. There was what the Goddess stood for and then there was the connection she had with her children. Mothers almost always voted against wars and violence, but if it came to it, she would die—or kill—to protect her daughters.

''I'm all for a positive and non-confrontational attitude,'' he said, ''but sometimes you can't smile away or run from a threat. When your back is to the wall, when somebody is in your face, you need another option.''

''A gun.''

''If that's what it takes. 'Your right to swing your fist ends where my nose begins.' ''

"Will Rogers," she said.

He nodded. "Yeah." Then, "I'll get the carrier."

He ambled toward the door, a loose-jointed walk. He closed the door behind him.

"Who was *that*?"

Moon turned. Dawn stood in the doorway.

"You aren't supposed to eavesdrop on people, you know."

"Mom, you were standing there talking to a strange man who had a *gun*. Was I supposed to go to my room and pretend I didn't see you?"

Moon shook her head. "He's a courier. He's going to take the silver box to the main temple."

"I still think we should keep it."

"It's not a toy."

"We don't know what it is. Maybe it's here because the Goddess wanted it to *be* here."

Moon repressed a sigh. Trust her children to throw the Goddess in her face when it suited them. She had already thought of that. She had contacted all of the attendees who'd been here that night; none of them admitted to leaving the object. How had it gotten here?

Maybe she should ask it.

She smiled.

Green sat on one of the four stools in front of Juan's Lonchería just off Figueroa. The shack was about the size of a small bathroom, an open-air wooden framed roof on four-by-four posts with just enough room for the grill and a cook inside. How it had gotten past any city inspectors was probably in the realm of the miraculous—or the exceptionally venal—but the burritos were the best in Little Mexico. Green ate a shredded-pork-and-refried-bean combo on a huge flour tortilla, and the hot sauce made tears run down his cheek.

"Okay, Padre?" Juan said.

"Excellent, Juan. *Está bien*."

"Gracias."

Juan turned away and saw a street dog on its hind legs, digging at the plastic garbage can next to the stand. He grabbed an empty Coke can and threw it at the dog. *"Vamos, perro."*

The plastic container sailed by the dog, missing cleanly.

The dog glanced over at Juan, unworried. It didn't pause in its digging.

All street dogs looked alike, Green thought, as he took another big bite of the burrito. Short haired, brown or mottled, maybe twenty, twenty-two kilos. Ribs showing, wary but not going to run unless there was a real threat.

Juan was angered by the dog's refusal to be afraid of him. *"¡Ah, perro, no me jodas! ¡Vete pa'l carrajo!"*

Juan grabbed a skinned pork bone lying next to the grill and threw it at the dog. It flew hard but the dog knew what it was. He jumped, caught the bone as if he were a shortstop fielding a line drive, then turned and hurried away. Nice catch, puppy.

Green fought the urge to grin around the fiery bite of burrito. Juan thought Green's command of his language was a lot more limited than it really was. But Green knew enough Spanglish and street Spanish to understand that Juan had told the dog not to fuck with him and to go to hell. He'd probably be embarrassed to curse in front of a man of the cloth if he thought he'd be understood.

Great burrito. He sipped at the Coke, washed down the final bite of the pork and tortilla. He slid a couple extra noodle bills under his paper plate and waved at Juan. "See you later, *amigo*."

"Vaya con Dios, Padre."

He was about to take his first step when he saw the Catholic coming toward him, smiling.

The burrito grew heavy in his stomach.

"Reverend Green."

"Father Sims. Going to lunch?"

"No, looking for you, actually."

Too much to hope for, he supposed. He smiled. It was an effort. "What can I do for you, Father?"

"Well, you could call me Leo, for starters. This title business gets a little unwieldy at times."

"Don't I know it. All right. Leo. What's up?"

It was a bit chilly, but the sun was out and the winter day seemed more like autumn or early spring. Green had never gotten used to the palm trees and climate here. The two men walked along Figueroa, past shops whose signs were Spanish first and every so often, English. The area could have been transplanted from Tijuana without any big changes, except the locals had more money. Not much more, but some.

There were some gangsters, Bandidos Locos they called themselves, gathered into a group next to a shop that sold cheap electronics. The boys and girls wore gang rags, in this case, red silk flight jackets with black wrist cuffs, the letters BL on the jacket backs, over boot-cut black spandex pants. The pants were skintight to the knee, then flared into wide bell cuffs cut to fall across the instep of flamenco boots, also in black, and to touch the concrete in back of the heels. Very precise, as rigid as military uniforms.

The *bandidos* waved at Father Sims in his priest's weeds and he nodded and waved back. They nodded at Green— he was okay, nobody would pull a knife and take his wallet because he was a holy man, too, only not quite as holy as the Catholic, of course. The *bandidos* had learned the hard lesson, Don't shit in your own nest, and there was seldom any trouble anywhere close to MacArthur Park, at least not from them.

"Let me ask you a hypothetical question, Walter."

Green kept the smile in place but it was an effort. The burrito that had grown heavy now turned to lead. The Jesuits and their hypothetical questions. *Lord, how have I offended Thee to deserve this?*

"Suppose for a moment that you were able to prove that Christianity was valid."

"Father—uh, Leo—"

"No, hold on a second, I'm not talking about faith, here. I mean *evidence*. Suppose you were given a . . . tool that would demonstrate to a reasonable man or woman that your religion was valid. Maybe not a hundred percent, but a compelling argument. You could walk up to an atheist, say, wave this at him, and he would blink and nod and understand—and likely agree with you."

"I'd say I'd been given a miracle and I would commence to using it high, wide, and repeatedly," Green said. He could play this game. "Though I can't see how faith can be translated into logic or science without divine intervention."

"Well, truthfully, neither can I. But you would say that if such a thing existed, it would be . . . valuable?"

"Beyond price. If I—or any other of the Lord's workers—could walk down the street converting everybody we met, it would be worth all the money in the world and any other world you might happen across that used money."

"I will agree."

They walked in silence for a few meters. Green had had enough of these hypothetical conversations with the Catholic to know there was a point to this exercise. Normally he would have been patient and waited for him to get to it, but the two-ton burrito was rumbling, causing other, better-digested meals to move along the pipe, and he needed to get back to his room to use the facilities. So he said, "All right, Father Sims—Leo—drop the other shoe."

Sims grinned. "You would have made a good Jesuit, Walter. Okay, if you allow that a strong proof of Christianity would be the greatest boon to the Church since our Savior Himself, then how damaging do you think the opposite would be?"

"Excuse me?"

"A mirror to the truth that Christianity is the true path for mankind."

"Are you talking about something that would *dis*prove our faith?"

"Let's say it would cast great doubt upon it."

"That's absurd."

"Of course it is. We're hypothetically speaking here, remember?"

Green shook his head. The man didn't have enough to do, that was apparent. Next he'd be asking how many angels could dance on the head of a pin, or how long eternity was. But to finish the game and get back to his room, Green said, "It would be worse than anything I can imagine."

"I agree."

"Did you spin this whole thing up just to make my lunch go sour, Leo?"

"I wish that were the case. Unfortunately, I have a source who says this scenario is not as farfetched as it might seem."

"I don't believe it for a second."

"Well, I can't say I believe it, either. But something has come to my attention that I have to pass along to somebody, and you are one of the sharpest political infighters in the game. I'm going to need some help and I'm afraid if I bring it to my own people, they'll bury it."

That must have come hard, Green realized. For the Catholic to turn to a *Baptist* for help. That was as amazing as anything Green could think of, and fairly scary.

"All right, Leo. What are we talking about here?"

"I hope we're talking about a hoax, Walter. I pray we are."

Fixedness means a dead hand. Pliability is a living hand. You must bear this in mind.

—Miyamoto Musashi, *The Water Book, A Book of Five Rings*

9

WITH THE PACKAGE crowed and locked to his belt, Long went into work mode. *Applied paranoia*, Marvin had called it.

When he'd finished his classroom work and gone into the field in New Orleans, his first and best teacher had been Marvin Robertson, a black ex–Marine topkick who'd left the service after twenty and joined IC. Being jarheads, they had something in common, plus Marvin knew Long's father. Long always suspected his father had told the retired Marine to look after him, and he certainly did. Marvin had taught him how to move, in public, on the street, in a crowded building, everything he'd needed to know. He'd taught him the tai chi form, an exercise the older man did every morning, rain or shine. And he'd taught him the basic rules to their game.

The first and most important rule was simple: Once you pick up your package and until it is delivered, you assume nothing about anybody. Little old lady, guy in a wheelchair, Girl Scout, it doesn't matter, they could be out to kill you and take your package. IC didn't give a shit if you got killed, but you fucking better not lose your package—even if you were dead, they'd send somebody to meet you at the Gates of Hell to kick your ass for screwing up.

The job was simple: Deliver the package. If you had an 0900 due time, you'd better be there thirty minutes early. There were no excuses for being late, either, none, period. Flat tire on your car? Figure it into the schedule. Your plane crashed? Better hope you got cooked crisp in the jet fuel barbecue. Earthquake? Volcano? Hurricane? Didn't matter. International Couriers had failed to deliver three times in thirty-six years and all three of the guys who screwed up were dead. Two of them died protecting their packages, guns working; the third was a thief and the rumor was that IC had hunted him down and killed him themselves. *Don't expect nothin',* Marvin had taught him, *but be prepared for everything.* The second your hand touched that package and you took delivery, you watched everybody until you signed it over. *Don't trust me, don't trust your girlfriend, don't trust your own mother.*

Mostly the lessons had taken. Long had worked IC for four years, from when he left the service in 2013 until '17, when he punched out Dobbins for a fuckup that nearly got Long killed. Quit or get fired, they told him, you can't beat up the supervisors no matter what. So he quit and started his own business. Met Sienna the following year . . .

No. Don't think about her. Now is not the time.

He scanned faces and cars as he went to his own car. While still across the street, he pulled the hound from his jacket and clicked it on, waved it back and forth at the Salvo. The sniffer would pick up any constant or regularly intermittent electronic signal emanating from the car; more, it would send a wide-spectrum pulse at the vehicle, the bands most commonly used in triggering tracking or explosive devices. If somebody had bugged his car while he was inside, or decided to put a radio-controlled bomb under the seat, the sniffer should tell him—or blow his car up.

Nothing.

Another control would start the car. He used it. The motor rumbled to life, ran smoothly.

He put the hound away and walked across the street. He bent and shined a small but powerful flashlight under the frame, moved to the exhaust pipe, and looked inside. It seemed to be clean. The car was locked, the alarm working and the hood still zipped shut. He opened the car, got inside, pulled away from the curb. Checked the mirror, made a mental note of the cars and bikes he saw.

He drove toward the airport, taking surface streets, planning on driving on Burnside to Sandy. He used his com to call and book a seat on the next flight to San Francisco. He had forty-five minutes and it was about a twenty-minute drive this time of day. Should be no problem. Once he got there, he would book the next flight out and let the first one go without him. You couldn't be too careful.

He was driving through the red-light district, a row of massage parlors and topless bars just across the Willamette, when he caught the van following him. He gave it half a block, then pulled his car over to the curb. He shut the engine off, got out, and walked into the nearest store, a yellow-and-red-painted porno shop with XXX over the door and a sign that said "Live Girls on CD." Well, unless you were into necrophilia, that was better than the alternative.

Inside, he picked up a CD-ROM from a slot under a holo of a man with a giant dick getting it sucked by a naked woman with a blond ponytail. He walked to the counter, paid for the disc, then went back outside.

He went through the hound routine again, though he kept it in his pocket. Probably they had been on him since he'd left the temple with his package, but in case they hadn't, no point in showing them he was on to them. Better the devil you knew than the one you didn't.

He tossed the disc into the backseat and pulled away from the curb.

If they had money and if they had any sense, he wouldn't see the van behind him again. A good automobile surveillance took at least three cars. Four were better, five better still. It could be done by a sharp op by him- or herself, but if you had to do it one on one, that meant whoever was paying you was cheap. That, or you had to set up in a real hurry and didn't have time to install your brackets. With three or four tails, you could avoid electronicking a subject. If your quarry got hinky about a tail, you had that car drop off and somebody else take over. You rotated cars anyway, so the subject never saw the same vehicle behind him for more than a few minutes. Everybody on your team kept in contact via com and you ran parallel or ahead or way back, only one or two cars in actual visual contact, especially during the daylight hours. SOP.

A block away, Long saw the van behind him. It was over a lane and trying to hide behind a beat-up twenty-year-old Chevy full of teenagers, but he had the plate number and it was the same. If they'd caught his reservation for the San Francisco jet, they'd stay back, knowing where he was going. If not, they'd have to stay close to keep from losing him.

He pulled his phone, tapped in the scramble code.

"Call encrypted," the vox chip said.

Even if they heard him call out now, they wouldn't be able to tell who he contacted or what was said—the code was his own and based on the name of his favorite nurse when he'd been in the hospital during the war.

"Yeah?"

"Danny?"

"Hey, Huey Alphonse. What can I do you for?"

"I need a license plate run."

"Shoot."

Long gave him the plate number.

"Oregon?"

"Yes."

"Hold on a sec."

Danny would be making magic with his computer, tap-
ping into the DMV mainframe, a trick he could do, he said,
with one hemisphere tied behind his back.

"Here you go. A rental, from Avis. Guy's name is . . .
J. E. Hoover, and he's listed as working for something
called Research Consultants, out of Washington, D.C. Got
a corporate Visa card, Virginia driver's license that expires
on his birthday in 2032. Nice-looking guy. He's thirty-five,
I like my tube steak a little younger. Though I'd make an
exception in your case, Long."

"Can you run the company?"

"Take a couple of minutes."

"Call me back. Scramble your call, Danny."

"Ooh. Sounds serious."

"Could be nothing. You know me."

"Not as well as I'd like. Back at you in a couple."

They discommed and Long put the phone onto the seat
next to him. Somebody with a sense of humor, calling himself "J. E. Hoover."

He drove carefully, watching. If there were other cars on
him, he couldn't spot them, just the van. And it could be
a coincidence, the guy might just be going to the airport
himself for a business trip, happened to stop at the same
time Long did.

Right.

Five minutes passed. Ten. He was nearly to the turn for
the airport and Danny hadn't called back.

The phone *cheeped*.

"Yeah?"

"You might be right about scrambling the call, boyo.
Research Consultants is a dummy. I tracked 'em backward
through three more dummies before I ran into a wall. A
fort, actually."

"Did they tag you?"

"Shee-it, no way. I'm Mr. Premature Ejaculation, in and
out before you know you been had. But it wasn't from lack
of trying. The security at the fort was real good, Longo.

Talking fedhead or military level.''

"Thanks, Danny. I owe you.''

"Nah, I already took it out of your account. Later, Long.''

Long glanced at the rearview mirror. The van was still back there. A tiny little alarm bell *chinged* in his mind. If somebody had that kind of back story on a fake company, Visa card and wards on the computer trace, then they had money, public or private. So either there were other cars watching him and they were real good, or this was a hurry-up deal.

He'd give odds that whatever it was in the packet he was carrying, it was of interest to the feds, and that's who was on him. And since they hadn't just pulled him over and offered to take it off his hands, that also meant there was something loopy about it.

Not good.

Well. If they had legal grounds, he'd hear about them before he got to San Francisco. If not, then it was his job to collect and deliver, and that was just what he planned to do.

The Catholic was perturbed and well he should be, Green thought. Even if the whole thing was some kind of big hoax, it was dangerous. If all the thousands who thought they owned a piece of the true cross actually had one, it would have had to have been the size of a sequoia. And others who still believed that somebody besides Oswald pulled the trigger on JFK. People loved conspiracies and mysteries and if there weren't any good ones around, then somebody would make one up. They'd been doing so for thousands of years. They'd buy into it and that would be bad.

He and the Jesuit were in his office, the door closed, his secretary fielding calls and visitors.

"You're sure about this, Leo?''

"That it's real? No, of course not. That the government

thinks it's real enough to send a couple of NSA operatives out to collect it? That I'm sure of.''

Green nodded. The council had its own intelligence agents and the Jesuit was in charge of them. Who better? Catholics had always been adept at knowing what went on in their territories and Jesuits were the smart ones. Catholics had the property and money and they knew they couldn't take it with them, so they spent whatever it took to keep themselves in control. Didn't always work; they couldn't shut up Henry VIII or Martin Luther and they'd long ago lost the battles against birth control and abortion, but they had a lot of experience in delaying tactics. The Protestant arm had learned much from the Catholics when it came to keeping a finger on the public pulse. While you might not always be able to duck an incoming blow, if you knew about it in advance, you had a better chance. Warned was armed. If you didn't pay attention to the secular as well as the divine, you were apt to find yourself behind the eight ball.

"All right. What do you think we should do?"

While Sims looked perturbed, there was another way he was enjoying all this cloak-and-dagger stuff. The man loved intrigue. He'd have been right at home with the early Gregories; he'd have been a fine drinking buddy to Machiavelli. "We've got to check it out," Sims said. "If the feds think there is enough here to work it, we can't let it slide."

Green leaned back in the old wooden teacher's chair. It creaked under his weight. "They've got the jump on us, don't they?"

"Maybe not. My informants lead me to believe the item has been moved. It is being taken to the Embrace of the Goddess Temple in San Francisco."

Green shook his head. "Those women are getting to be a pain in the butt. Every time I turn around I'm hearing them complain about male-dominated this and evil patriarchal that.''

"Can't really blame them," he said. "The Jews pretty

much coopted the Goddess right down the line. Until Yahweh came along, the women had a hand on the tiller, at least some of the time.''

''I realize there were injustices in the early days,'' Green said, ''but that was then and this is now.''

''True.''

Green sighed. He didn't much care for this part of the game but it was necessary. The Jesuit could have done this business on his own, not said a word and gotten away with it. He was so twisted they'd have to screw him into the ground when he died, and when he went to Hell, he'd wind up running the place. But that kind of bent had its drawbacks. He would probably assume that Green had his own spies in place watching and it was better to pretend to be forthcoming than sneak around and get caught. Wheels within wheels within wheels. Spare me, Lord.

''All right. See what you can do.''

He grinned. ''Consider it done, Walter.''

Allah loveth not the treacherous.

—Al-Hajj Muhammad Shakarzâdeh, (A translation of his rendering
of that which cannot be translated) *Spoils of War,
The Glorious Koran*

10

WENTWORTH KNOTTED HIS tie in front of the hotel
room mirror. Reflected from behind him on the bed, the
dancer—Thalia, she called herself, though that was not her
real name—lay naked and languid on the bed, recovering
from her second orgasm.

He finished the knot, adjusted the center pleat, and
smoothed the dark blue silk. Eighty-five dollars if it was a
penny, a gift from his wife, who had excellent taste if not
much passion—at least not for him.

"Thursday?" Thalia said.

"No, I've got a reception at the Korean Embassy Thursday. Friday."

"Seven?"

"Right."

"Great. See you then," she said. She arched her back,
stretched, and scissored her legs open and shut slowly.

Wentworth smiled into the mirror at her image. The
woman was uninhibited and was willing to do virtually anything he wanted. He was a simple man when it came to

sex: nothing kinky, the usual three holes in varied positions was all he needed, so it wasn't as if she had to work too hard. And he took the time to get her off, too. She earned fifteen hundred a week as a "consultant;" had her free time for herself, even had a little clout, if she used it with care and caution and not too frequently. It was better than dancing in a nude club for tips and the occasional well-heeled customer who wanted to touch as well as look. She had a lover who was in his late twenties, a health club manager with muscles who kept her company most nights when Wentworth wasn't around. For three or four sessions a week, some of them noon quickies, Thalia could hardly complain.

He turned and gave her a brief smile. "Say hello to Matt for me," he said.

Her own smile froze for a second, then increased a little. "All right, I will."

He'd surprised her with the comment but she was bright enough to realize almost immediately that he had had her checked out. And he'd let her know she wasn't getting anything past him with her testosterone boy-toy. They were sophisticated adults here—she provided what he wanted, he paid for it, and everybody was happy. They weren't talking about love or marriage or romance, simply an equitable exchange. Though he surely was getting the better of the deal. Money didn't mean much to him. Even if nobody ever added to it, his family wealth would last his grandchildren's children all their lives, assuming nobody pissed it away before it got to them. And nobody would—the Wentworths were old money, and they knew how to keep it. If he needed it, he could lay his hands on five million of his own, all legal and aboveboard. His wife's family was nearly as well off as his. Thus he was able to stay a Boy Scout in Washington, insofar as graft went. He would never think to siphon any of the Agency's money off into his accounts. He wasn't a crook.

Sleeping with an exotic dancer wasn't frowned upon in

his circles; a mistress was almost a necessity for a man in his position. His previous *amor por dinero* had been an ex–call girl with a master's in American history. She had decided to marry a congressman from her home state and get out of the business. Too bad. Thalia had a better body, but was not as cerebral as Victoria had been.

Certainly his wife, the cool-as-ice Marsha, wouldn't kick too hard if she found out about his latest interest—that twenty-three-year-old assistant tennis pro at their club filled *her* needs when she felt them. Currently. The tennis jock was but one of a long list of Marsha Wentworth's own toys. He didn't begrudge her. Their fifteen-year-old marriage was primarily a joining of powerful families. They had produced the two required children; he and Marsha had managed to remain relatively cordial throughout. They each had their own lives.

He shrugged into his jacket, adjusted it over the shoulder holster, and headed for the door. He was relaxed, showered, ready to work.

Nguyen stood in the hall, hands held in front of his groin, waiting.

Nguyen was twenty-five. He had a black belt in one of the more nasty combat arts, was a crack shot with the 9-mm SIG P-210-6 he carried and he was absolutely loyal to Wentworth. The Vietnamese chauffeur and bodyguard had been working in a Saigon brothel at twelve when Wentworth found him and bought him out. He'd sent the boy to schools, had him trained not only as a fighter and a driver, but in the ways of polite society. Nguyen had a degree in business and politics, could converse intelligently on dozens of topics, and made more money working for Wentworth than he would as a corporate manager. Nguyen didn't seem to have any ambition past taking care of Wentworth, which was exactly what the head of the PSS wanted. Nguyen was single, had his sexual needs attended to by a reputable call-girl service, and his only luxuries were tailored suits and expensive guns. His single living relative was a widowed aunt who still resided in Vietnam, to whom Nguyen sent enough money each month to live upon quite comfortably.

"Buttonhook called," Nguyen said.

Wentworth nodded. He seldom took his com into a room with a woman he was going to fuck. The buzzing could be very distracting. Plus Buttonhook was one of his *sub rosa* wetwork ops and all of those calls went to Nguyen's scrambled line. He was nominally a bodyguard and chauffeur, but Nguyen also ran the wetwork section for Wentworth.

"And . . . ?"

"He's going to wait until the package is delivered to obtain it."

"His reasons?"

"Security will be easier at the destination. The courier on the job is armed and a shooter. He has four confirmed kills, a couple more suspected, and is an ex-Marine: Silver Star for bravery, Purple Heart at Guantanamo."

"Buttonhook is smarter than we thought."

"He'd have to be," Nguyen said. He grinned his thin-lipped, tight grin.

"Well. Whatever. Keep me apprised."

"Of course."

Long parked his car in the short-term lot, top level of the structure, and hurried across the skybridge to the main terminal building. He wanted to get a look at the man following him before he boarded the jet to San Francisco and he'd need a little distance to do it right. He took the tiny spotting scope from the armored glovebox and slipped it into his pocket. The scope was a 10X Leupold Mini, small enough to cover in his hand so that somebody standing to his side would see only his fist pressed to his forehead.

With the influx and egress of passengers to shield him in the terminal, he turned and looked back at the open sky-bridge to the parking structure. He had gotten a glimpse of the tail earlier, enough to mark him as male, with short dark hair, in a blue synlon or Gore-Tex windbreaker. If the man didn't change clothes before he left his car—not likely since he'd be in a hurry—he should be able to spot him.

There he was.

Long raised the scope.

He got a quick but good look at the man, noticing the set of his ears, the color of his eyes—blue—and a quick pan down to check out his hands. Ears and hands were hard to disguise. Unless the guy put on a mask, gloves, and a hat, he should be able to spot him later. If he did disguise himself in a major way, he'd stand out in San Francisco, where the temperature was relatively warm compared to Portland.

Long put the scope away and sauntered toward the ticket counter. He didn't notice anybody else watching him. If they knew where he was going, then one man here was enough. It was the watchers on the other end he'd have to worry about picking out, assuming they knew where he was going. Worst-case scenario said he had to figure on that.

He passed his credit card to the ticket clerk, watched her run it through the scanner. He booked the next flight—no point in waiting since he *knew* he had a tail.

"I'm declaring a firearm," he said.

She nodded. "License number?"

He gave it to her.

She read the number carefully into the computer, looked at the response on the flatscreen. "Please go through the detector station on your left, M. Long."

He nodded. He'd done this before.

"Your flight will be boarding in five minutes; it leaves in twenty minutes," she said. "Concourse G, gate 14A."

Long nodded again.

"Have a nice trip."

He didn't look back as he walked toward the security station. The armed airport cop wasn't one Long knew. He looked up and saw him approaching. "Your ID, please."

Long presented his card.

"Courier, huh?"

"Yes."

"Interesting work, I bet."

"Now and then it is."

The guard had a keyboard connected to his terminal. He tapped in a sequence and waited a second for the response. "Okay, there you are. . . . Wow, you carry a wheelgun? Kinda limits your firepower, don't it?"

" 'Six for sure,' " Long said.

"Yeah, I suppose."

"Your pistol ever hang up?" Long asked. "Stovepipe or a failure to feed, any kind of malfunction in practice?"

"Sure. But only once or twice every two or three hundred rounds."

"My revolver has never jammed, not in twenty years and maybe twenty thousand rounds."

"Hunh."

Long smiled. If the cop had ever had a weapon freeze in a firefight, he'd be more impressed.

He walked down the corridor. He paused at the gift shop a hundred feet along the corridor and pretended to look at a CD magazine display. He used his peripheral vision and saw that his tail also went through the security checkpoint. And *he* did it without slowing down, save to wave his ID at the cop.

Old Blue Windbreaker was official, sure enough. Cop, Fed, something.

Long wondered what that meant.

You can be a Master even if every shot does not hit.

—Eugen Herrigel, *Zen in the Art of Archery*

11

GREEN FELT HIS step lighten as he approached the front door to his home. The old concrete walk was cracked and it had patches of half-frozen St. Augustine grass growing up through the gaps. The front porch needed painting again, seemed like he'd just done that, but it had been almost ten years. The risers on the front steps creaked under his weight, as did the old pine boards of the porch itself. He could afford to hire somebody to fix things but he never did. Loretta did the yard work herself and he would tend to the house upkeep and repair eventually, probably during the coming summer. When he got some time off.

He opened the front door and got a whiff of supper: pork cutlets, spinach, red beans, and rice. The house was warm and the winter chill tried to follow him in but didn't get very far. He shut the door and put his suitcase down.

"Loretta?"

She came out of the kitchen wiping her hands on her apron. She was a fine-looking woman, the years had been kinder to her than to him. Some white in the hair, a few extra pounds top and bottom but she still had a shapely, womanly form, comfortable and pleasing to his eyes. Rubenesque.

"Hey, honey. Welcome home."

He smiled at her and held his arms out wide.

She came to him, stood on her toes, and they hugged.

Now he was home.

She leaned away from him, looked up at his face. "What's wrong?"

"What are you talking about?"

"Something's wrong."

Lord, how was it she could do that? Just *look* at him and know he had something on his mind? Didn't matter if he pretended otherwise, if he laughed or tried to work around it, she almost always *knew*.

"I'll tell you about it over supper."

"All right. It'll be ready in about fifteen minutes."

He nodded and went to put his suitcase in the bedroom.

"Any good mail?"

"Mostly just bills. Your personal stuff is on your dresser. Couple letters from the baby, your friend Jerry in France, like that."

"Let me make a pit stop and clean up and I'll be right out."

He went to the bathroom, emptied his full bladder—he never could pee on a plane, all that bouncing around—then washed his hands and face. Felt better. He pulled off his shoes, found his old buckskin slippers with the fake fur lining, and put them on. Tugged his shirttail out and let it hang over his pants, untied his tie and took it off, unbuttoned his top button.

He padded into the kitchen. The house had a dining room but they never used it except for company. When it was just them or one of the kids coming by, they ate in the kitchen at the old wooden table Loretta had refinished twenty years ago. In this house, the kitchen was where people always seemed to wind up anyhow.

Loretta had the table set and was loading his plate with rice and beans, piling them up high next to the spinach and breaded pork chop already there. Pork wasn't good for you and they didn't eat it much anymore, except on special occasions. Like when he'd been gone for weeks and finally made it home.

He went to the refrigerator and got the carton of milk, filled glasses for Loretta and himself. Loretta did the cooking, and he washed the dishes and cleaned up afterward; they'd always thought that was fair. Mostly they split the household duties right down the middle, though he hadn't been holding up his end too well lately.

They sat. Bowed their heads. He said, "Lord, thank you for this food and the place in which it was prepared, and thank you for all the joy you have allowed us in this house. Amen."

"Amen."

They caught up on personal stuff for a few minutes.

"Bradley and Lashanda are coming by Sunday with the children for dinner. Lashanda says that little Dirisha got the lead in her school play."

"Figures. That child is a born actress." Dirisha was the youngest of the grandchildren, she was fifteen. She was a beautiful girl, looked just like Brad, who looked just like Loretta, far as Walter was concerned.

"Rowena got offered a job in Birmingham, that big law firm she interviewed with last month. Associate, with a shot at partner in five years at the most, she says."

"She gonna take it?" He chewed on a bite of the pork. Delicious. "This is real good, sweetie."

"Thank you. She doesn't know. They'll give her a car and an expense account and the pay is higher than the other place, but she still isn't sure she wants to work in a big firm."

"Well, least she's got a choice. What did the baby have to say?"

The baby was Shanti, who was off at school at the U of

A. Green had been forty when she'd been born and she was just shy of her nineteenth birthday. If he and Loretta lived to be a hundred and ten and Shanti made it to her eighties, she'd always be the baby.

"You think I opened your mail and read it?" She sounded amazed.

He laughed but didn't say anything. She'd been opening his mail since before they were married.

"She's fine. Hates chemistry, loves astronomy, met a new boy who writes poetry, hasn't washed her clothes in two weeks, could use a little more money next month."

"Sounds normal. What about Jerry?"

"He says a French doctor stuck a laser up his butt two weeks ago and burned off his hemorrhoids and that he took his first painless dump in twenty years yesterday. He is a crude man, Walter, I don't see why you bother with him."

He laughed again. "Nobody twisted your arm and made you read that letter."

"Puhhh!"

"Honey, next to some of the people I have to deal with, Jerry is a star in the Lord's crown."

They ate in silence for a moment. She looked at him, but didn't say anything. She waited.

He sighed. "All right."

He told her what the Catholic had told him, the whole thing. When he was done, he raised one eyebrow at her and said, "What do you think?"

He knew her pretty well, his wife of thirty-seven years, but as she had throughout their time together, she surprised him yet again. Loretta: mother of his four children, daughter of the pastor who'd been Green's first employer when he'd come fresh out of Bible college full of fire and brimstone; as good a Christian woman who had ever drawn breath. She looked at him and said, "If he's right about this, then you all have to stop it. If you got to move mountains with a teaspoon or smite a legion of the ungodly, whatever it takes, best you do it. You're God's instrument,

Walter, and this sound like the Devil's handiwork for sure.''

He nodded. She was right, of course , and that was how he saw it himself, but this was Old Testament stuff and Loretta had always been more of a peace-and-harmony New Testament person in her ways. Even when she'd been teaching all those hard gang children in the public schools, she'd spared the rod and kept her open hand extended to them. She was not weak, but certainly gentle.

He nodded. "It could be the Catholic is mistaken, but I can't say I put much hope in that—when it comes to this kind of thing, he seldom is wrong. He's got eyes and ears all over the place.''

"When will you know?''

"Pretty soon. The Catholic is putting his people on it. Don't be surprised if the private line rings this weekend.''

"Well, better to know than not,'' she said.

A moment passed as they thought about the problem. Then she said, "Go on, eat your supper before it gets cold.''

He ate.

The courier had been gone for only an hour when the house security announced a visitor. Moon, in the kitchen, looked at the monitor and saw a well-dressed man standing on the porch, smiling at the cam.

"Yes?''

"M. Moon? I'm Peter Lewellyn? My girl sister Sarah attends your meetings?''

Moon blinked at the image on the monitor. One of those people who made every sentence into a question. "Yes?''

"If I might have moment of your time?''

"Of course. Just a second.''

She walked from the kitchen toward the front door. Sarah Lewellyn. The name sounded vaguely familiar, though she couldn't place the woman immediately. Must be one of the new attendees.

She opened the door. Peter Lewellyn wore a dark blue silk unitard with a fake shirt and tie printed on the front, as well as a matching blue jacket untabbed and open. Blue patent leather shoes. He looked to be about thirty, had well-groomed short hair, and a thin mustache, both mouse brown.

"What can I do for you, M. Lewellyn?"

"I won't trouble you? My sister left something here the other day? I need to pick it up?"

She had a sudden cold flash: the book.

"See, I'm a computer engineer at Tek. We . . . ah . . . that is, the R and D unit I work in—we've been developing a new piece of hardware, a player for a new kind of inter-active encyclopedia game program, and well, Sarah bor-rowed it and accidentally misplaced it? She, ah, remembers having it here but not afterward? I thought I'd check to see if you found it?"

He was lying.

She couldn't have said how she knew for sure, but he was. If his sister had been here the night the book had turned up, she didn't remember her; moreover, she had called everybody who had logged in that evening to ask about the book when she'd found it and nobody had known anything about it.

What did it mean?

Well, it meant she wasn't going to tell this liar anything.

"I'm sorry, M. Lewellyn, but I didn't find your device." That was true, she was sure enough. She had found *a* device but she would bet a fortune it did not belong to this man.

"Ah, well, sorry to have bothered you? If you, ah, come across it, please give me a call?" He handed her a card.

She watched him walk away and the cold she felt didn't come from the Portland winter.

In the backseat of the armored but inconspicuous Chrys-ler, Wentworth looked at his watch. He wore a Rolex that looked plain but was something other than it seemed. To a casual viewer, the timepiece was stainless steel; it was actually carved from a block of platinum, had a titanium band, and the face cover was denscris, a new type of glass harder than steel. The watch had been a wedding gift from his father-in-law. Fifteen years ago it had cost about the same as a new Mercedes Electric and was worth more than that now.

Almost six and already dark, another snowy night. Crappy weather lately. The car's tires threw slush as it rolled through the city. He had a meeting with Congressman Walker in half an hour, dinner scheduled with General Miller at eight, a liaison with Thalia at ten. Another long day.

From up front, Nguyen said, "Call coming in from Buttonhook. You want to listen?"

Wentworth shrugged. "Why not?"

Nguyen touched a control on the dash.

"Go ahead, Buttonhook."

"A slight change in plans," the scrambled but undistorted voice said. "I just got a call from Cola in San Francisco. Somebody pulled the welcome mat at our subject's destination. Place is crawling with security, six, seven hardwared beefos prowling the perimeter. A couple of high-viz lawyers inside, too. Our package gets through the door, it's going to be dicey to pry loose."

"Interesting," Nguyen said. "What are you going to do?"

"We'll have to take it before it gets inside."

Wentworth glanced up and saw Nguyen watching him in the rearview mirror. Wentworth shrugged.

Nguyen said, "Whatever."

Buttonhook discommed and Nguyen flicked a glance at the mirror again. "Maybe there's something to this," the driver said.

"Maybe. Gray is no fool. But in the grand cosmic scheme of things, how important can it be?"

"We'll find out when Buttonhook delivers it."

"I suppose. Never a dull moment, hey?"

"No, sir."

Wentworth leaned back against the seat. No rest for the guardians of the republic, was there?

... yea, the sharp pointed arrow, and the quiver, and the dart and the javelin and all preparations for war.

And thus being prepared to meet the Lamanites, they did not prosper against us. . . .

—Joseph Smith, his translation of *The Book of Jerom,* 8–9

12

LONG DROVE THE Chevy rental electric past the Burlingame exit, watching the mirror to see if Windbreaker was still behind him. He was.

He slid the paddle holster around so it was easier to reach, and unsnapped the safety. He didn't want to use the gun and he wouldn't if he had a choice, but Long figured it was a whole lot easier to explain to a judge why you'd pulled a weapon on a fed or cop than it was to explain to Saint Peter why you hadn't. Yeah, it was all borrowed time, but he wasn't ready to pay it back without doing a little of what it took to keep it.

He was feeling a little antsy. He'd worked out this morning, done his tai chi fist exercises and the long form, stretched afterward, yoga asanas for twenty minutes. Even so, there was nothing like being followed by somebody you didn't know for a reason you didn't know to tighten you up.

He headed for the New Bay Bridge, built after the quake that took out the old one a few years back. Supposed to be proof against a nine-pointer, but engineers were always optimistic about such construction. The 7.5 quake in L.A. last year had leveled freeways and buildings supposedly able to withstand it, shattered plastcrete and twisted arm-thick steel rebar like boiled spaghetti.

He punched the toll into his rental's computer, saw it logged, and drove through the automatic pay lane. The sky was clear, the winter sun bright against the blue, and traffic was light. He didn't care much for San Francisco, too many people in too small a space and it was foggy a lot more often than in Portland, but as big cities went, it was better than a lot of them.

The temple was close to downtown, just off one of the new trolley lines installed for the Chinese tourists looking for the Frisco of the old movies they'd watched. With any luck, he'd be in and out in a hurry and whoever took delivery of his package could worry about Windbreaker and his friends. It was just another job, he'd had worse—nobody had shot at him on this one yet.

He got off the freeway and took surface streets, let the car's vox chip guide him through the turns toward his destination.

The building didn't look like what he thought of as a temple; it was a four-story cube, like any small office building; modern, plain vanilla synstone, and a parking garage underneath. No Doric columns, no statues of gods or goddesses holding up the roof, not a gargoyle in sight.

There were two large men in suits standing near the front entrance, trying not to look conspicuous. The pair had the look of cops or well-trained guards, and the way they moved made him think they were armed. A man with a gun carried himself differently than an unarmed man.

Long drove past, planning to circle the block. Were these two with Windbreaker? Or were they working for the temple? No way to tell by looking.

He spotted another one on the side of the building by an exit-only door as he looped around the corner. Hmm. Very interesting. If the muscle was Windbreaker's, then he was going to have trouble getting into the building. He had a local com number for the temple and he could call to try and see what was what. If the temple's lines were patent, that would help, but since he didn't know anybody inside, somebody could rascal the call, intercept it, and he wouldn't know it.

Hey, is it safe to come in?

Sure, pal, no problem. Right through the door.

Maybe not.

He could pull into the underground garage and see if there was any kind of security on the elevator, but the idea of bottling himself up like that didn't appeal a whole lot, either. If they had the doors up top covered, they'd have the garage entrances dogged down, too.

Well. What to do?

The question was answered for him.

Windbreaker began to come up from behind, just about the time Long spotted the front tail. A brown package-delivery van cut across the two lanes on the one-way street to move in front of him. He could be wrong, it might be a coincidence, but he didn't think so. It looked as if they were building a box, a standard street maneuver used in assassinations. When they got to a place where the road narrowed, the van would slew sideways and block the road ahead, Windbreaker would put his car into a skid and barricade the lane behind. Unless there was room on the sidewalk, he'd be forced to leave the car, and if he had to do so, they'd be ready.

Long looked around. Was it just the two of them? Or were there others? He couldn't spot any more watchers.

Half a block ahead, a delivery truck, its back open and hydraulic lift down, blocked one of the two lanes. If he were in the van, that's where he'd do it, right where there wasn't enough room to take to the walk, which was narrow—and full of pedestrians.

Long took a deep breath, let half of it out. He'd done

okay in the defensive driving course he'd taken at the antiterrorist school in Connecticut a few summers back. Now was a good time to see if it worked. The Chevy electric didn't have much in the way of guts, but it was what he had to work with.

He stomped on the accelerator.

"That's the private line," Loretta said.

Green nodded. "I'll get it."

"Could be the baby or one of the children."

"Could be."

But it wasn't.

"Walter. It's Leo."

"Leo. What's up?"

"There's been a complication."

Green's belly lurched. "I see."

Wentworth was halfway through his dinner, an excellent broiled catfish with hazelnut butter and honey mustard sauce, when Nguyen appeared from a dark recess of the restaurant and stood where he could be seen. He didn't wave or waggle his eyebrows or anything but that he was suddenly apparent meant there was some kind of problem.

To the general, Wentworth said, "Excuse me a minute, would you, Louie? I need to hit the men's room."

The general, his own mouth full of rare prime rib, merely nodded.

When Wentworth stood, Nguyen turned and walked away.

Once they determined they were alone in the men's room and Nguyen did a fast sweep with his sniffer to make sure the place wasn't bugged, Wentworth said, "What?"

"Buttonhook called."

"And . . . ?"

Nguyen shook his head.

That was never a good sign.

•   •   •

The Chevy didn't have any power but Long had surprise with him. He was halfway around the van before the driver checked her mirror and saw him. Before the startled woman could react, Long twisted the wheel and slammed into the van. The woman's instinctive reaction was to turn away from him and the delivery truck was right in her way. She tried to swing her van back into the lane but he was ready. He rammed the Chevy into the van's front door.

She had the size and weight but he had momentum. It wasn't enough to move the van much—just enough so it caught the right rear bumper of the parked truck. The front of the van exploded, a spray of fiberglass and tempered plastic, the left headlight glass shattered into a fountain of glittery chips. The van's rear end swung around and smacked into Long's Chevy but it was more like a hard shove than an impact, and the rental car overgained the motor and jumped forward.

The careening van continued to spin and wound up blocking the lane behind Long.

Windbreaker plowed into the van at speed.

It was loud and messy and Long found himself pounding the Chevy's steering wheel and yelling, "Eat that, you fuckers! Eat *that*!"

The Chevy's driver's-side panels were cracked and splintered and the safety bars bent but the car was drivable. The question was, Where was he going to drive *to*? He couldn't risk the temple, not knowing who the thugs outside were. Losing a package was worse than being late, but in this case, the package didn't have a ticking clock anyhow, it didn't have to be delivered today. He would find a quiet spot and call his client, get some information from her on how to contact the deliveree. They could set something up.

And as for the tails he'd picked up? Cops or not, he'd lost them for the moment. If they wanted him bad enough, they'd find him again. Might not be good for his business, what he'd just done, but as far as a jury would be concerned, Windbreaker and the woman in the van hadn't identified themselves as anybody official. A reasonable person in fear for his or her safety in the same situation could be expected to sympathize with Long, right?

He hoped.

He drove.

Normally Moon didn't bother cleaning either of the girls' rooms. Unless it spilled out into the halls, she allowed them to live in whatever disarray they wanted. Dawn had left a trail of dirty socks and underwear from the upstairs bathroom to her own room, however, and rather than wait for her to come home from school, Moon intended to gather the clothes and dump them in the middle of her daughter's bed.

The sight of a large naked man with an erection so startled her she gasped.

Even as she did so, she recognized the image as a hologram. She let out a sigh of relief, then frowned. The hologram was frozen over the set. Moon shook her head, picked up the headset lying next to the holoproj unit, and slipped them on. "Run program," she said.

The image of the well-hung man came to life. Smiled at her. "Hey, baby. You look good. Good enough to eat."

The image took a step toward her.

"Tell me what you want."

"I'd like you to go fuck yourself."

The image froze for a moment. A voice said, "Unable to execute that command. Please try another."

"Freeze picture," Moon said.

The rampant man obeyed, still smiling.

Moon went to her daughter's bed and lifted the mattress. She knew she shouldn't be snooping around in Dawn's room, she wouldn't like the girls in her room, but this new discovery was a surprise and a worry.

Nothing under the mattress. She bent and looked under the bed.

Enough clutter there for a family of junkers. Shoes, old

potato chip canisters, drink cans, wadded socks. Amazing what a slob her child was.

There was a squarish plastic box with less dust on it than the other crap stashed under the bed. Moon pulled the box out and opened it.

There it was. An electronic dildo, with a built-in vibrator, clit massager and wireless caster control.

The device was simple enough. You plugged it into yourself, dialed in the desired size, and it expanded to fit and press. The sexual toy would be linked to the pornoproj, so that when the image touched you, the device would respond. You could lie back in bed and enjoy electronic sex without any risks.

Sweet Goddess. Dawn was twelve years old. How did she get something like this?

The com buzzed.

Moon shook her head again, put the toy back into its box, and carefully replaced it beneath the bed.

She padded down the hallway and downstairs, picked up the com in the kitchen on the fourth buzz. The com would have already told the caller she was home and would answer shortly. "Yes?"

It was Long. She had a shaky screen with his pix on it. From the angle, it looked as if he'd unplugged the minicam from his com unit and stuck it onto the dashboard of a car he was driving.

"Ah, hello."

"M. Moon. I'm in San Francisco, not far from the temple."

"That's good."

"Not really. Somebody tried to stop me from going inside. I assume they are interested in the package."

"Are you okay?"

He looked surprised to hear her ask. "Yeah, fine. They had a little traffic accident. But there are other people posted on the doors, guys with guns who aren't smiling a whole lot. I need to know if they are with the ones following me or if they belong to the temple.''

"I can call and find out.''

"Can you vox and TV-ID your person on the inside?''

"I-I think so. Why?''

"The guys following me might be able to swipe the temple's phone feed. I need to be sure whoever is giving us directions is on our side.''

Moon felt a lump in her throat and her belly fluttered. "I'll call. Your number . . . ?''

"Incoming is offnet at the moment. I don't want anybody tracing me. I'll call you back in ten minutes.''

"All right.''

She broke the connection and frowned at the phone. She didn't like this, not at all. Things were getting more complicated.

Better call and see if she could simplify them.

"We're sorry, we cannot complete your call at this time. Please check the code and retry.''

Moon nibbled at her lower lip. Carefully tapped the code into the com again.

"We're sorry, we cannot complete—''

She canceled the input. The third time, she used voxax mode, spoke the number aloud.

"We're sorry—''

There were probably a dozen good, logical reasons the call failed to go through. A relay station on the blink. An overload on the system somewhere, a computer glitch. Some idiot with a jackhammer fixing a sidewalk cut an underground cable. It happened.

But it seemed to be a sign that it would happen just now.

Still using the voxax, Moon said, "Com, connect me with Bretcher's Deli in San Francisco, California, U.S.A.''

Bretcher's was next door to the Temple, she used to eat there frequently when she'd been in her last months of study. The old man who ran the place had really liked her, said she reminded him of his second wife. She didn't recall the number but the com's routecomp would find it for her.

"Bretcher's Deli. Saul speaking."

"Hi, Sollie. This is Miranda Moon."

"Miranda! How's it going? Haven't seen you in a while. What, three, four years?"

"I've moved up to Portland, Sollie. Listen, I've been trying to call the Embrace and can't get through. Is somebody working on the road or phones or something?"

She didn't have visual—Sollie didn't like it in his business—but she could almost see him shrug. "Who can say? Nobody I see, although there are all kinds of big ugly golems walking up and down on the walk in the front. Looks like a convention of arm-breakers. The ladies owe somebody money?"

"I don't think so, Sollie. Listen, can you do me a favor? Send one of your boys up to see if they can find Lila Starshine, have her call me?"

"Sure, sweetie. No problem."

She gave him her number and thanked him, then discommed.

If Lila was there, she'd find a way to call. Until then, she'd just have to wait.

The Goddess must have decided her life was too smooth lately. She'd thrown a few wrinkles into her path, that was for sure.

It is evil that dies; good dies not.

—Mary Baker Eddy, *Footsteps of Truth*

13

WHEN HE HUNG up the phone, Green saw Loretta looking at him, one eyebrow raised. "Bad news?"

"Maybe."

She didn't say anything.

"The delivery man arrived at the temple in San Francisco like he was supposed to. The Catholic's—*our*—people said the two federal agents who were supposed to stop the courier and collect the package before he got inside screwed up and lost him. Nobody knows exactly where he is at the moment."

"That doesn't sound good."

Green nodded. "You right about that. The feds shut down the com lines to the Embrace of the Goddess Temple until they could get a scanner set up to record all the calls."

She didn't ask how the Catholic knew this, but took it for granted that he did know. "That doesn't sound too smart. The courier might call to tell them where he is and they'd miss it."

"No, it's actually pretty swift. If he gets a busy signal,

he'll call back, but if he gets in before they're set up to hear, *then* they'd miss him.''

"Ah. So what now?"

"The Jesuit's agents are monitoring the situation. Some of them are out looking, others are keeping track of what the feds know. In the meantime, all we can do is wait."

He looked at her. "I don't much like any of this, Loretta. It doesn't feel right."

"I imagine that's what Job said about his boils," she said. "But it was the Lord's will. He will guide you in this, Walter."

"I sure hope so."

Driving south toward San Jose, Long punched up Moon's number. He hoped she'd been able to get through to the temple; even so, if the guys chasing him were feds, things would start to get a little more tricky. They knew who he was and they knew who'd sent him. If they wanted what was in his packet bad enough, they'd have a tap on Moon's line by now, figuring he would call her or vice versa. So even if she had gotten through to the temple and her people, anything she told him had to be considered public information. He had an encryption leech on his com and he could back-walk it to her end to total the scramble but it was only a commercial unit. It would hold up against a kid hacker with a home computer, but a fed code cracker running one of the new wetlight chip mainframes could break his little Radio Shack unit faster than Long could quick-draw his revolver. If he and Moon set up a meeting without using some kind of one-time-only code a listener couldn't possibly know, the feds would be there waiting for him. If they were feds.

If, if, if.

Another problem was, since he and Moon didn't know much about each other they could use as a basis for a code, how to do it? She'd grown up in Montana but a fed would know that. He carried a .357 and they'd know that, too.

Did they know her uncle was a deputy in Butte? Or that his revolver had ivory grips? And even if they didn't, what good would that do him?

Hey, tell your priestess to meet me at the place where my gun stocks originally came from.

Where would that be? The zoo? Or the elephant grave-yard?

Or maybe: *Meet me at the place where your uncle worked.*

How many sheriff substations were there in the bay area? More than one.

Wait. The daughter, the one who'd gone out . . .

"Hello?"

"Moon. I'm going to send a scramble bounce to your com. Hold on a second."

He sent the code, waited for five seconds, then said, "Listen, we have to assume we are being overheard by somebody who can understand what we're saying. Did you get the information?"

"Not yet. The lines are blocked. I have a messenger hand-delivering my request. I expect a call back soon."

"All right. Here's the deal. You remember where your daughter went when I was there?"

"Yes."

"There's a place equivalent to that in San Francisco. Do you understand?"

"Yes."

"Can you convey that to your people here without saying it aloud? Some common experience?"

"I . . . I think so."

"Good. Tell them I'll meet them there in three hours."

"All . . . All right."

"I'll call you after I've made the delivery."

"Okay. Be careful. Somebody was here today looking for the . . . package. He lied about it being his."

"I'll be careful. Best you take precautions yourself. Dis-com."

He cut the connection, looked for a freeway exit. Probably they hadn't been on long enough to do a trace but they might have gotten a heading on the call and if so, he was about to be going the opposite way. He needed a new car, too. This one was on a list and they might already have the local cops looking for it.

He left the freeway and looked for a used-car dealership. He had chunks of money banked under a couple of pseudonyms. A couple of hundred noodle from one of those accounts would buy him a junker; anything with wheels that would run for a few days would do. After that, he would make his way to the San Francisco Museum of Science and Industry and hope that nobody had been following Moon's daughter when she went to OMSI with her boyfriend earlier in the day. He also had to hope that Moon could clue the location to her people without giving it away. She seemed bright; maybe this would work out after all.

Just ahead on the left was a used-car place. Long started looking for a place to hide the rental car so it wouldn't be found right away. There was a shopping mall a few blocks past the dealership, one with a big holoproj movie house in it. He pulled the Chevy into the lot and parked it between two pocket vans. There'd be cars parked here all day and probably some left all night. People who met in the movie and left together in one vehicle, night workers, like that. The best place to hide a grain of sand was on the beach. He got out, locked the car, removed the plastic license plates from the front and back. He dropped those into a Dumpster on the way to the used-car lot. By the time somebody got around to reporting the Chevy, having it towed and getting the serial number run, he ought to be long gone.

At least that was the plan.

He walked to the car lot, the package on his belt carefully hidden under his jacket.

•   •   •

Moon's com buzzed ten minutes after she talked to Long and she grabbed it. "Hello?"

"Miranda, it's Lila."

"Where are you calling from?"

"The deli. Something's wrong with our phones."

"Something's wrong with this one, too. Extra ears."

"Ah. I see."

"Listen, that thing I was sending down? There's been a complication. The temple is being watched."

"We know."

"My courier has a place to meet you. I can't say where but you remember that lecture we went to four years ago? The one where we met the big blond guy?"

"The one with the great glutes? He was a—"

"Don't say it!"

"All right. Go ahead."

"Remember where he worked?"

"Yeah."

"Well, if he'd been Einstein and working in the same kind of place, do you know where that would be?"

The blond had been a catalog researcher at the Museum of Natural History. It was a stretch.

"Lila?"

"I don't . . ."

"Or if he'd been Henry Ford?"

There was a pause. A scientist and an industrialist. Those were as narrow as she could get without giving it away. Even so, a sharp listener might figure it out, given enough time.

"Oh. Oh, I see. Yes, I think I know the place you're talking about."

"Have somebody there in three hours. Make sure they aren't followed and give them the code word we agreed on earlier. My courier will meet them."

"All right. Go with the Goddess, sister."

"And you, sister."

Moon cradled the com. Lila could send twenty people

out at once, wait a few minutes, and send out twenty more. Unless the watchers blanketed the temple, they couldn't follow them all. If she had gotten the clues, somebody would be at the museum to meet Long. After that, they could relax.

But she didn't feel relaxed at the moment. She wanted her children home, with the door locked. This whole situation was more than she needed to be responsible for, and it now felt very ugly.

"When Buttonhook gets back, I want you to cut off his balls and have them bronzed for my desk," Wentworth said.

Nguyen nodded. "All right."

"It was a joke," Wentworth said.

They were in the limo again, splashing through the hardening slush as the night's temperature dropped well below freezing. He didn't much feel like going to poke Thalia but she was on his to-do list and since he was paying for it, he might as well enjoy it. Besides, it would relieve some of his tensions. If he'd learned anything in his years in the power capital of the world, it was that when you couldn't do anything about something bothering you, it didn't pay to worry about it. It didn't help and you might as well leave it alone until you could fix it. Easier said than done, but he worked at it.

"Send in half a dozen of our West Coast ops. Buttonhook can still call the shots but I want it nailed down."

Nguyen nodded. "I'll do it."

"Give me an hour with Thalia, then pick me up."

Nguyen nodded again.

Wentworth smiled at the back of his driver's head. He was better than a dog, absolutely faithful and a helluva lot smarter and meaner. Nguyen was his wrist hawk; he would fly and put his talons into any target Wentworth wanted clawed. Faithful retainers like that were worth a lot. The family had always had such men and sometimes women.

They were necessary for those who guarded the republic. His father, when he'd been ambassador to Spain, had picked up a Basque driver who'd served him in that capacity for twenty years. Now the Basque's son drove his father's limo and the Basque was head of security for the family's computer company, of which the senior Wentworth was chairman of the board and CEO. If the old man asked him to, the Basque would still kill a man with his hands and then jump off a tall building when he was done. That was loyalty. Those were the kinds of servants upon whose backs empires had been built.

"Okay. I guess that covers things. Let's go see my dancer."

And Thalia? Well, she was the kind of servant upon whose bellies legions of bastards had been sired. Wrong-side-of-the-blanket sons who couldn't inherit but who also could be molded into razor-edged tools to serve the family.

His own first sexual experience had been in the arms of the young Cuban maid who worked in the family's summer home on the cape. Although young was a relative term. Juanita had been twenty-two and he'd been but fourteen. He'd paid her five hundred dollars, and while she had taken advantage of his ignorance regarding how much such sex should cost, it had been worth every penny. She had been his first but he had been at the end of a fair line for her favors; her experience had exhausted him in short order. Unlike his father, who had sired a bastard son from such a liaison with a Norwegian maid thirty years earlier, Wentworth's first romp hadn't produced anything other than ecstatic exhaustion.

He had finally hunted down and met his younger half-brother a few years back, without telling his father he knew of the man. John had a job running an import business owned by the family, and like Nguyen and the Basque, was grateful for the privilege. He was a simple square-head, big and happy and not too bright, but he loved the old man and would do anything for him. Amazing.

Wentworth was glad he got the family's name. And the power and prestige that went with it. He'd done okay on his own, with only a word from his father to help him along now and then, but it was expected that he would do well. He had gotten the name, and that carried certain responsibilities. His father, his grandfather, his great-grandfather, all had been advisers to presidents, had been ambassadors, captains of industry, men of stature. It was the Wentworth legacy. In a few more years when he was seasoned, he would take over the family businesses and the primary responsibilities for power brokering. Like his father, he would sit on the boards of major corporations, whisper into the ears of the movers and shakers, and be a somewhat shadowy kingmaker. He would find an old Harvard classmate who had languished in some law professorship or business school deanship and elevate him to the federal bench or maybe the Senate. He would oil the machinery that ran the world. That was his destiny.

But first, he had to go and screw the brains out of his exotic dancer. The Wentworths had a reputation to maintain in that arena, too. . . .

When [an] opponent pushes, the judo expert pulls.
The aikido expert turns.

—Oscar Ratti, Adele Westbrook, *Secrets of the Samurai*

14

IT TOOK MOON about five minutes to decide to call
the girls. They were both in class, on the evening schedule
this month, so their coms would be set to vibrate and not
buzz; nor could they talk to her until their classes were
done, but she left messages for them to call her as soon as
possible.

Dawn called first.

"What's up, Mama bird?"

"I want you to come straight home after school."

"Sure. Any particular reason?"

"It has to do with that thing we found."

"Oh. Okay."

"Be careful."

Ten minutes later, Alyssa called.

"You called?"

"Yes. Come straight home after school."

"Jeez, Mom, I can't, I'm supposed to go to the library
to meet—"

"It's not open for discussion, Lissy."

"What's wrong?"

"I want you here until a certain package is delivered."

"Huh? I thought that would be done by now."

"There was a problem."

"Well, it doesn't have anything to do with me—"

"First bus home," Moon said, her voice tight.

There was a short stretch of silence. Moon could almost hear the anger bubbling in her daughter. When she spoke, the words carried it clearly: "All right!"

When she discommed, Moon felt better. If her children were angry with her, she could live with that. It wouldn't be the first time. But if something happened to them . . .

She felt restless, she wanted to get up and move, but pacing around the temple wouldn't help anything and she didn't want to go outside into the cold evening.

The girls didn't understand how she felt about them. Oh, she was pretty sure they knew she loved them, whatever that meant to children their age. But they didn't know about the nights she'd lain awake worrying if she had done the right thing punishing them for some minor grief; or the fear she'd felt when they caught a virus and ran a fever; or the dread that somehow she had utterly failed them as a parent. They didn't want to know. When she'd tried to tell them she wasn't perfect, that she had doubts and fears, they shut her down. Parents are supposed to be all-wise, all-knowing, slotted neatly in their niches so children didn't have to think about them. There's Mom. She does Mom things. She doesn't come awake in a cold sweat from a nightmare in which something has menaced her offspring.

Moon wandered into the kitchen, opened the fridge, looked for something to eat. Nothing appealed.

It really was a two-person job, raising kids. Not that she wanted to be married, held in thrall to somebody like Martin. There was a man who had all the features of a decent human being. Attractive, though you really couldn't judge by that; studying to become a minister, a man of God. But he never quite made it into the New Testament, at least not while she had known him. Being beaten by someone who used the Bible as a justification had soured her on her husband and on any religion that would allow him to hit her. Yeah, she missed the intimacy, the companionship, the sex. But not the other.

She shut the fridge. Ran her hands through her hair. Shook her head, as if doing so would rid her of the bad memories. It didn't.

So there they had been, she and Martin and Alyssa, in Loveland, Colorado. They'd gotten married just before Alyssa was born. Moon—still using the name Lea Quinn back then—dropped out of the Colorado Bible Institute to take care of the baby while Martin went on to get his divinity degree. After he'd been confirmed and offered a job as an assistant pastor in the Holy Flock Church in nearby Boulder, she had thought things would change.

They changed, all right. Martin discovered amphetamines. Mixed with the alcohol he already enjoyed too well, it became a nasty combination. He became like a pet tiger—purring and playful one second, ready to claw you bloody the next.

Dawn was born in 2018. When she was four, Martin came home from church in a rage over something one of his parishioners said. He started drinking scotch, used it to wash down three Dexedrine caplets. Dawn said something else that set him off. He grabbed her from where she sat eating supper, jerked her by one arm hard enough to snap a forearm bone, and shook her, yelling in her face.

It was the final straw. Moon exploded into a rage of her own. She picked up a kitchen chair and smashed Martin until he was unconscious.

By the time he awoke, she and the children were gone.

He'd tried to get them back. Sent flowers, profuse apologies, promises that it would never happen again. She'd heard it all before. And as long as it had been only her he'd abused, she had put up with it. She'd thought the flaw was in her. If she'd been better, he wouldn't be so angry.

The Bible backed him up, after all. The man was the master of the house, his word was law.

But the look in her daughter's eyes when Martin snatched her up and snapped the thin bone in her arm was enough to offset all the holy books ever written. There ought to be a commandment that said, ''Thou shalt not molest thy wife and children.'' And there wasn't.

Supposedly, Martin had undergone treatment for his addictions. Supposedly, he was a different man now, repentant, doing good work in his church, clean and sober. But even if that were so, even if she could forgive him the awful violence he had perpetrated upon her and her children, forgiveness was not trust. She would never be able to see his face without remembering Dawn's terrified expression as her father shook her, oblivious to the girl's screams, to her sister's screams, to his wife's screams.

Moon sighed. *Calm down. It was eight years ago. It shouldn't have the power to enrage after all this time.*

But it still did. The wound had scabbed over but not healed under the crust. It was the old war, the brain versus the heart. Her mind gave her the reasons for Martin's weakness, and knew it was the drugs that altered him from the mild and loving man she'd lost her virginity to into the monster he became. She could understand that, intellectually. But emotionally, her bond with her children had been and still was too strong to allow her to feel anything but anger at what he had done.

Some crimes get you a life sentence, no matter how understanding your judge and jury might want to be.

Martin had earned his incarceration in the prison of her soul and there was no parole earned for whatever he had done or become since he'd put himself there. As much as Moon did not want that anger within her, it was there, and she'd had to learn to live with it. Mostly by not thinking about it. But at a time like this, when she was afraid for her daughters, it all came back to her.

She hoped with a passion that Long would be able to rid

them of the package today, so they could get back to their normal lives. Once that was gone, they would be free again.

The new San Francisco Museum of Science and Industry perched on the shore of small inlet of the bay, a finger of water that curled around the place almost like a big C. The rebuilt BART had a stop there, and there were a huge parking lot and winding tree-lined walks, so people could park and enjoy a stroll around the place.

Long arrived at the museum grounds more than an hour ahead of his meeting time. He walked around, looking as much like a tourist as he could, staring out over the white-capped gray water, smiling at other pedestrians who risked the stiff, chilly breeze off the bay. He was just ahead of a horde of primary school children being shepherded by a teacher and a couple of parent volunteers.

He stopped to look at an old prototype of a seawater engine, a tall and spindly power generator that produced electricity from the temperature differences between the surface and the depths dozens of meters below. The children were more interested in a vertical wind generator that spun and creaked in the fresh air currents. The device looked as if a pair of parentheses had stuck their points into a pole.

The children oohed and ahhed and then were herded along. He let them swirl around him and continued to look at the sea engine after they had grown bored and moved on.

He didn't know what his contact would look like but they would have the code he needed to transfer the package and they would know him by description. At least he hoped they would. The wind chill off the water might freeze his ears off if he had to spend too much time wandering around outside. He planned to cycle back to the front entrance every so often, but not to go inside. He didn't intend to bottle himself up any more than he had to, and as it was, there was just the one road in and out of the grounds, unless he wanted to try to swipe a boat and leave that way.

Because it was windy, he had zipped his jacket up, both to keep warm and to keep his holstered gun from showing.

"Hold it!" somebody behind him said.

Long turned and found himself facing the man who'd followed him from the Portland airport. The man had a suppressed big-bore pistol pointed at Long's chest. He held it one-handed, in his right hand.

The children were behind him and Long didn't want the man to start shooting; one of them might be hit. Looked as if the game were over and he'd lost. Well, there was nothing to be done. He'd been wool gathering, not paying enough attention, and they'd sneaked in on him. He hadn't expected it, there was no reason to, but he was pissed at himself nonetheless. There must be a leak at the temple. Somebody had given him up. He had thought about it, but he should have given the possibility more weight.

He moved his hands away from his body, palms out and fingers spread, to show he wasn't a threat.

"You got me," he said.

The guy in the windbreaker smiled. "I sure as hell do," he said.

Then he shot him.

The bullet hit just to the left of his sternum. If he hadn't zipped the jacket up, he'd have taken the round in the heart. It felt as if he'd been thumped in the chest with a bowling ball, but the spidersilk held—he *saw* the deformed slug pop back out through the hole in the leather and bounce on the sidewalk. There was some noise but not much; the suppressor stoppered most of it.

Long moved. He shoved off to his right, hard, forcing the shooter to swing his gun hand across his body. At the same time, he pulled his jacket hem up with his left hand and made the draw with his right, a move he'd practiced hundreds of times against the one instance it would be needed.

The shooter capped off another round. It hit Long low,

on the left side, got mostly jacket and only a little of him, just above the hip bone.

Long had his Smith out. He swung it up and squeezed the trigger.

The shooter was also wearing armor under his windbreaker, enough to stop Long's bullet, but it startled him to get tagged and he lurched backward.

Long's second round hit the shooter just below his hairline. It took the back of his head off when it exited. He saw the blood and brain and bone spray in a thick, slurried mist.

The sound of Long's weapon going off set the children to screaming.

Long dropped into a running crouch, gun hand leading, and did a fast 360, looking for the others. There would be more than one.

He spotted two of them angling across the grassy grounds, about a hundred meters away. So, Windbreaker had wanted to take him alone. He'd made his backup stay out of play. Not smart.

He didn't want to do any more shooting and he didn't want the men after him to do so, either. If they got close enough, they could aim for his head as easy as he could, and he wouldn't have the advantage of surprise or firepower on his side.

But the two running toward him were holding their weapons down, pointed at the ground, and he thanked whatever gods there were that the pair maybe didn't want to hit a six-year-old on a class outing.

Long turned, angled away from the two incoming men, and leaped over a short hedge designed to keep people off the lawn. He took three or four fast steps and a sharp dogleg to his left. Part of an old Atlas booster blocked his view of the two runners and he stayed in its cover and sprinted in a straight line as fast as he could.

One down, two behind him. Probably others, he had to assume that. They'd be blocking the road or covering his

car, at the very least, so there wasn't any point in trying to
reach his beat-up vehicle.

He circled around a display of electric trolley cars and
cut back toward the parking lot. They would be watching
his car, but—would they be watching their own transportation? If they were still using the van that Windbreaker
had been in earlier, it would be easy enough to spot. The
fresh damage to it would make it stand out. If they weren't,
he was probably screwed, unless somebody had left a key
or a card in their car for him to borrow. And he wouldn't
have much time to look for that. He knew what Windbreaker's car looked like, as well as the package van. If he spotted either of them, he would try for those. If not, he'd see
what he could see.

His two pursuers lost contact; he couldn't see them, anyway, but they'd be connected to each other and any other
members of the team by short-hop radio. He couldn't give
them time to get anything set up. The only way out of this
was to be past them before they could gather their wits.

Easier said than done.

He ran. Had time for a strange and only remotely connected thought: He was going to run out of spare barrels
at this rate. . . .

Wentworth considered strangling the woman. Not that
she had said anything; not even a hint of a smile had played
on her face, but she had been witness to his . . . failure to
perform.

It wasn't failure in the sense that many men would consider it so. The first session had gone well, they had
stripped and grabbed each other and he had fucked her
hard, gushed into her, discharged quite happily.

But after fifteen minutes had passed, he hadn't been able
to summon any more desire. She had tried to rouse him,
with her mouth and hands, but nothing happened. He covered it by telling her he didn't have time for anything else,
he had business, and he'd shoved her away and hurried to

the shower to clean up, but he knew *she* knew.

She was a beautiful and sexually talented woman who would do whatever he wanted and he hadn't been able to make himself hard again.

That had never happened to him before.

Sure, the days when he could come five or six times in one night were long past, but he'd never had trouble getting an erection even if he hadn't been able to climax a third or even a second time.

Tonight, however, he had remained limp.

It worried him. Was it some aberration? Or was it the beginning of something?

He dressed quickly, eager to leave. He was tired, he'd had a busy week, he had much on his mind. Such things were distracting. He would see to his rest, make sure he caught up on his vitamins, and work at the gym. That would take care of it. It was just a fluke. He was a young man, vital. Stronger than he'd been at twenty.

"When will I see you again?"

"I'll call," he said as he left the room.

Nguyen waited in the hall, leaning against the wall. When he saw Wentworth, he pushed away and came to a kind of parade rest.

"Let's go," Wentworth said.

Nguyen nodded once, a choppy, military bow. "We got a call from the West Coast," he said.

"And . . . ?"

"Buttonhook ran the courier down. He tried to take him, they were at the Museum of Science and Industry. Made his team wait while he cowboyed it on his own."

Wentworth shook his head. "Grandstand play. What happened?"

"Buttonhook shot the guy, twice. He must have been wearing protection. He shook off the hits, then gave Buttonhook two back. One stopped on the body armor. He put the second right between the eyes, took the back of Buttonhook's head off."

"Shit."

Nguyen didn't speak to that.

"What else?"

"They lost him."

Shit!

When an elephant falls, do not place yourself under
him to hold him up. . . .

—Jean Herbert, *Introduction to Asia*

15

"HE'S KILLING PEOPLE," the Catholic said.

"What? Who?" Green wasn't sure he'd heard the man
right.

"The feds tried to capture the courier. Actually, according to my sources, they shot first and apparently didn't plan
to ask any questions. Some hero opened up on him with a
gun while they were in the middle of a group of school-
children at a museum in San Francisco."

"Dear Lord."

"Yes. The fed's haste cost him. The courier fired back.
Blew the man's head off." There was a brief pause. "None
of the children were hurt. And this courier is more adept
than the feds, apparently."

"Who isn't?" Green said, stalling while he tried to figure
out what this all meant. "Have the local police been called
in?"

"No. The feds are keeping it to themselves. The dead
man has been . . . removed and the whole thing brushed under the carpet of national security."

The Catholic's voice on the phone was calm, but Green could sense the undercurrent of excitement. Even though the opponent in his game was currently ahead, the Jesuit in the man enjoyed playing almost as much as he did winning. That was the thing about intellectuals, they could rationalize anything. Just as easy for them to play Devil's advocate as it was to speak for God.

"I'll be back on the coast tomorrow," Green said.

"Good. Meanwhile, I think we should perhaps take a more active role in this. If the feds are willing to go to these extremes, we can't do any less."

"Whatever you feel is necessary."

They broke the connection. Green stared at the phone.

From the kitchen, Loretta said, "That the Catholic again?"

"Yeah. The feds tried to take the courier out. He got one of them instead."

"Serves them right."

"A man was killed, Loretta."

"A man who tried to shoot another man first?" she said. She'd been listening to every word, like she usually did. "Eye for an eye, tooth for a tooth."

Green shook his head. This was all beyond what he ever imagined he would be doing in defense of the faith. Guns, federal agents, mysterious devices that might rock the foundations of Christianity. He had come a long way from the First Baptist in Tuscaloosa.

Too far, maybe.

"Walter?"

He sighed. "I wonder what my daddy would have said about all this?"

"You know exactly what he would have said. The Lord works in mysterious ways and His laborers ought not to expect an easy walk in His service. He never promised there'd be angels mowing a path for you through the wilderness."

He nodded. "You're right. We weren't put on this Earth

to loll about. Whatever it takes is whatever it takes. I just
wish I could see a little further down the road sometimes.''

"Don't we all? You just remember who you are and why
you're here and you'll be fine. You always try do the right
thing, that's the important thing.''

"I'll be going back to California tomorrow. I don't want
to get too far away from the Catholic for too long on this.
He's got his own ends to serve.''

"Of course," she said.

He envied her her certainty. With Loretta, doubt was
always a six-day hike away. It didn't dog her heels, nipping
at them like it did his.

Getting away from the museum had been anticlimactic.
Long spotted Windbreaker's car—obviously made of
sterner stuff than the delivery van it had plowed into back
at the temple—parked in the lot. It wasn't locked, that was
good, but the vehicle didn't have the keys in it. Then again,
neither did it have an armored ignition. Long set himself
and kicked the dashboard until it split. Managed to trip the
air bag with his third or fourth shot, which expanded, then
deflated and hung from the steering wheel like a used silver
condom. He ripped the cracked plastic dash apart, found
the electronics, short-circuited the key switch with a piece
of wire from the radio, and started the car.

He drove with his left hand, his S&W held low and ready
in his right, but he must have been ahead of them. Nobody
tried to stop him as he pulled from the lot onto the street.
Nobody tried to follow him, either on foot or in another
car.

When he was five klicks away, he holstered his gun and
breathed a little slower.

Well. Now what?

First thing was, he'd have to get rid of the car. Sooner
or later somebody would miss it and if they had official
clout, they'd put out a description of it. Him, too, maybe.

Who *were* these guys? If they were some kind of cops—

and they had to be—what would that mean? Was he going to go down for shooting one of their agents? Or were they just going to pot him on sight, like Windbreaker had tried at the museum? That was a big worry, that he might have to spend the rest of his life on the run, however much life he had left. Serious trouble.

Maybe he should hole up somewhere and consider giving them the package.

He hated it that the thought came up, but come up it did. He had a gut feeling that all this could be made to go away if he arranged to give them what they were willing to kill for. Maybe they'd take him out anyway, but maybe not. He could structure it, cover his ass, lawyers, press, whatever. Secret agencies didn't like a lot of light shined on them, maybe he could make it bright enough so they'd scuttle back to their own hole once they got what they wanted.

Then again, maybe not. A man had to draw the line somewhere. Long didn't have much he could be really proud of except one thing: He always did his job. The medals in the war? They didn't mean he was a hero, they meant the Marines had acknowledged he had done what they'd paid him to do. And he'd never lost a package, never failed to take it where the client wanted. It wasn't much, but it was what he had, what he did. What he was. If he rolled over and gave his package up, he might survive, but the cost . . . ?

No. Fuck 'em. If he died, then it would be doing what he did. A man had to look at himself in the mirror.

Well. He grinned at the rearview mirror in his stolen car. For as long as he *could* look at himself.

His instinct was to get out of this town, to go home. How he was going to get there might be iffy. Commercial air flights were out, as were bullet trains and jet boats. He could get to his money, safely stashed under other names. Rent a car, maybe, or charter a private plane under a pseudonym.

What would he do when he got there? He could give the

package back to Moon and tell her it was more trouble than
it was worth, although he didn't see himself doing that. He
could ask her if she still wanted it delivered, given the
problems. There wasn't a ticking clock so he wasn't late
but he had certainly hit a potholed detour.

Hell, he could find a quiet spot and pop the seal on the
carrier and see what all the fuss was about, too. That was
another powerful urge, but he he didn't think he would give
in to it. Not yet, anyhow. Maybe if he took a bullet and
was going to check out, he'd do it. Just to know.

He grinned again. Lots of options. For now.

Dawn made it home first and Moon fretted until Alyssa
arrived twenty minutes later. She had missed the first bus,
she said. Probably on purpose. Another time, Moon would
have nailed her for it, but not today. That they were both
here safe was all that mattered.

"Go pack a bag," she said to the girls. "Enough for a
day or two."

"Where are we going?" Dawn asked.

"I don't know. Maybe a little scenic trip up the gorge,
maybe we'll run down to Eugene and visit the ashram."

"In the car?"

"Yes, in the car."

Alyssa brightened, lost her petulant look. Said, "Can I
drive?"

"Maybe. We'll see."

They seldom used the car, a sturdy but somewhat beat-
up Mazda that spent most of its time stored in a garage
eight blocks away. What with the price of fuel and the
license fees, it was cheaper and easier to take pubtrans or
a bike just about anywhere. But if you wanted to get off
the beaten track, the car was nice. When the girls had been
a few years younger, they had liked camping and hiking.
All the gear was in the Mazda's trunk: the old rip-stop
flimsytent, the sleeping bags, the little bottle-fed stove and
mantle lamp. They hadn't used them for a while, not since

they'd gone to the Goddess Gathering in Idaho last year.
Probably had mold growing on them by now.

"Is everything okay, Mom?" Dawn asked.

"I think so. The courier had some problems."

Alyssa said, "Is he okay? He was kinda cute. Nice
buns."

Moon stared at her daughter.

"Well, he was. You noticed, I saw you."

Moon shook her head. She wasn't ready to be Alyssa's
friend yet, not to have this kind of discussion, certainly.

"Just go get packed. We'll get something to eat along
the way."

The girls hurried off to their rooms and Moon went to
her own room. Maybe she was being paranoid. Then again,
Long had definitely been worried the last time she'd talked
to him and she should have heard from Lila Starshine by
now, had he been able to meet her and deliver the package.
Maybe she was turning into an old lady, seeing things under
her bed, but when it came to her kids, she wasn't going to
take the chance. If it were nothing, then they'd get a little
day trip out of it and no harm done. If there *were* any
dangers lurking, maybe it would be better to be elsewhere
if they came to call. Better safe than sorry. That wasn't the
Embrace's official policy, to duck and cover, but Alyssa
and Dawn weren't the Embrace's children, they were hers.
They came first. Always.

Nguyen stood stoically in a modified parade rest next to
the couch while Wentworth sat in his horsehide chair and
fumed. This whole incident with Buttonhook and this ex-
Marine courier was bad for business. Fortunately, he had a
big enough hammer to squash the immediate problem of it
going public. The San Francisco cops had been taken out
of the equation; the local media hadn't gotten anything,
since the eyewitnesses had been spirited away by Buttonhook's team and cajoled or threatened to secrecy. Nobody
had gotten a vidcam on the incident. The blanket had a few

holes in it and eventually the heat might leak out, but it would do for now.

The big problem was that the mission had failed, and while that shouldn't have anything to do with the validity of it in the first place, it did. Wentworth was now convinced that Gray's discovery was more important than he'd first assumed.

He looked at the computer image over his desk. It was the bio of the courier. Huey Long. Somebody had a warped sense of humor—or maybe, since the man's parents lived in Louisiana, some kind of admiration for the crooked politician whose name the courier wore.

To Nguyen, Wentworth said, "All right. You have the stats on this guy. Go out there and collect him. And whatever he's carrying that's worth a dead agent. Get what we need and get rid of what we don't."

Nguyen smiled his snake-lipped smile. He loved going into the field. "I'll leave on the next flight out."

"No. Go out to the Air Force base. I'll have them scramble a jet for you. San Francisco, right?"

"No. Portland."

"But our guy is in the Bay Area."

"Maybe now. Not for long. I wouldn't be."

"Fine. Whatever."

He waved and Nguyen left. He'd find the courier, Wentworth didn't doubt it for a second. And that would be the end of this little problem.

He leaned back in the chair and allowed the machineries to work on him. It didn't help much, he was still tense. A bad week, coming off a not-so-great month before. He couldn't let this one little bit of business get him down, he had too much work to do.

He grinned and shook his head. Maybe he should have gone to collect the courier himself. He'd been a pretty good field man in his day. And there was nothing like a waltz with Death to stoke the old fires, get the blood coursing, to get your edge honed. He had danced with the Reaper a few times, gone balls out and managed to walk away.

He relaxed a little into the chair. First time he risked his life, he'd been pushing seventeen. In New York, on a roof-top.

It was the last day of March, a windy spring day, as Ford pounded up the stairs to the roof access, two steps behind Jimmy Thornton.

The armed building guard was two flights down, scream-ing at them.

"Stop, you fuckers! Stop or I will shoot your asses!"

Sixteen-year-old Jimmy hit the metal-sheathed door, cursed, managed to get the latch undone. He shoved the thing open. It slammed against the backstop.

The roof was flat, covered with a thick layer of old tar. The six-story apartment building in Queens was one of half a dozen the same height in the immediate area. Ford and Jimmy had picked it at random, gone inside, and started spraying glitter-paint graffiti on the walls. They hadn't seen the guard but he'd shown up waving a pistol and they'd run.

Ford's old man would shit if he had to bail him out again, only a week after the last time.

"Fuck!" Jimmy said. "Now what?"

The nearest building to the one they were on was fifteen feet away. They could probably make the jump, but if they missed, they'd fall six floors to the alley. Not a real thrilling thought.

Ford looked around. Somebody was building what looked like a greenhouse on the roof. There were boards, plastic sheeting, tools. And a big extension ladder.

"Grab one of those two-by-fours, a short one!" Ford ordered. "Hurry!"

Jimmy wasn't a leader. He went. Came back with a six-foot length of wood. Ford, meanwhile, had found a hammer and a couple of long nails. "What are you gonna do, smack the guard with it?"

''No, stupid. Shut the door!''

Inside the angled kiosk, the guard continued to bellow. ''You fuckers! I'll kill you!'' He was dark, not too old, Indian or Pakistani or something, he had an accent Ford couldn't place. He wore a white turban and a uniform, had a long beard. And he was almost to the door.

Jimmy shoved the door shut and Ford ran to it, wedged the two-by-four under the knob and jammed the other end of the board into the roof tar. He set one of the nails against the base of the wooden slat and hammered it into the roof. Started a second nail.

Just in time. The wog guard hit the door.

The board vibrated and bowed slightly but held, and the door stayed shut.

''Fuck! Fuck you! You are dead, you understand? Dead! Dead!''

Unseen, the guard slammed into the door again. And again.

''It ain't gonna hold forever! How will we get down?''

''The ladder. Help me get it across the gap.''

The two teenagers hurried to where the ladder stood on one edge. It had a rope they could pull to extend it, and Ford hustled to extrude the ladder to its full length.

''Fuckers! Fuckers!'' the guard's muffled rage filtered through the door as he continued to slam his shoulder into it.

''Come on, let's move!''

They half dragged, half carried the heavy ladder to the edge of the roof, managed to get it over the parapet. The roof next to theirs was maybe a foot lower.

''Okay,'' Ford said. ''On three, we shove it across. Don't let go of the end.''

They backed up, caught the opposite end of the ladder, pushed it. Once it was halfway, it started to tilt downward.

''Hard, go, push!''

The opposite end of the ladder thunked down on the roof of the building next door.

"Little fucking bastards! I spit on your mothers!"

"Go, go!"

Jimmy hopped onto the parapet. Looked down, then at Ford. "Christ, man, I don't know about this!"

"Look, that raghead is gonna come through the door any second! If you won't go, get the hell out of my way!"

Without waiting, Ford hoisted himself up on the parapet. He put one foot on the nearest round wooden rung, then stepped out and onto the next rung. "Hey, it's no sweat. Just take it slow and steady!" He walked across the drop, concentrated on the rounded rungs. He was pumped and excited, flying on natural speed, but there came a moment halfway across when he knew that if he fell, he would die. Poof, end of story, *adios*, Fordy boy, and give my best to the Devil.

The fear blossomed like a mushroom cloud and threatened to overwhelm him, to choke him, to topple him from the ladder and into the air.

No. He fought it, beat it, hurried the last few feet and jumped. Hit the roof, rolled, came up laughing. "Come on, man, it's easy!"

Jimmy looked at the door where the guard continued to bang, then started out on the ladder.

He was halfway across and grinning when the guard's efforts paid off. The two-by-four prop popped from the handle and the door flew open. The guard tumbled out of the kiosk and fell. The thump he made hitting the roof was enough to get Jimmy's attention. Jimmy turned to look behind him—

And missed the next rung. He fell.

But he was okay, because he fell forward, onto the ladder, his hands within centimeters of the roof's edge. He could crawl the rest of the way in a couple of seconds. He pushed himself up to his hands and knees and started forward—

As the guard reached the parapet and grabbed the ladder. "Stop, I say, you must stop!"

He must have moved the ladder a little. Not much, because Ford never remembered seeing it move, but Jimmy put his hand down on empty space instead of the ladder. And this time when he fell, he twisted a little. His left shoulder hit the ladder's upright and he bounced, rolled to his left, off the ladder and into the warm spring air.

He screamed all the way down.

The guard stared over the edge, stunned.

Ford Wentworth turned and ran for all he was worth.

He had never felt so alive.

In his office, the chair was beginning to win the battle against his stiff back. Wentworth shook his head at the memory. Too bad, Jimmy. Better you than me.

Better you than me.

Fear is the first time you can't get it up twice.
Terror is the second time you can't get it up once.

—Anonymous

16

LONG LEANED BACK in the Honda Raptor's cushioned leatherette seat and watched northern California zip below him. The Honda was an eight-passenger double-engine prop job that would take him from San Francisco to Portland in something just under three hours, according to the pilot. It cost a whole lot more than flying commercial, but given his current situation, cost was the least of his worries. He could understand the appeal of being rich when it came to things like being ferried around in a private plane. He'd never particularly cared about having money, but certainly it had its uses. Like now.

There was a small bar built into the Honda, with a little cooler and several kinds of wine, beer, and liquor. Probably was some smoke or other semilegal substances tucked away somewhere, too. But until this was sorted out, he wouldn't be chemically altering his consciousness in any way that might slow him down, mentally or physically. Back in Cuba before he'd been wounded, he'd known guys or gals who'd go out on patrol, stop a couple hundred meters into the woods or a cane field, then plop down to toke or pop their favorite recreational chem. They'd sit stoned for a couple of hours, enjoying the high. Or sometimes couples would suck squirts of HnH—Hot 'n' Happy—and spend the time fucking each other's brains out. After a while, the chemmers would hoof back to base. *Geez, we looked all over the place, Sarge, didn't see nuthin'.*

The idea of being so blasted on smoke or happy or skin poppers that ol' Pablo could sneak up on you and lop your head off with a big cane knife didn't appeal to Long. He was pretty sure the Marines had lost a few troops that way. It wasn't a survival characteristic.

If whoever was after his package wanted him, they were going to have to take him down cold sober.

" 'Bout another hour," the pilot called back to him. The passenger cabin was cordoned off from the control area, but the barrier was no more than a piece of thick cloth, strung from a wire like an old shower curtain.

"Thanks," Long said.

So he had an hour to worry about what he was going to do when he got back to Portland. He had a couple of ideas but was going to have to proceed carefully. He wouldn't be able to risk using his own car and he wouldn't be able to go home, at least not directly. He lived in Old Beaverton, on a quiet gated street of sixty-year-old homes. The high concrete razor-wire-topped walls and electric gates kept all but the residents and the most athletic burglars out of The Village, whose housing was a blend of single-family dwellings, linked condos, and quadraplex apartments. There were shops and markets an easy walk away outside the gates, and the sound-muffling walls and sculpted hillocks next to them kept most of the traffic noise from Murray's eight lanes out. A lot of the residents were retired; there were few families with small children, and while it wasn't a rich man's neighborhood, neither was it a place the poor could afford to live. If he used his keycard to get in past the gates, a computer would know it and so would anybody who could get access to the gatecomp.

He could go over a wall after dark and sneak through some backyards, if he was careful to avoid the ones with dogs. The locks on his house were mechanical and not run by the house computer, and the alarm system wasn't hard-wired to a monitoring computer—it called for help only if there was a breach, and he could disarm it without anybody knowing. Unless they had watchers surrounding the house, he could get in, if he was careful.

And if he didn't get spotted skulking around by The Vigilante.

Long smiled.

The Vigilante was one of his neighbors, a seventy-five-year-old man who lived alone, save for his dog, a big malamute. His wife had died a couple of years back and his kids all lived out of state. Every evening, usually around midnight, The Vigilante walked the dog and took stock of the neighborhood. Long himself was a night person and prone to walk off his insomnia, and on those nights when he strolled down to the park or up past the primary school, he'd always seen The Vigilante. They had a nodding acquaintance. A couple of times they'd passed each other on the bridge over the duck pond at the park. The lighting was pretty good there and Long had gotten a fair look at the older man. He carried a waterproof yellow plastic diver's flashlight in one hand, a small and powerful lamp that could cast a bright fifty-meter beam, though he usually kept it turned off. Though Long had never seen it, he was pretty sure the man also had a weapon of some kind on his right hip. In cool weather, The Vigilante wore a coat or jacket and even in the summer, a vest or shirt with the tails out, hiding his belt. Could be a gun or a gas canister or maybe a prod. He was a self-appointed watchman, Long had decided, who went on his nightly patrol to protect his streets. A rainy night a year or so back, a couple of kids had hopped the fence and broken into the neighborhood club-house. The cops had arrived and captured the would-be thieves just as Long happened to pass the park. The Vigilante had been standing there under a golf umbrella with his big dog, watching. Long found out from the cops that the old man had spotted the kids and commed it in. It must have made his year.

Long wondered how many neighborhoods had men like The Vigilante, walking the streets late at night, watching, protecting, serving without glory or recompense. Probably more than a few.

No doubt anybody sneaking around and watching Long's house would find him- or herself being scoped by The Vigilante pretty quick. Could make for an interesting turf battle. It would make a nasty report if a sub rosa federal op waved a gun at the wrong time and got cooked for his trouble by somebody's great-grandfather out walking his dog. . . .

Well. That wasn't high on Long's list of worries right now, either.

One thing at a time.

One of her flock had a house on the beach and Moon decided to go there. She had a standing invitation to use the place in the off season, and this was as off as it got. With the air temperature just above freezing and a wet, stiff wind driving the chill factor lower, it didn't make for crowds out walking on the beach. Moon had the entry codes—she'd held a couple of retreats there with the owner's blessing, though she'd never taken the girls.

Or, in this case, been taken by the girls. Alyssa drove, an experience that Moon was sure added gray to her hair at five times the normal rate. At least that.

They were in the hilly section of the Sunset Highway, climbing in the Coast Range where the road had narrowed to four lanes and no divider. As the Mazda chugged up the grade, Alyssa allowed it to drift over the yellow center line.

A big truck approached from the opposite direction.

"Honey, you might want to edge over this way a little,"

Moon said. She tried to keep her voice light and relaxed, but there was panic behind the words. Her right hand lay on the door's armrest, though rest wasn't part of the equation. Her fingers were white from the power of her grip, and she had her right foot pressed so hard against an imaginary brake she thought the floor might give way.

Alyssa, as stiff as if she were covered in plaster, jerked the wheel to the right and lurched the car across two lanes and onto the road's shoulder, which, fortunately, was paved at this spot.

"Hey, feekbrain! What are you doing?" Dawn yelled from the backseat. She'd been listening to music over the plug-in headset and not paying attention, and the sudden turn had banged her head against the window.

Alyssa ignored her sister and compensated, wheeled the Mazda back toward the middle of the road, where she straddled the dotted lane line. Fortunately, there wasn't any traffic on their side of the highway.

"Relax, baby, you're doing fine."

Alyssa hunched over the wheel, still stiff as an arthritic robot, her own fingers bloodlessly white from their clamped grip. If she concentrated any harder, she was apt to blow an artery.

For her part, Moon would rather do a thousand sit-ups than ride two minutes as a passenger while her daughter drove. How did parents get through this kind of thing? How could they smile and pretend everything was okay when what they had to feel was utter, stark terror? When teaching a child to drive, patience was not only a virtue, it was a necessity.

Not much longer now. With any luck—maybe with a lot of luck—they'd be at the beach in less than an hour.

The car drifted to the right, then back to the left before it stabilized in the left lane.

"Remember what I told you, sweetie. If you look at the hood and see that little ornament in the center, it should be lined up with the lane lines, okay?"

"Okay," Alyssa said. She didn't look at Moon but continued her determined stare over the wheel.

Goddess, give me strength!

In the backseat, Dawn's head bobbed up and down to the beat of the music. It was so loud it leaked from the earphones and into the front seat, where Moon had to pretend to ignore the thumping noise. What an awful racket, all those electronic instruments and heavy primal rhythms. These kids today.

She grinned in spite of her fear. Never thought she'd ever hear herself think that. So far, she'd been able to keep from saying it aloud to the girls, but if she wasn't careful, it was going to slip out. And when that happened, she knew the next time she passed a mirror, she would see her mother looking out of it and smiling in victory.

None of this was addressing the thing that really bothered her, the courier and his problems, plus the guy who had come poking around the temple. But there wasn't anything she could do about that right at this moment, and she *was* taking the girls to a safer place. One thing at a time.

"Something to drink, Reverend?"

Green smiled at the cabin attendant, a pretty young woman who might be twenty-five. The rumble of the Boeing wide-body cruising along several kilometers up had lulled him back into a half doze. He was one of a dozen passengers in the first-class section. "No, thank you. How far out are we?"

"We should be arriving in LAX airspace within the hour."

"Thanks."

She went to attend to the two Hollywood people behind him. Green looked through the window at the landscape, cold and wintry. Must be Arizona, maybe New Mexico. He'd caught the shuttle from Alabama to New Orleans, switched to the bigger jet there, managed to get a little sleep as they flew over Texas. The drone of the plane's engines coupled with the babble from the Hollywood people had put him out. The Hollywood people—a writer and a producer, as near as he could tell from their overloud conversation—had spent the taxi and liftoff talking about a movie deal they were putting together. Once the flying auditorium had lumbered into the air—he never quite trusted something big enough to carry almost five hundred people across the sky to manage that, to actually *fly*—he'd drifted into slumber listening to them earnestly and obscenely discuss "gross points" this and "back end" that, in voices designed to carry. They wanted everybody on the jet to know they were movers and shakers. He'd met a lot of men like them over the years. Men who thought the sun wouldn't come up in the morning if they didn't make the deal for a new television show or movie, as if what they did was supremely important. Men who would never say "nigger" or "kike" or "wop" for fear of offending somebody, but who would use "motherfucker" and "cocksucker" in voices loud enough to raise the dead, never dreaming anybody would be upset by that. Another example of how family values had declined. Once upon a time, you didn't hear language like that in public. Certainly not from God-fearing men. Once the attendant started the champagne coming, they'd eased up some. Green had tuned out the words and allowed the speech to become background noise, and it had put him right into dreamland.

He grinned. He'd been in a few conversations on airplanes that might have bored his neighbors into a trance. Cast not that first stone, Brother Green.

He had other things to think about besides a couple of loudmouthed Hollywood folks. This game the Jesuit had gotten them into was turning into something more than they'd expected. That the feds were willing to shoot people and risk their own had to mean something. It didn't necessarily follow that what it meant was what the Jesuit believed—or said he believed—but it did mean *some*thing. Something they couldn't risk not knowing. Sure, the church had kept a few secrets over the years, especially the Catholics. And the feds had a few of their own they kept buried real deep, but the nature of people was such that sooner or later, all secrets were revealed. Might take fifty years, but guilt had a way of loosening a man's tongue. Sometimes it waited until he was on his deathbed, but nothing really major was going to stay covered up forever. Secret radiation and chemical tests with a paper trail so narrow you needed a microscope to see it had come to light fifty or seventy-five years after the fact. The forbidden texts discovered with the Dead Sea Scrolls in the late forties had been in the Israeli vaults for almost eighty years before somebody rolled over and gave them up. If this *thing* the Jesuit was talking about existed and it wasn't destroyed, sooner or later, it was going to show up, too. That was the way of things.

Green sighed. Well. There wasn't much else he could do right at this moment, was there? He'd get back to Los Angeles, talk to the Catholic, figure out what they knew and what they didn't know.

One thing at a time.

Marsha was in the study when Wentworth arrived home. The door was open, so he entered. She was at her desk. She glanced up, gave him a cool smile, said, "Good evening, Ford," then went back to what she was doing. Handwriting a note to one of her family or sorority sisters, no doubt, most of whom she kept in touch with. Without looking at him again, she said, "How was your day?"

He slipped off his jacket, tossed it onto the hand-stitched green leather couch, shrugged out of the shoulder holster. He started to drop the gun onto the couch, caught the quick glance from his wife, and moved to the antique credenza instead. He opened the sideboard's storage drawer and carefully put the pistol and holster into it, closed it. Said, "Fine. The usual. How are the kids?"

"Fine. Kennedy is going on a field trip to Aruba next

week. Jennifer has gotten a part in her class production. She's playing Desdemona."

"*Othello?* For twelve-year-olds?"

"She *is* in the advanced class, Ford."

He shrugged. "I suppose."

She finished her note, folded it, slipped it into an envelope, pressed the seal shut. Put the letter into one of the pigeonholes and carefully closed the foldout shelf of the desk. A desk that had once belonged to Mary Todd Lincoln and had, for a time, stood in the White House.

"You really ought to use e-mail," he said.

She gave him another of her frosty smiles. "For ordering a plumber to fix the toilets, certainly. To answer a wedding invitation? I hardly think so."

"What are your plans for the evening?"

She stood. She wore a silk dress, cut loose and flowing, a pale blue and flowered print. She'd kept her figure, what she'd had of it. She'd always been on the thin side and an unkind appraisal might use the word "bony." Her hair was a nice honey gold without any gray, courtesy of a two-hundred-noodle-a-pop stylist in a Virginia salon. Her skin was lightly tanned and still flawless. She never went outside without sunblock. Still a very attractive woman for her age.

"I have a DAR meeting at eight. We're having dinner at Alberto's. Are you going to dine in?"

"Yes. I've got some work to catch up on."

"I'll have cook make you something."

"Thank you."

She moved to where he stood, put her hands on his shoulders, leaned in, and kissed him on the cheek. "I won't be late. I should be home by midnight."

"Have a good meeting, dear."

They traded polite smiles, and she flowed away in a swirl of designer silks that probably cost as much as the Lincoln desk.

Wentworth loosened his tie, untabbed the top stay of his shirt. The DAR meeting would run for an hour. Then the women who wanted to do so would go home and the others would go to spend a couple of hours with their lovers. Marsha's tennis pro would already be installed in a room at the new George Washington Hotel, twirling a bottle of expensive champagne in the ice bucket, waiting for her. No performance anxiety there, not at that age. He would probably bang her three or four times before she showered and came home. She'd sleep well tonight. Likely a lot better than Wentworth himself would rest, given his own recent adventures in the sexual arena.

He went down the hall to his office. Not his main worry at the moment, his carnal shortcomings. Though a session on the stair climber or rower might help him lose a bit of his work tension. Yes. Maybe he'd work out before he cranked up the computer and tried to get some work done. Muscular activity was an anodyne for stress, not to mention that it promoted the production of testosterone. A session in the house gym, yes, that was what he would do. He hadn't worked out in what? A week? Not a good idea to get behind and have to be constantly restarting. Nguyen would be in Portland by now, and the problem of the dead-eye pistol-packing courier would be on the way to being solved. He could afford a thirty-minute session to work up a sweat. No point in letting himself go to pot. The paperwork would wait that long.

One thing at a time. That was the ticket.

One thing at a time.

No one need think that the world can be ruled without blood. The civil sword shall and must be red and bloody.

—Martin Luther, *Werke*, Volume XV

17

IT WAS NEARLY eleven P.M. before Long went over the wall into his own neighborhood. He'd taken a bus from the airport, leaving his car in the lot, watched or not. He hadn't spotted anybody keeping an eye on his old clunker but they would have had plenty of time for bugging it.

Once he was in his own general area, he went into a small pub six blocks away from the entrance to The Village and ate a light supper, washed down with a soft drink. He watched a soccer game on the holoproj in the pub, cheered with the others as Canada kicked Chile's butt in the internationals in Mexico City.

Just after ten-thirty, he made his way out of the pub and down a side street that meandered through an open neighborhood before it looped back to Murray, not far from his house. There were several spots where the children and teeners had blunted and mashed the razor wire on top of the three-meter-high wall, places adults normally wouldn't notice. He found one of those secret spots, behind a medium-sized fir tree that hid it from the street. The branches of the tree were worn smooth from climbers and easy to scale. The sharp wire had been rearranged so a careful ascent wouldn't snag anything.

A police cruiser went by on the street, its electric motor humming slightly off key, the driver not even glancing in the tree's direction.

Long worked his way through the wire, then hung by his fingertips and dropped. The soft ground was only a few centimeters below his feet. He flexed his knees and landed easily.

Lying in the high grass at the base of the concrete wall was a long, notched four-by-four board. Long looked at it and saw how it worked. When you were ready to leave, you stood the board up and propped it at a slight angle against the wall. You could put your toes into the notches if your feet weren't too big, climb up high enough to grab the top of the wall, then kick the board over so it fell into the unmowed weeds at the wall's base again. The makeshift ladder would be almost invisible unless you knew where to look, and even then, you might not know it for what it was. Clever.

His house was only three in from Murray and the people on the corner next to the concrete wall didn't have a dog—currently. They'd had a yappy little miniature poodle but he had gotten loose somehow a few weeks back and tried to cross Murray during evening rush hour. Why on Earth the dog wanted to do that didn't make much sense. He had made it almost to the third lane when a bus squashed him. Not a minipoo survival characteristic, crossing a major street in heavy traffic, and the breed was probably better off that Nipsy didn't live to father any copies of himself.

There was a small community garden plot just inside the fence. Long hurried across the fallow ground. He hopped the privacy fence into his neighbors' backyard, a two-meter wooden-slat affair, and crouched low, near the back of the lot. Like most of the houses in the area, they probably had security lights, but they'd be set high, to keep from being tripped by their dog—unless they'd reset them since the pooch's escape. As long as he stayed low, he'd probably be all right.

The house next to his did have a dog, but it was a barker and they usually kept it inside after nine or ten at night, earlier when it was really cold out. Since it was cold and relatively late at the moment, he figured he'd be okay there.

He was right.

He made it into his own backyard without lights or noisy dogs. At the northeast corner of his lot was a stand of ever-green shrubbery, San Jose juniper, a couple of smallish fir trees, a rhododendron bush. He came over the fence into the thick foliage, found a relatively comfortable spot, and sat. The ground was cold under his butt but he could live with that. The cold kept the spiders and the insects quiet.

He sat and waited.

At midnight, according to his pocket watch, he was pretty sure he was alone in the yard. He had to consider that there might be somebody in the house. His security system was a standard commercial one, good for petty thieves, but not likely to stutter-step a well-equipped federal op. Still, if he were going in, there didn't seem much point in waiting any longer. Nobody had coughed or flushed a toilet or flashed a light and the house felt empty.

His own security lights would go on once he got within a few feet of the door, but they were only sixty-watters, they shouldn't be real visible from the front of the house. He'd have to risk that, too.

He moved.

The lamps blossomed as he hurried to the back door. He used his key to unlock the bolt, quickly stepped inside, and killed the lights.

Home sweet home.

How safe it was, he was about to find out.

The girls were asleep, tired from their long walk on the windy beach and full from the fish house take-out. Moon sat in the old overstuffed chair in the small living room, the lights off, in front of a wall of glass, watching the breakers foam over the sand a couple hundred meters away. It was overcast but some of the houses along the row had outside lights and the combined glow was enough to reveal the greenish white surf and little else. Far in the distance she saw the running lights of a ship paralleling the coast.

The sound of the waves was a basic, soothing, swooshy rumble, a prehistoric call to something deep inside. She always slept well at the beach, once she went to sleep. She was tired, but not quite ready to let go of her consciousness yet.

The house had that stale, unlived-in smell, and the wind tapped etheric fingertips against the glass, then grasped and shook the structure gently, moaning quietly as it slipped past the first man-made barriers on its way inland. The night air was wet—droplets congealed from the mist and spray and ran down the outside of the double-paned windows—but it wasn't really raining. It was the kind of gloomy weather that made you want to curl up in front of a fire with a lover and a bottle of wine, the kind of weather that made you happy, even smug, to be inside and dry.

It had been a long time since she'd had a lover. More than a year. Sean had been five years younger than she, a gentle, quiet man, a teacher and a poet. He'd attended a lecture at the mega-bookstore, Powell's, had come up to speak to her after her talk. The Goddess interested him, he'd said. He wanted to get in touch with his feminine side. He was polite. The girls liked him.

Moon smiled into the semidarkness covering the beach. What he'd really wanted to get in touch with was *her* feminine side, to immerse himself in hot carnal congress, but that had been okay. She knew she could handle him; she decided how and when the relationship happened. She had been in control. He got what he wanted, she got what she wanted and each was pleased.

Since her husband, men like Sean were the ones she

chose when she felt the need for one. There had been only a few and none of them had lasted long. She got lonely, and the feel of a warm body next to her in bed, the touch of lips on hers, the simple holding of hands, those were things she took pleasure in. And the sex, too. She liked it okay, though she restrained her passion, never quite letting go. You had to really trust somebody to do that, to let them see you that way, and since Martin, she hadn't been able to release herself with a man. When they'd first become lovers, she and Martin had rolled around and knocked furniture over. Done it outside under bushes, in the library, in trains or plane rest rooms, in cars, once on the backseat of a nearly empty bus. She had been lusty, no other way to put it, and a couple of times she'd climaxed so hard she nearly passed out from pure bliss. It had been raw, primal, unthinking. Her brain shut down and her body took over and the ride was like falling off a mountain and splashing in a deep and sparkling pool of warm and bubbly pleasure.

A long time ago, those energies. They'd stopped cold the first time Martin struck her in anger; they were not something she expected to ever find again. That type of abandonment required faith, and she didn't think it was in her to ever have that much faith in a man again.

Too bad. But she'd learned to live with it. She could always find men like Sean, men who would let her lead, who would follow and be satisfied with that. She could get what she needed from them without risking herself and that was how it was. It might not be star-crossed passion and blinding satori but it was safe. If that wasn't enough, they could move on.

She'd tried to keep from passing her fears along to the girls and in that, she seemed to have succeeded. On the one hand, she wanted to warn them of the risks; on the other hand, she knew they had to find out about life on their own. And maybe, Goddess willing, they would be lucky and not wind up with a man like their father. Maybe.

Another gust of wind inquired at the glass, was denied
admittance, moved on. A fire, a bottle of wine, and a lover:
those sounded nice, but tonight, it was going to be bed and
a book. Not her first choice, but not so bad, all things considered.

She arose from the chair and moved through the quiet
house to her room.

Reason is the enemy of faith.

Green believed it was Martin Luther who'd said that, not
Dr. King but the man he'd been named for. He didn't believe it was strictly true, but he understood the crux of it.
A man who demanded a logical reason for everything in
the universe, who couldn't accept God and His infinite wisdom, His plan, well, that man was a full vessel. He might
call himself a ''freethinker'' but the truth was, nothing
could be poured into his soul, for it was already filled with
human ego and pride that demanded Man be supreme and
God merely a wishful fantasy.

Green stood at the window of his hotel suite, looking at
the city ten stories below. It was a vast edifice, the city of
Los Angeles—supposedly the city of the angels—a mon-
ument to man's ability to curl his thumb and use tools. But
without God, it wasn't anything more than a glorified ant-
hill, a termite mound, a nest of sticks woven by a bower
bird or a dam built by beaver. He felt sorry for men who
saw nothing past themselves. Such men were, no matter
how clever, how adept with their busy fingers, damned.
Doomed to spend Eternity in darkness, without the light of
salvation. The ultimate tragedy.

He turned away from the view of the city, the shining
jewels of neon and argon and filaments of electrified metal.
It was his calling to save those men, to bring them to the
true light, the holy supernal glow of the Lord, filtered
through the perfect lens of Jesus Christ, God's only son.

Not likely to do much converting at two in the morning,
though. L.A., like other megaplexes, never truly slept.

It ran day and night, but trying to gather a crowd on a corner at this hour to deliver the word, well, that wasn't his path.

His path. He chuckled.

He'd never wanted to be anything other than a country preacher, heating up the congregation on Sunday morning from his pulpit, or ministering to the sick in the local hospital. He'd always assumed he'd spend his time doing just that, along with putting the departed to rest in sanctified ground and dunking babies and converts to wash away their sins. But the Lord hadn't let him off that easy. The Lord had given him a skill: he could move people with his voice and he could organize things in his mind, on paper, in a database. And that was his blessing and his curse. He showed a talent and he was called on by others to use that talent in the service of his church and of his Father. One thing led to another and here he was, pushing sixty, as high as a Baptist minister was likely to get in the secular world. And it was his ability to reason, backed by his faith, that had brought him here.

He wasn't a Jesuit, somebody who delighted in playing mind games. But there wasn't anything wrong with his brain, his ability to add two and two and come up with four. And as long as there was faith behind that, he didn't see that logic and faith were enemies.

You had to start with the basic premise, of course, but after that, logic was logic, no matter who wielded it. It was what you chose to use it for that mattered. God or the Devil, good or evil, those were your choices. You didn't get to sit on the fence. The Lord of the Flies was always out there in one disguise or another, laughing, waiting for his chance to shove the unwary off into the mud. You needed to be on the right side of that fence so you could see Lucifer and his gang coming, to know that you were armored in the power of God and thus invulnerable.

How did atheists sleep at night, not knowing they had

souls that would outlive their frail bodies? How could a man face death and the endless stretch of eternity without knowing he was going to be saved? Even if you didn't believe in Hell as a real place, to be dead and gone with no hope of redemption, no chance of resurrection, to think you went out like a snuffed candle . . . ?

It was beyond him, the answer to that question.

He went back to bed, to try to get a few hours' sleep before the sun came up and kick-started another day. The Father of Lies was out there, up to no good, and best that Walter Green get prepared to do battle with him. One more time.

It took Long only a few minutes to figure out he was alone in the house. Even so, he didn't plan to stay in it long. He hurried to the admit hatch to his crawl space, opened it. There was a powerful flashlight secured under the lid. He unclamped the light and switched it on. The safe was buried in the ground beneath the house, a heavy concrete box with a carbon-fiber door and a thumbprint reader lock. It was under the black plastic moisture shield and you wouldn't see it unless you knew where to look. Inside the safe were a few items he wanted.

He skipped the new barrel for his handgun—they knew who he was and if they wanted to throw a net over the country and get him, they could. If the wandering federal-asaurus put its massive foot on you and let its full weight come down, you were going to get crushed, period. It didn't quite feel like that was happening yet.

There were several legally established IDs, credit that went with each, and a com in one of those names that ought not to be linked to him. He'd have to put a new battery in the com but it ought to be in order otherwise.

There was a keycard to an electric cart, a vehicle he kept stored under yet another name in a garage a few klicks away. He grinned as he fingered the little plastic strip.

There had been a time when he'd thought he was more than a little paranoid for having such things. But Marvin had been right. Better to have it and not need it than to need it and not have it. Marvin was off the street these days, in management down in New Orleans, but Long would offer long odds that his old teacher still had his back door getaway package in place. "Life is funny," he used to say. "Never know but what it's gonna smack you when you aren't looking. Best to have something to land on when it knocks you down."

Thank you, Marvin.

It didn't take long. He pocketed his gear, shut the safe, covered it again. Slid the crawl space cover back into place. A diligent search would find it, but he had what he wanted now.

He cruised through the house, moving slowly and carefully. Time to leave. He hoped he would be able to come back someday.

He planned to leave the same way he'd come in, only he heard the next-door neighbor's dog barking.

Well. Apparently they had let the beast out. A big German shepherd that still woofed at Long every time he and it were both out back at the same time. Hopping the side fence into the yard with Spica didn't much appeal. Neither did trying to go over the back fence. The people behind him, the Scates, didn't own an animal; unfortunately, their yard was awash in motion detectors wired to lights, sirens, and the local police. They'd had a break-in once and any thieves who thought they were going to sneak up on the Scates undetected were in for a big surprise.

Long stood by the back door, considering his options. The woman who lived on the other side of his place, to the west, had cats. He could climb the fence along the back edge—she wasn't as security conscious as the Scates were—and circle back to the street in front. If there were any watchers parked in their cars keeping an eye on his house, he could spot them from the bushes in front of his neighbor's house. Maybe go the other direction to the west gate and leave that way.

Yes. That would do.

He shut the back lights off, opened the door and slipped out. The fence was easy enough, the trip across his neighbor's backyard uneventful. He circled through her side yard, past the recycling bins, and made it to her big rhododendron bush out front.

The street in front of their homes was quiet. No cars parked there he didn't recognize as belonging. Nobody moving. The row of alternating pine and Douglas fir trees planted in the common strip along the sidewalk stood silent and still.

Maybe the watchers—if there were any—were set up on the gate, thinking he'd come in that way. If it were him, he'd be watching the house, but unless they were inside one of the houses across the street or under a bush as he was, he couldn't spot anybody.

Okay. He'd ease out and move west, keeping to the front yards as much as possible. Once he was a few houses away, he could cross the street, loop through the neighborhood, find anther place to climb the wall. He'd work his way to the garage, charge his car, and get out of town. Call the client and arrange to meet her and discuss the problem. Good a plan as any.

Long moved from beneath the rhody bush and angled toward the sidewalk. Behind him, he heard a small thump, like somebody dropping something heavy onto the ground. He spun—

And found himself facing a short Vietnamese man pointing a pistol at him.

The man was five meters away. He must have been up in one of the trees. Long hadn't considered that.

The man said, "This'll punch through whatever armor you're wearing. Blink and I'll shoot."

He'd never be able to get to his own gun in time.

"Come on down, Harvey."

Another thump as a second man dropped from the next tree in the line. This one was bigger and he also had a gun.

Damn.

During great stress and especially in the perception of deadly danger, time can become plastic; can stretch as does taffy on a hot summer's day, turning seconds into hours, even days.

—Hans Ludwig Wöller, *The Psychology of Threat*

18

"GET HIS GUN, Harvey," the Vietnamese said. "Under the jacket on his right hip."

The streetlight glow was more than enough for Long to see the little Oriental smile.

"That'd be a .357 revolver, right? Snub-nosed Smith and Wesson?"

Long didn't say anything. This guy was a fed and they were rhetorical questions—he obviously had computer access to Long's license to carry.

"You got a couple of lucky breaks to get this far, but you're out of your league here. Game's over. Let's have the carrier."

His pistol didn't waver a centimeter as he spoke. Long noted the piece was a top-of-the-line SIG.

He didn't have much choice. He could draw against a leveled gun and that would sure as hell get him killed. He didn't doubt that the Vietnamese's projectiles would hole his spidersilk. Maybe if he gave them the package, they'd let him live. A sudden move would damn sure be stupid—

but he was thinking about it, wondering what his chances
were. If he lunged to the side as he made his draw,
maybe—

A dog started barking across the street, a big dog with a
deep voice. Long couldn't see it but it was close enough
so it must be in the bushes. It must have hopped a fence
or broken a leash and was probably chasing a raccoon or
a possum. Both Harvey and the Vietnamese flicked glances
in that direction. Both men frowned.

While they were looking for the dog, the Vigilante appeared out of nowhere and shot the Vietnamese in the ass.

The Vietnamese convulsed. His pistol clattered onto the
sidewalk and he fell and juddered violently.

Some part of Long's mind recognized the spasmodic
twitchings as the result of a Taser impact, of high voltage
coursing through the fallen man's muscles.

Harvey spotted the Vigilante and started to turn. He
snapped his gun up and out in a classic isosceles stance,
arms straight, both hands on the pistol. He meant to plink
the old man, no doubt about it, and the Taser was a single-
shot weapon.

The old man hit the button on the flashlight he carried.
The bright beam splashed over the gunman, made him
squint. That bought the old man another second, maybe
two, but no more. Even if the light was held out away from
his body, all Harvey had to do was draw a horizontal line;
his pistol had enough ammo to cover the whole street.

Then again, Harvey was only a couple of meters away
from Long.

Long jumped, snapped his hands around in a three-
quarter circle, left hand braced against his right wrist, and
smacked Harvey square on the ribs under his left armpit.

The move was a speeded-up tai chi technique with the
innocuous name of "press wrist forward." It was a powerful appliance, but slow, and not something he would normally use in a fight. But with the man not paying attention,
it was perfect.

All of Long's weight focused on a spot the size of a quarter at the point of his bent right wrist and the impact knocked Harvey completely off his feet. He slammed the curb on his left shoulder and slid into the street, tearing cloth and dragging bark chips with him. By the time he managed to raise his head, Long was there. He kicked Harvey's temple with his heel, almost a stomp, and the downed man went boneless; his outflung arm sent his pistol sailing halfway across the road. It clattered loudly on the hard surface. No way to treat a decent gun, even a plastic one.

"Nice move," The Vigilante said.

On the ground, the Vietnamese stopped twitching and lay still. He might have been conscious, though Long didn't think so. The man's eyes were closed and he sure wasn't going anywhere for a few minutes.

Long moved to where The Vigilante stood.

"Sheila! Quiet!"

The dog stopped barking.

"Come here!"

The malamute emerged from the bushes and hurried across the street to The Vigilante, her tail wagging.

"Good puppy," he said. He bent and scratched behind the dog's ear.

Long looked at the old man. "Thanks. You probably saved my life. But you need to clear off. These guys are feds."

"Fuck 'em," the old man said. He grinned. "Fed or not, that little gook was going to plow you under. He had the look."

"I appreciate it. Listen, I don't think they got a good hit on you. Best you get home and lay low for a while before they get ambulatory again. Nice shooting with that thing." He nodded at the Taser.

"I was in the Army reserves when Desert Storm went down," the old man said. "Spent me a few months over there. No big deal. Probably ten good guys with squirrel rifles could have kicked Saddam's ass, but I potted me a few camel riders who tried to kill me. I know when somebody needs shootin'. You were in the service, weren't you?''

"Marines, in Cuba."

"Yeah, I figured. One of them damned jarheads."

Long nodded. "If I get out of this mess, maybe you and I can get together and swap war stories over a beer. I'll buy."

"Look forward to it, son. You don't think we should finish these suckers off?"

"Probably not a good idea; bring a lot of heat if we did that." He extended his hand. "We've never officially met. I'm Hal Long."

The old man shook Long's hand, a dry and firm grip. "Thomas Carson. My friends call me Tom."

"Pleased to meet you, Tom. Better take off. I'm going to."

"You take care, Long."

"You, too."

"C'mon, Sheila. Let's go home."

Long heard the pride in Carson's voice. He might be old, but by God, he was still a man.

Long smiled as he hurried away from the fallen feds.

Even though it was almost five in the morning and he normally would have been asleep, Wentworth was lying awake in bed when his com chirped. It was the private tone, only three people had the number, officially: the President, Gray, and Nguyen.

"Wentworth."

"Nguyen here."

"You got him?"

"No. We caught him outside his house but he's got help. Somebody tasered me from behind. When I woke up, Harvey was lying in the street with his skull fractured. He'll live but he's still out. Even if he saw who did us, he might not remember when he does come to. I didn't get a look at them."

"Shit." This was bad. The courier might be tapped into some kind of underground organization. God only knew which one it might be.

"What about the woman, the priestess?"

"I sent a man to check her out. She's gone, she and her kids. She's got a car, we found a storage space for it, but it's not there. I'd guess she took her daughters and went to ground."

"With Long?"

"I don't think so. She pulled her car out of the garage while Long was still in San Francisco."

"Maybe she went to pick him up."

"Doesn't scan that way. He had to have flown or taken the maglev to make it here so fast. No record on a commercial flight, nobody answering his description bought a ticket on the express maglev from the Bay Area to Portland, so he must have rented a private plane. We're working on that but the airport's traffic log doesn't show the priestess's car in or out."

"All right. What are you going to do?"

"I will run him down." The tone of Nguyen's voice was cold, a breath of liquid oxygen wafting from the com. He was pissed.

"All right. Call me when you get something."

"I will."

Wentworth stared into the darkness at the ceiling. Well. He wasn't going back to sleep now. Shit.

Green got the call around six A.M. He was in the chair next to the window reading in Judges when the com chimed. The Lord was favoring the Israelites again. There was a big battle, which the Israelites won. Sisera, the leader of the beaten army, ditched his chariot and ran. Came upon Jael, the wife of Heber the Kenite. He was on the run, looking for a place to hide. So Jael smiled sweetly, put him in her tent, covered him up, gave him a bottle of milk. And when Sisera was sleeping, exhausted, too tired to wake up, she found herself a long nail and a hammer, went back into the tent, and drove that spike through Sisera's temples. Nailed that sucker to the ground, stone-cold dead.

Don't let them give you to the women.

The com kept complaining. He picked it up.

"Yes?"

It was the Catholic. He said, "The feds tracked Long to his house in Oregon. Apparently there was some kind of shoot-out on the street and Long escaped."

"Dear Lord. More killings."

"Nobody died this time. Long apparently has some kind of help. The agents trying to take him were overcome by his confederates."

The signal was audio only but Green could almost see the Catholic smiling. More players to complicate the game. He'd love it.

"Do we know who these confederates might be?"

"Not yet."

"Any ideas of where the courier might have gotten to?"

"We're working on that, too."

"I see. Well. Keep me posted."

"Of course."

Green sundered the connection. Wheels within wheels within wheels. He didn't like any of it, hadn't from the start, and it was only getting worse. Maybe he was relying too much on the Catholic's abilities. Maybe he ought to check things out on his own. There were other resources available to him.

The Jesuits weren't the only ones who knew how to play twisted games.

Moon made coffee. While it was dripping, she stretched out on the rug in the living room and did yoga. She wasn't an adept, but she could manage fifteen or twenty poses once a day, enough to keep her supple. She relaxed into the asanas, allowed her breathing to slow, concentrated on moving precisely. The smell of the brewing coffee filled the room. She was at her best in the mornings, just after the sun rose, when it was quiet and she was alone. The girls would sleep until ten or eleven, left alone, and she planned to let them. To enjoy the quiet time.

She sat in spinal twist to the left, her elbow braced inside her knee, hand wrapped around her ankle. The sea, the sky, the land were all variations on gray, only the white of the surf's foam to break the monochromatic palette. That and a few gulls who stood on the wet sand or swooped on the wet air, thinking whatever it was gulls thought.

Her com chimed from the kitchen counter where she'd left it.

She released the asana and stood, stretched her low back, then padded into the kitchen. She'd had the robot at the phone company screen and record all her incoming calls except for one, so she knew who it was. She picked up the com, tucked it under her ear and shoulder, poured coffee from the glass beaker into a stoneware mug.

"Long?"

"If they are listening, it'll take a trace forty-five seconds to get a GPS on you," he said. "I've got a scrambler and a misdirect but I want to be off-line by then. Where are you?"

"At a friend's beach house."

"Give me the address."

"You're in Portland?"

"Yes. The address."

She rattled it off.

"I'll be there in two hours. Don't make any more calls. Discom."

He clicked off.

Moon put the com down. Sipped at the coffee. She'd planned to check her messages, to see if Lila had called her. That probably wouldn't hurt anything.

Then again, maybe it would. Long was coming here.

She'd wait until she heard what he had to say first. He'd arrive before the girls woke up.

She took the coffee back into the living room, put it on the short table next to the chair, sat on the rug. Coffee and yoga weren't supposed to go together, the teachers frowned on chemicals generally, but Moon had learned a long time ago not to be a fanatic about such things. Extremism generally led to trouble and she could do without that.

She began spinal twist to the opposite side.

Back when she'd been a student in San Francisco, there had been a girl in her dorm who'd been gung-ho about almost everything. Cathy arose every morning and drank half a gallon of salt water, then vomited it back up. That was to clean her insides out, she said. She would inhale through her nose a fat and fuzzy kind of string, also soaked in salt water, and cough the end out, so she had a line running into her nostril and out of her mouth. She moved this back and forth as if she were drying her backside with a towel, did both nostrils. She then sat in a tub of water, and with a muscle control Moon envied, drew the warm liquid up into her anus and vagina, then expelled that, too.

Cathy cleaned *every*thing out.

Among other things, she ate only "pure" foods. On her days off, she would spend half the morning making a list of what she wanted from the organic market, then the other half getting prepared psychically to go out into the world with all its tribulations. Once actually in the store, it always took her nearly an hour to select a couple of apples or a banana. She would examine every piece of fruit in the bin before making her choice. That done, she'd spend the rest of the day recovering from the rigors of the trip—the pollution, the bad auras, the negative city vibes, the half-block walk from the temple.

The temple cooks were fairly strict themselves, octolavo-vegetarian fare only, no meat, fish, poultry. Lots of beans, cheese, rice, eggs, vegetables.

Moon unknotted the spinal twist and moved into lion pose.

She grinned at the memory. A diet high in beans and eggs and veggies made for a lot of gas. Sometimes during group meditation, it sounded like a band full of tuba players warming up. And stink? Goddess. They used to joke about what would happen if somebody lit a match in the dorm. Probably wipe out half a city block.

Once, one of the cooks got creative with the bean casserole, actually put in some decent spices. Sage, thyme, rosemary, cilantro, even a bit of curry.

Cathy got sick. Went to bed for two days. Continued her daily all-orifices cleansing. Got somewhat better but still dragged around for a week. Looked as if she were in the final stages of plague. Then one morning she came into the dorm and sat on the end of Moon's cot and told her she had finally managed to bring up the flake of rosemary that had been making her sick. It had been in her system for a week, she said, and now that it was out, she could begin to recover. She held her hand out and there was a spot of moldy green half the size of a pinhead on her palm. It didn't look like any rosemary Moon had ever seen and the idea that it could have lain in Cathy's stomach undigested and not washed out by the daily deluge of brine didn't make much sense, either. But even if it were true, Moon felt a great surge of pity for the woman. Somebody that sensitive, that anal retentive, that *fanatic* was not going to be happy in *this* world. She'd have to mellow or she'd never survive. Cathy made the princess and the pea seem like a drunk who could sleep on a bed of nails without feeling it.

She finished lion and began to stretch her legs in preparation for lotus. Paused to take a sip of the cooling coffee. If the yogis didn't like her drinking while she worked out, well, fuck 'em. It was her life.

And although much has been written foolishly about the antagonism of science and religion, there is, indeed, no such antagonism.

—H. G. Wells, *The Outline of History*, Book VI

19

THE QUICK CHARGE in Long's battery was running low when he reached the coast. He debated with himself about pulling into a public plug somewhere and recharging, but decided against it. He should have enough to reach the house where Moon was supposedly staying. His cart's computer map wasn't the latest version but the roads couldn't have changed that much in the last five years. If push came to shove, he could download a revised atlas under the pseudonym but he didn't think it would come to that.

He headed south along the coast highway, away from Seaside, staying in the slow lanes, trying to look innocuous when a state patrol unit whipped past him. A light rain began to fall through the fog and the day struggled to put forth any light. He kept his lamps switched on as he rolled toward Cannon Beach. Moon's place was, if his map could be trusted, just south of there, before you got to Cape Falcon. Not far.

When he got to the neighborhood, he made one pass through it, looking for watchers. He didn't see any, but after his experience of last night, he couldn't assume there weren't any.

He circled back, pulled the electric into the gravel driveway of the house whose number matched the one Moon had given him. Sat quietly in the car for a minute, listening to the cooling motor click.

He unsnapped his gun's strap and got out.

Nobody started shooting.

Moon met him at the door.

"Girls are still asleep," she said. "You want to come in for coffee?"

He'd been in the car for hours and was stiff. What he wanted to do was work the kinks out of his back and legs, then sleep for a week. She was dressed in sweats and walking shoes, had a windbreaker over her arm. He got the hint.

"What say we walk a little?" he said. "Stretch out?"

"Okay."

She slipped the jacket on and he followed her down a sandy path edged with wind-flattened saw grass to the beach. The rain wasn't much and it was a little breezy but not really that cold. They moved through the damp and mushy sand to where the tide had smoothed and packed the grit harder, making it easier to walk on.

Neither of them spoke for several hundred meters.

"Okay," he said. "Here's the deal. Somebody wants your package. I don't know for certain but I would bet big money at long odds that I'm being chased by the federal government in one of its security agency forms. FBI, CIA, NSA, whoever.

"I went to deliver the package at the temple and the place was crawling with armed men. After somebody tried to smash my car, I called you and set up that meeting at the museum.

"Somebody told them I was coming. They started shooting."

He touched the hole in the front of his jacket where the bullet had pierced the leather but stopped on the armored lining. It was almost an unconscious move.

"I shot back. One of them is dead."

He watched her for a reaction, saw the tightening around her eyes and mouth. She didn't say anything but waited for him to continue.

He did so.

"So I rented a plane and flew back to Oregon. Sneaked home and got a few things, but ran into more of these guys outside my front door. Nobody got killed but that was luck."

He stopped walking, looked at her. "Do you think anybody followed you here?"

"I didn't see anybody."

Her voice was, like her face, tight. A hint of worry in it, not a lot.

"Could somebody maybe have attached a tracking device to your vehicle?"

She shook her head. "I don't think so. The car was in a garage and the door was covered with dust and spiderwebs, looked like they'd been there since we used it last. I guess it's possible."

He nodded. "Okay. That's the situation, far as I know it. The question is, how bad do you want me to try and deliver this thing?" He patted the carrier.

She sighed, shook her head again. "You'd go back there again?"

"That's what you pay me for. But the reason I'm here is—and it's none of my business, so you can tell me to butt out if you want—if I were you, I'd have some doubts about the people I was sending this thing to."

"What do you mean?"

"I wasn't followed to the museum. They shouldn't have known where I was going in advance but they were in place and waiting by the time I got there. So, unless you gave me up . . ." He paused. Watched a gull slide past them sideways on a wet breeze, its harsh cry dopplering away in the wind. Good air for kite flying, if it weren't so wet and nasty.

She was bright enough to finish his sentence. Said, "Then either somebody figured it out from what I said or whoever I told must have told somebody else."

He shrugged. "They could have tapped the call."

She watched a second gull drift by. "Even so, I was very oblique. If they could figure it out from what I said, they'd have to be very sharp. I suppose that's possible, too."

He nodded, let her finish working it out.

"But if they didn't, then Lila told them—or told somebody who told them."

"Yeah. Either way, that place, those people, they've been . . . compromised. And even though my job is just supposed to be pick up and deliver, it seems to me you might want to rethink this. Whatever is in this carrier is worth killing people for, at least somebody thinks so, and while that doesn't make it valuable by itself, if it's the feds doing the shooting, that means something."

"Yes. It does."

She turned back toward the ocean. He waited for a moment, silent.

Finally, she said, "I guess maybe I don't want you to deliver to the temple after all."

"Okay."

"Listen, can we go back to the house and talk? I mean, I know you don't owe me anything, but I could use some advice from somebody who knows about this kind of stuff."

He nodded. "Okay."

Well, yes, one of the first lessons in this game was not to get involved, but hell, he was shooting guys and being shot at, and the truth was, he really wanted to know more about why. If he was going to be plowed for protecting his package, that was fine, but it *would* make a difference whether it was somebody's old socks or something of great value, even though it wasn't supposed to.

So when she said, "I think maybe you ought to know what's in that carrier on your belt," he didn't argue. He wanted to know.

Moon led the courier back to the house, watching him look for trouble. His gaze was like the gulls', flitting, shifting, sliding from side to side, never staying in one spot but taking it all in. She was willing to bet that if somebody jumped out from behind a bush and yelled "Boo!" he would be real sorry he did. Long was wound tight, ready to spring, and she wouldn't want to be in front of him when he let go.

It was hard for her to believe that Lila would have sold her out. They'd been like sisters, she the younger, Lila the older. Shared all their secrets, been willing to do anything to help each other.

That was then. Time had passed and she had only been in sporadic contact with Lila. Who knew what forces had shaped her since, what burdens she now bore? She would rather believe Lila had misplaced her own trust, that somebody had betrayed her, not that she had done so to Moon.

Either way, it didn't seem like a good idea to send Long back into the killing fields. Yes, he was a professional courier, but she still felt bad about having involved him as much as she had. And maybe he had some ideas.

The girls were still asleep when they got back to the house. She removed her jacket, took Long's. He wore his gun and she saw that the snap on the holster was open. That one little detail was enough to make her shiver. The game had turned uglier, and it hadn't been pretty to begin with.

"Coffee?"

"Please."

She busied herself in the kitchen, pouring the ground coffee into the gold cone, adding bottled water to the heating tank. The machine began its cycle and she moved back to where Long stood looking out at the beach. He wasn't watching the ocean, she saw, but once again scanning the land.

"Coffee'll be ready in a couple of minutes."

He didn't speak to that.

For a moment, she couldn't think of anything to say, either. She considered waking the girls so that they could be part of the discussion, but until she had an idea of what she was going to do, maybe it was better to leave them out of it. No point in worrying them any more than she had to.

Long said, "Here," and passed the carrier to her. "Put your thumb on the black plastic plate," he said.

She did so and the lid popped open on a concealed spring, revealing the contents. Moon sighed and reached into the carrier, caught the silver brick with her thumb and forefinger and eased it out. It came all too easily. She held it up for Long to see.

"What is it?"

"I think maybe it must be Pandora's box," she said.

The wisest man is usually one who fancies himself least so.

—Nicolas Boileau-Despréaux, *Satire*

20

GREEN SAT IN the dentist's waiting room, reading an old magazine. It was a dog-eared copy of something called *Modern Mythos,* a kind of New Age thing, and was a couple of years old. No big deal. Once, when he'd been in college, he'd gone into a doctor's office in Mobile and found a copy of a *National Geographic* magazine from August 1943. Of course, that had been a long time ago, in the late '80s, but still, forty-five years old, now *that* was an ancient waiting room magazine. There had been two pictures in it that he still remembered: One was of a South African native riding an ostrich, a small man wearing a brim-down pork-pie hat with a feather in it. The other picture was of a Japanese woman in a traditional costume, holding a basket full of eggs on the end of a long stick over a plume of vapor spewing up from between two rocks. She was boiling those eggs in the live steam that arose from a natural thermal vent. Many families in the area did not have stoves, the caption said, but cooked their rice over holes punched directly in the ground.

Amazing those images had stayed with him all this time.

"Reverend Green?"

He looked up from the article on creation myths—an article that dared to include Genesis, thereby damning the writer—at the receptionist behind the counter.

"Dr. Gray will see you now."

Green smiled at the young man, and went to see Gray. He didn't know if the man was actually a dentist or not, he supposed it was possible, but he didn't think it was likely, even though the setup here seemed perfect.

"Ah, Reverend, good to see you again."

"Gray." He was an average-sized man, innocuous looking, white haired, probably in his early sixties. Gray had ruddy skin and a healthy air about him.

"Family okay?"

"Fine. Listen, I'll get right to the point. I've got a problem—"

"That thing in the temple in Portland," Gray said. It was not a question.

"Sweet Jesus, how did you know that?"

Gray smiled. "I get around."

"The Jesuit is supposedly on top of it," Green said. He hesitated.

"But it never hurts to cover all your bases?"

Green shook his head. The man was too clever by half. Then again, that was exactly why Green needed his help. "Exactly," he said.

Gray smiled.

It wasn't as if he didn't have other things to do, Wentworth thought, but this whole business out in the Pacific Northwest was beginning to grate painfully upon him. He had a bad feeling about it.

He sat in his office, staring at the pulsing cursor on his computer, focused infinitely past it. It had been simpler when he'd been a younger man. As a hot and upcoming agent in the FBI in Kansas City, he'd been in the right place at the right time. He had been the man who had flung himself in front of the visiting Pope Pius when a crazed gunman had opened up with a sawed-off .22 rifle. Wentworth's brand-new issue vest had stopped three of the four rounds that hit him, slowed the last one enough so it punched only a tiny hole in his right pectoral and came to rest against a rib. The shooter had considered that the pontiff himself might be wearing a vest, and thus had put the noses of the little bullets into a pencil sharpener and pointed them so they'd go through. Wentworth's ceramic-weave armor had mostly worked, but one of the needle-pointed lead pellets slipped past. He'd put five from his own service pistol into the shooter before the guy hit the ground; the loony hadn't been wearing any protection. The would-be assassin died before the ambulance got there.

But the Pope was safe and Wentworth was the hero of millions of Catholics around the world, including Leonard Harvey, then director of the FBI. As a result, Wentworth came out of surgery already promoted to special agent at large and assigned to Baltimore, where he could be trotted down to be shown off to visiting dignitaries in D.C. whenever the need arose.

"Madame Prime Minister, may I present Mr. Ford Wentworth, the man who saved Pius the Seventeenth from that assassin. . . ."

They'd gotten a lot of political mileage out of that, and it had put him on a fast track. Shortly thereafter he was able to jump to the CIA as a bureau chief in Saigon, where he did two years before joining the National Security Agency in 2018. Then Benjamin Morris was elected President of the United States. An old friend of Wentworth's father, Morris offered Wentworth the position of chief for the newly formed President's Special Section of the NSA. At thirty-two, he was at the acme of his profession. He had risen like a helium balloon and there were men below him who would have killed to have ascended the ladder of success half so quickly.

He grinned. Too bad for them.

But now, he was the man at the top and the buck did stop with him. And this particular bill had an unpleasant feel and smell to it. He'd been in the game long enough to know that big crises from little problems grew—look at Watergate, the Pakistani Bribery Scandal, the Night Hawk Missile Snafu. Each had started out as some little bit of business; a break-in, a pork-barrel junket, a line of mangled computer code. And each had been unexpectedly brought into the light by chance: a rent-a-cop who caught a bunch of CIA-trained ops; a reporter for some yahoo weekly in Virginia who snapped a picture of a powerful senator on a Hawaiian beach with a gunrunner; a kid hacker who downloaded a supposedly top-secret file and discovered major fraud that went right to the Pentagon. Bad luck for those involved, but there it was.

This whole thing had that stink about it, the tip of the iceberg that might lead to a hidden mountain. If Nguyen didn't clean it up in the next couple of days, Wentworth was going to hop on a jet and go take care of it himself. No way was he going to get caught flat-footed on something like this. No way.

"Ask it something," Moon said.

Long looked at her. She'd set the shimmery little block on the coffee table and was looking at him. He raised an eyebrow.

"Go ahead. Anything you want—except where it came from. It won't tell you that."

He shook his head. What kind of game was she playing here?

"Humor me, Long."

"Okay." He looked at the block. "When and where was I born?"

And the little brick said, in a clear and deep masculine tone, in pure unaccented American newscasterspeak: "Fourteen March 1989, four forty-five A.M. local time, Alexandria, Louisiana, U.S.A.''

Long blinked. ''It's a computer,'' he said. ''Voxax, some kind of encyclopedia program. Nice toy, but birth certificates are a matter of public record. So what?''

''And how did it know who you were, so it could pick *your* birthday?''

Even as she asked him that, the same question popped into his mind. Had to be some kind of trick. She must have a hidden remote.

''Listen to this,'' she said. ''Is the Shroud of Turin real?''

''If by real you mean: Does it exist as an artifact? Yes. The artifact is Z-twist woven linen, three-to-one herringbone twill, approximately four and one-half meters in length by one and one-tenth meters wide with the representation of a crucified human figure upon it.

''If by real you mean: Is the image upon the cloth an imprint of Jesus of Nazareth transferred there shortly after his death by some unexplained supernatural phenomenon? No.''

''Well, what is it, then?''

The box said, ''The shroud is a collaboration created initially by two artists from the English Abbey of Meaux; the sculptor Paul de Vergy and the painter N.F.N., N.M.I. Ashe, under the direction of Geoffrey de Charnys. In A.D. 1354 Ashe painted the initial image by the application of heated iron oxides in the English daub-watercolor style upon the cloth as it lay over a wooden statue of Jesus of Nazareth carved by de Vergy.

''This drawing was secretly altered by Leonardo da Vinci in A.D. 1514 using the *sfumato* technique, under the direction of the Duke of Savoy. In A.D. 1532 a fire at Chambéry, where the shroud was stored, caused a scorching and partial bleaching of the cloth and pigments, altering the image.''

Sounded real, but Long didn't know. It could have made it all up.

"Ready for a big one? Try this: Is there a God? Or Goddess?"

And the voice said, "If by God or Goddess you mean an omnipotent, omniscient, anthropomorphic originator and ruler of the universe as represented by major human religions, no.

"If by God or Goddess you mean an intelligent force behind the creation of the cosmos, yes."

Moon said, "And where would this force be?"

"You can't get there from here," the block said.

Long smiled. "A philosophical dictionary program. With a sense of humor. Impressive."

She shook her head. "What are the winning lottery numbers for tomorrow's Powerball game?"

The voice rattled off six numbers.

Long looked at her skeptically.

She said, "I don't blame you. But I asked it the same question the night before the last lotto drawing, a full day before the little balls got whirled around in their cage and spat out on live television. It got those right. Six for six."

"You're kidding."

"Nope. And I didn't even buy a ticket. Look, ask it something I can't know, something you've never told anybody."

Long thought about it for a moment. No matter how smart this little gimmick was, unless it could read minds, it would miss his next question. Nobody alive knew but him. "Okay, little block, try this one: What was Sienna's pet name for me?"

"Long Enough," it said.

He stared at the box. Had it turned into a fire-breathing dragon and flown around the room blowing smoke rings, he could not have been more amazed. His voice, when he found it, was husky. "Where the hell did you come from?"

No answer.

"Told you, it won't say."

"Are you some kind of computer?"

"Yes."

"What . . . what kind?"

"The same kind as you are," the box said. "A biogenetically encoded electrochemical enzymatic-hormonal holographic processor."

"Excuse me?"

"What part didn't you understand, Mr. Long?"

Unless he'd lost his marbles, this little shiny block was, at the very least, an artificial intelligence—an AI—which would be pretty damned impressive. Scientists had been working on such things a long time, were getting closer, but last he heard, there weren't any that could pass the Turing test. And sure as hell none that could tell the future or could somehow read minds. That wasn't just impressive—it was flat out impossible.

Because such a thing would be the most valuable thing on the planet.

It scared the hell out of Long.

No wonder Moon had wanted to get rid of the thing.

"Holy shit," he said.

"Yeah," Moon said. "Exactly."

Part
Two

And after much Time had flowed the God and Goddess looked upon that which they had wrought and were moved to compassion. They created then the *Bibliokaas,* that their children might find some measure of peace.

—*The Book of Life,* C10, v. 1

He wasn't what he first seemed to be—but then, nobody is what they first seem to be.

—Charles Hart Benford, *The Orange Impostor*

21

LONG ROLLED OVER in bed and pressed himself against
Sienna's warm and naked backside. Outside, the center of
a late-evening summer thunderstorm rumbled its way closer
to their condo. The thunder followed closer on the strobes
through the bedroom's curtains. He'd left the window open
a crack before he turned off the light and the damp breeze
stirred the heavy cloth in little ripples, bringing the smell
of the approaching rain into the room.

Asleep, Sienna pushed back against him and he felt himself stir. Had a mind of its own, all right.

Sienna would probably sleep through the rain, unless
lightning actually struck the building. She went to bed late,
was a late riser, and slept like the dead between the two.
Long, who usually slept in himself when he didn't have to
get up, had discovered after Mary Louise had been born
that he could and did come out of a sound slumber if the
baby so much as squeaked during the night. When she
awoke in the mornings, usually around six, the noises she
made stirring in her crib were enough to get him up. It had

been that way since her arrival almost two years before. Unlike her mother, Mary Louise was a light sleeper and the thunder would have already gotten her up—except that she was in Baltimore for a week with Sienna's mother.

Long hadn't much liked that, letting the baby go visit her grandmother by herself.

"She's not a baby, Hal," Sienna had said. "She's a toddler."

"Still . . ."

Sienna laughed. "She managed to raise Bette and me just fine, or do you have any complaints about us?"

Bette was Sienna's twin sister and, no, he didn't have any complaints about the Woodruff women, thank you.

"It's only a week. We can use a break. We can screw all night and sleep all day."

"Well. If you put it that way . . ."

He missed his daughter, but Sienna was right. Her mother adored Mary Louise, would take care of her as well as anybody, probably spoil her. The child's feet would never touch the ground, Jane and Sienna's father Richard and Bette would carry the little girl everywhere. That's what doting grandparents and aunts were for, wasn't it?

Another splash of lightning, an almost immediate boom, and the light and sound were a signal for the rain to begin. As it often did in subtropical Louisiana, it started as a downpour, fat drops hitting the roof, drumming like tiny wet fists on the aluminum tiles.

It was a comforting sound. Long had always liked the sound of rain on the roof, liked watching the water pour in torrents from the overfilled gutters, spilling in thin sheets, drenching everything.

Half-awake now, Sienna pressed the crack of her ass against him in little shoves: one, two, three.

Long grinned. Here he was, in bed with the most beautiful woman in the world, a black-haired, blue-eyed Dutch-Irish-Italian genius who'd gotten her master's degree in biochemistry from MIT at nineteen; a woman who, despite her intelligence, had a major flaw—she had fallen in love with Hal Long. Talk about a blind spot. It still amazed him every time he thought about it.

He didn't see how life could get much better than this.

He pressed against her—

Long snapped awake as though jerked from sleep by a mad giant. He blinked, saw Moon sitting in the chair across from him, watching in silence.

"Sorry," he said. "I must have dozed off."

She nodded.

"How long was I out?"

"A couple of hours."

He shook his head. "Really?"

"The girls are still asleep. It's almost noon."

Long's mouth felt like dried leather and he needed to pee. "Bathroom?"

"Down the hall." She pointed.

He stood. His shoulders crackled as he stretched. He rotated his neck, did a squat. His knees popped like silenced pistols. He headed for the bathroom.

Moon watched Long amble toward the bathroom. The man had been through a lot. It showed on his face, in his movements. Given the seriousness of the magic block that sat and shimmered on the coffee table, he'd taken things pretty well, she thought. He was just a courier, a highly paid delivery man, really, but something about him made her feel more secure. Maybe it was the gun and his willingness to use it. Maybe it was just because he was a man, full of testosterone and pride, two of the most dangerous—but fascinating—elements on the planet. Maybe it was because when they'd met, he'd been worried about her daughter going into town on a bus. Whatever it was, there was a kind of comfort about it, she was more relaxed than she would have expected to be around a stranger, especially a strange man. He could be violent, if what he'd told her

was true, but somehow she couldn't quite picture him drunk
or stoned and using his fists on her or her children. Maybe
that was it.

She heard the old plumbing rattle as he flushed the toilet.
The door opened and he padded back down the hall.
Looked at her, then the block. Pandora's box, she'd called
it, and she'd only been half joking. It was kind of like being
handed an atomic bomb. Yeah, where it came from was
important, but not so much as what to do with it.

And what to do with it before it went off . . .

Before he could say what was obviously on his mind,
Alyssa walked into the room behind him. And because she
didn't know he was here—or maybe because she did—she
wore what she slept in—nothing.

Long turned and saw the naked young woman behind
him.

Now, the Goddess was not ashamed of her bodies, and
neither were her followers. Nudity was considered healthy
and natural, and during warm days, clothes were optional
for temple services. But to have her fifteen-year-old sexually active daughter stand stark bare in front of a man she
didn't know did cause Moon to clench. Alyssa was a beautiful child, and like it or not, wore a woman's body, complete with full breasts, thick pubic hair, and the desires that
went with both. And she thought Long was cute.

"Hi," Alyssa said. She scratched a spot under her left
nipple. She flashed him a big, half-awake smile. She wasn't
an adult but she knew her nudity would have some effect
on Long, and she was pushing it to see what it would be.

Moon looked at Long. He was a man, how could he not
respond to Alyssa? Moon's belly knotted into a fist.

A tiny smile flitted over his face, the smallest of grins.
"Morning," he said. Then he turned around and looked at
Moon.

What she saw in his face made her want to leap up and
hug him.

He gave her a little more of the grin, not much, but in

it she read volumes: He had looked upon her naked daughter, acknowledged her attractive—and, if Moon read her right, *available*—beauty, and then quietly told her mother he wasn't going to take advantage of it. She thought. It was a lot to read into a look.

"So," he said, "why don't we ask *it* what we ought to do?"

Alyssa, not sure of what *she* ought to do, turned away and shuffled down the hall toward the bathroom.

"Thank you," Moon said after Alyssa was gone.

He nodded. Said, "I had a daughter. She'd have been twelve on her next birthday. I don't molest children."

"You saw her. Alyssa is not exactly a child."

"But she is. Big enough is not necessarily old enough."

Moon repressed the sigh. A man with morals. Another point in his favor.

The little part of her that worried about such things piped up: *What is this, a contest? Favor-shmavor, you aren't getting* involved *with this guy! He isn't your type! This one won't be controlled.*

Moon didn't ask about Long's daughter. Instead, she looked at the shining curse that had befallen her. "Sure. Why not?"

Long smiled. "Okay, little friend, you have all the answers. How do we get out of this mess you've gotten us into?"

And the brick said, "Run away."

Moon laughed, she couldn't help it. Ask it about a religious artifact and it gave you chapter and verse; ask it a life-or-death question, and it said, "Run away." It was funny.

Long chuckled and looked at her. "I think you're wrong," he said. "Not Pandora's box. Cassandra's."

Wentworth got a call from his man in Aruba. It seemed that his son, Kennedy, had, at the tender age of fourteen, been deflowered. A local girl, a young woman of the evening. Not to worry, Wentworth's op said, the trull was healthy, her medical card was up-to-date, and from her account, Kennedy had acquitted himself well. His first round went off predictably early but the second and third shots were apparently on target.

Wentworth grinned. A chip off the old block, so it seemed.

"What did it cost him?"

"Hundred and fifty noodle," the op said.

Wentworth nodded silently. Boy was smarter than he had been. "Thanks for the call. Nothing on the record."

"Of course not."

They discommed. Well, at least that wasn't something he had to worry about anymore. Up until today, he'd wondered if maybe Kennedy hadn't been leaning toward boys, there hadn't been any interest evidenced in girls, no pornoproj's in his computer, no female friends come by to study, nothing like that. Not that Wentworth considered being gay a moral problem, he could give a rat's ass, but in high-level political circles, it was still something of a handicap. Wentworth didn't care if a man stuck his dick into a polar bear, as long as it didn't affect his ability to do his job. Ah, but the Great Unwashed out there tended to cling to traditional values, and like leeches on a dying man, they were oblivious to the health of their victim. Wentworth had experimented in prep school—in an all-boy school many of his fellow students had—but it hadn't really done anything for him. Wrong chemistry and that was that. Just as well, as he had learned it was better to appear to be near the middle of the road when you were whispering into the ears of kings and presidents. Wife, family, dog, backyard grill, all the signs of "just like everybody else" in place. Purely a pragmatic choice. Why strew boulders in your own path?

One less thing to worry about, his son, but hardly a drop thus spilled from his overfull bucket.

He looked at his watch. Almost time for his visit to the

range. He tapped his intercom. "I'm going to The Gallery, Susan."

He opened the desk drawer, brought out his Coonan and holster, put it on, went through his ritual magazine switch, shrugging into his coat. Maybe a session in The Gallery would loosen him up.

More and more, Green's time was taken with secular business. Now that this event in Arizona was a go, there were a million details to be handled. Yes, the bid from Phoenix covered a lot of it—hotels, special permits, even reduced airline fares—but there were so many other things that had to come together. Security was a major chore; with all those different religions there were bound to be a few fanatics opposed to anything and everything outside their narrow views. VIP attendees from the religious and the business and governmental arenas had to be stroked. Too much to do, too little time to do it.

His secretary buzzed him. "I've got the papal deputy on line one. And Vice-President Mbutu of Zimbabwe due to arrive here in five minutes."

"Thanks, Larry. I'll take the call. If the VP gets here before I'm done, give him the dog-and-pony show."

"Copy, Walt."

Larry was a good assistant, he knew how to handle the bigwigs. The boy could make you think you were fascinating if you told him you had to go to the toilet.

As for all the stuff with the courier and the feds, well, that would just have to wait. The world didn't stop so you could take care of problems, it just kept spinning along. If you didn't learn to adjust on the run, you'd fall flat on your face a hundred times a day.

"Green here. How is it going, Mario?"

The Pope's deputy said, "Great, Walter. Got a UV-ten day here, sun blazing away, not a cloud or a wisp of smog in the sky. Too pretty to stay inside." Although the man was as Italian as spaghetti, he had no trace of an accent. A

Harvard man before he went into the church, born in Milan
but raised in Pittsburgh.

"I hear that. What can I do you for?"

"Well, His Eminence has a couple of concerns. . . ."

Green listened to the man with half his attention. A few
concerns here, a few more there, it wasn't going to be a
picnic, this conference. That it was going to happen at all
was major; he had to expect an avalanche of concerns before it came to pass.

Give me strength, Lord.

Let him who desires peace prepare for war.

—Vegetius, De Rei Militari III

22

WENTWORTH SNATCHED THE Coonan from his shoulder holster, swung it around and down, locked onto the target, and fired two-handed, a double tap. He thumbed the safety back on and reholstered the pistol, cocked and locked, looked at the monitor inset into the booth wall next to him. The first round hit in the solar plexus, the second round at the top of the heart, in a straight line about a dozen centimeters apart.

Pretty good shooting, Ford.

The target itself was self-sealing plastic, an image of a man pointing a gun at the shooter. It was set at ten meters and a fine grid of laser sensor beams crisscrossed the back of the poster. The hits were thus transmitted to the monitor so you could see immediately where you'd scored no matter how far away you set the target. The sidewalls of this booth were thick plastic, proof against handgun rounds. ADs— accidental discharges—were rare for shooters of his skill, but they didn't like shoulder holsters here and so made all those who wore them use armored booths when on the line.

Not a bad idea. When the gun came out of the holster it was pointed briefly to the side as it went through its arc toward the target lock. Wentworth trusted himself, but he didn't want to be standing next to some clown who might pull the trigger at the wrong time; it would be galling to be killed by an AD coming through the wall at the range.

The Gallery was more complex than simple target shooting. There were action stages in the back where one could shoot against a clock at moving targets, and Wentworth would move to those as soon as he practiced the basics. He always used full-power loads, even though they put more wear on his pistol and kicked some, even with the compensator. If you shot the same loads during practice as you would in actual combat, you wouldn't get any surprises. He'd known guys who used wimp charges at the range who, when they had to cook off high-powered ammunition in a street shooting, missed at spitting range because they weren't used to the recoil and ballistics. Stupid.

Not that he expected to have to use his piece for anything but targets ever again. He wasn't a field man, hadn't been for a long time. Directors of agencies didn't go around potting felons, that's what the help was for. Even this thing in the Northwest, he didn't really have the luxury of leaving the office and flitting off to take care of it himself, not really.

Then again, it did a man good to get out into the field once in a while. To get in touch with his roots.

He grinned. Snatched the Coonan from its rig again and fired another double tap—blam! blam!—at the invulnerable shooter. Put the gun away.

One in the heart, one in the throat.

His left earplug felt loose. He pulled it out, adjusted the control, and reinserted it. The plugs were silicone and custom molded for him, and each had a cut-out circuit that shut off high-decibel noise within a hundredth of a second or so while allowing normal-level sounds through. You had to protect your hearing, and a .357 made quite a racket going off, especially inside.

He thrust his hand under his jacket, found the smooth wooden grips of his pistol again.

The shots were a little slower, because he picked a smaller target.

Two to the head.

Didn't matter what kind of body armor you wore if somebody could do that to you.

"So what do you think?" Moon asked Long.

He listened to the sound of Alyssa in the shower down the hall, the rattling pipes, and shook his head. "Offhand, I'd say maybe the little box has got a good point. We should run away."

"We?"

"Yeah, well, like it or not, we're in this mess together. After my recent adventures with the bad guys—even if they are feds—I get the feeling they won't be real pleased with me. If they think I've still got the box, they'll delete me to get it. If they think I've stashed it somewhere, I'd bet they'd keep me alive long enough to pry that location out of me and then deep-six me. Until we can figure out something, it might be a good idea to take a vacation."

"Where? How?"

"I've got a little money stashed under aliases. Enough to lay low for a couple of months. I'd opt for somewhere I've never been and they won't think of right off the bat. You ever been to South Dakota? Or Maine?"

"You really think it's that serious?"

"They tried to kill me twice. What do you think?"

"I wish I'd never seen the damned thing."

"I hear that. But you did and I don't figure it'll be in your best interest to go home until we do something to divorce you from the little sucker." He glanced at the brick. "No offense, brick."

The computer did not speak to that.

She shook her head. "I don't know."

"You know. You packed up the kids and left town because you knew."

She sighed. "Yeah, I guess I do."

"So, starting now, no calls, no contact with anybody who could point them at us. Soon as my cart finishes charging, we'll pack up and go."

"Won't they, uh, have roadblocks up or something?"

"Possible. Although the feds hate to let local or state cops in on anything if they don't have to. As long as we don't log into the net anywhere using our IDs, they probably won't find us unless they trip over us."

Not yet, anyway. If they don't collect us soon, they might get over their reluctance to call for help, and then it'll be harder to hide. But he didn't say that part aloud.

Green was in the bathroom when Gray called via his private channel.

"Good news and bad news. The good news is that package you were looking for is still unlocated," Gray said.

"That's the good news?"

"You don't have it but neither do the feds. Have to take comfort where you can, Reverend."

"Uh-huh. What's the bad news?"

"Nobody has the slightest idea of where it might be. The courier disappeared and he could have gone any direction, including straight up. His car is at the airport, his house is empty and he hasn't used his ID or his com, hasn't gone anywhere he is known to go in Portland."

Green chewed on that for a few seconds. "So what do you think?"

"I think if it was me, I'd find myself a place to hide and stay in it until the middle of next summer."

"Think the courier is that bright?"

He could almost see the shrug. "Can't say, Walter. But he's managed to make the feds look like Keystone Kops so far. He doesn't have to be all that bright."

Green chewed at his lip. "This has turned into a lot bigger deal than I thought it would."

"Ain't that the truth. Bigger than you and everybody else thought."

"All right. Keep me up to speed."

"Copy that. Discom."

Green thumbed the off-button on his com, put it on the bathroom counter. Well, damn. The church had been around for a long time and had learned how to be patient, but knowing that didn't make waiting any easier. He'd done as much as he knew how to do. If the Lord wanted this thing, the Lord would show Walter Green how to do it.

Amen.

Long drove back to the highway, Moon and her daughters with him. They had debated briefly about taking her car and decided to leave it. It ought to stay in the beach house's carport more or less unnoticed until the house's owner came out there again. If the feds were running a place-of-interest list on Moon's known whereabouts, they might come across it, but probably not for days, maybe weeks. But they'd sure know the make and license number, and that was something Long didn't want to risk.

They made it to the highway and started to pull out when Long spotted the flashing lights of several approaching police vehicles. They were half a mile away and not running the sirens. In a hurry, but a quiet hurry.

"Can you drive?" he asked Alyssa.

"Sure."

"Quick, change places with me and drive. Head toward those lights." To Moon and Dawn, he said, "When we pull out, I want you to lay flat, out of sight."

"What?" Moon began.

"Don't ask, just do it. Might not be anything, but if they are looking for us, all we want them to see is a teenage girl alone in this cart."

Long opened the door, slid out, switched places with

Alyssa. The girl looked at him nervously, wiped her hands on her pants. "Just like your mother's car," he said.

Next to her older daughter, Moon scrunched down and twisted sideways. In the back, Long stuffed himself behind the front seats on the floor while Dawn stretched out on the backseat. Snug. Very snug. "Go," he said.

"Shouldn't you, you know, get your gun out or something?" Dawn said.

"No. If this doesn't work, I don't want any shooting. We give up. I don't think the feds'll do anything with local cops watching, and once they get what they want, probably they'll let us go."

Right. And I'll fly to the moon by blowing rocket smoke from my butt, too.

Alyssa pulled out onto the highway. The little cart jerked a couple of times, but smoothed out once she got rolling.

Long held his breath.

It didn't take long. Fifteen seconds later the colored lights strobed the inside of the car as the cops zipped past. He heard the brakes as they skidded and slowed to make the turn.

Even as that was happening, Alyssa said, "Oh, *shit*!" The car swerved, then whipped back into its own lane.

"Just keep it steady," Long said.

"Motherfucker!" Alyssa said. "Mother*fucker*!" She pounded on the steering wheel.

Her mother said, "Baby? What is it? Alyssa?"

When he sat up, he saw Alyssa was crying.

Through the tears, the girl said, "Django. *Django* was in one of those cars!"

"Pull over, right there," Long said.

Alyssa rolled the car under the canopy of a big fir tree.

"Dawn, sit in the front with Hal," Moon said. "Get in the back, baby." Moon helped her sobbing daughter into the backseat as Long took over the wheel.

Alyssa was in the depths of great grief. Her mother tried to comfort her. Long glanced over at Dawn.

"Her boyfriend," Dawn said.

"How did he know where to find us?"

Dawn looked down at her lap. Shook her head. "I—I don't know."

She knew, but she wasn't going to tell on her sister, he could see that. Alyssa had given her boyfriend a call. Told him where she was. He must know where the place was, enough so they brought him instead of asking directions.

So much for their big head start.

There were a lot of back roads in Oregon, ways to get out of the state without rolling down the interstate where you were too visible. The logical thing being here on the coast would be to go north toward Washington and Canada or south to California.

Long checked his map, then headed east.

> The Great Wheel turns and Karma does always come
> round. Take no meaning from this.
>
> —Oxajizen, *No Mind, All Mind*

23

THE DRIVE ACROSS Oregon gave them more than a few tense moments, but they were all false alarms. They were somewhere in Idaho as dawn approached. On a country road in a cool forest, clean and bright stars pinpointing the dark curtain overhead. There in the woods, they came across a motel.

The place was a pit, a motel hell, eighty years old if it was a day. A three-meter-tall painted wooden statue of a demonic-looking logger with a double-bladed ax stood spread-legged on the roof of the main lodge. The statue's paint had weathered considerably over the years, its beard bleached from black to dull gray, the cap, blue jeans, and checkered shirt mere ghosts of their original selves. There were rain streaks, bird shit, and patches of moss, fungus, and grime coating the thing. Entropy was winning; Paul Bunyan there looked as if he'd been dragged through a vat of tar and rolled in the dirt.

But they had empty cabins, it was off the beaten path, and the old lady running the desk was half-deaf and three-quarters blind. She had a reservation computer terminal on her desk but the screen itself was almost invisible under scratched and frosted glass. A holoproj in the room behind the desk blared with a soap opera, the sound so loud the stained front windows rattled under the blast.

Granny here wouldn't be turning anybody in. Assuming she could remember she'd ever seen them, they couldn't be much more than blurs to her. Long paid in cash, which was fine by her, she didn't like fooling with all that input and printouts and such, she informed them. Half the neighborhood must have heard her yelling.

They rented one cabin with three bedrooms in it. Long checked the place before he allowed Moon and her daughters inside.

If filth were dangerous, they'd all be dead before the sun came up, but otherwise, nobody lurked under the sprung beds or in the crumbling pressed-paper dressers. The black mold in the shower stall was fairly militant; it had crawled up the plastic curtain and walls at least a meter from the drain, but it probably wouldn't come after them while they slept. Though you'd want to shower with shoes on if you were desperate enough to risk it.

"Okay. It's clear."

The cabins on both sides were empty. Long tried the mechanical key in their locks and both doors opened. Figured. He'd prop something against the door in theirs before he went to sleep. Probably he'd slept in worse places, though he couldn't remember one right off.

He was on the porch, staring into the night, when Moon came out and moved to stand next to him.

"Alyssa's still pretty upset," she said.

He nodded. "I can understand that."

"She doesn't want to discuss it with me," Moon said. She sighed. "I wish children came with handbooks. I never know if I'm doing the right thing."

"Nobody ever does. You do the best you can with what you've got."

She shook her head. "Yeah."

"Maybe I can talk to her."

She looked away from the dark forest of firs and alder and up at him.

"Couldn't hurt," he said.

There came a *thump!* from the darkness. Long reached for his gun, stopped and listened. "Look over there," he said. "Corner of that cabin."

"What is it?"

"That white lump? An owl. That's what made the noise. When it landed."

"Sweet Goddess."

The tension eased a little.

"Dawn, come out here, please," Moon called.

The younger girl emerged. "Yeah?"

Moon looked at Long. "Go ahead. Your serve."

Long nodded. Walked into the cabin.

Inside, Alyssa sat on the ratty couch, her arms crossed, her posture so tight she looked as if she might explode. Her face was pinched into grim and white-lipped anger.

Long stood just inside in the doorway for a few seconds, not speaking. Finally, he said, "I'm sorry about Django."

"I can't believe he did it," she said.

He let it simmer for a minute. "It was a rotten thing to do."

"He said he would do anything for me, *any*thing! Instead, he spewed to the grabs!"

Long did a mental translation: Spewed to the grabs = Gave her up to the cools. Youth patois, ever changing. Not something you could keep up with unless you were on that cutting edge, where nobody his age could be, no matter how hard they might want to be. And he didn't want to be. Life was hard enough without having to go through adolescence twice.

"They must have put some pressure on him," Long offered.

"So fucking what? He said he was willing to *die* for me!"

He watched as she almost lost it, nearly slid down the face of the barren cliff that had appeared in her soul and into the sea of sadness below. But her anger kept the welling tears back. He could see it, feel it, almost touch it.

He took another step into the room, rubbed his hands along the sides of his jeans. Said, "Sucks, doesn't it?"

She pulled her stare away from eternity and looked at him. "How would you know?"

"When I was your age, my best friend was Woody Bramlett. We did everything together. Went to school, hung out, lived in each other's pockets. We joined the Marines, got sent to the same base for training. They used to let you do that, link up and buddy through basic and even advanced."

She stared at him, arms still knotted together, body still a coiled spring ready to let go. Nobody had ever been hurt this way before. Nobody could understand. Certainly not *him*.

"We finished basic, got shipped to the AMS in Pensacola. We trained together, took liberty together, got drunk and stoned together, picked up women together. We were not just friends. I would have cut off a hand for him."

Her crossed arms were a little looser, he had her interested, he thought.

"So fucking what?"

Well, maybe not too interested.

"So, there was a woman in our platoon. Tough, smart, good-looking. We weren't supposed to fraternize with each other, it was against regs. We were eighteen, nineteen, most of us. At that age, nothing really scares you, so I said to hell with the regs."

"What was her name?"

"Sandra Forrest."

"You remember that after what? Thirty years?"

He smiled. "Not quite that long. And some things you don't forget."

"Okay. So what happened?"

"Woody was interested, too. No surprise, we were together so much we thought alike, had similar tastes. I guess I would have been surprised if he hadn't wanted to get next to her.

"Anyway, we both started working her. It wasn't just sex, she would probably have slept with with either or both of us if she'd felt the urge. We didn't attach a whole lot of importance to the act. If it felt good, why not do it? It didn't hurt anybody, right?"

She nodded, but didn't speak.

"So I sang and danced and put on my happy face, tried to convince Sandy I was the best thing since AC electricity. When Woody got a chance, he did the same thing. It was about sex—but it was also about being the one picked. That make any sense to you?"

"Yeah."

Long wondered if he should have taken this road. Talking about this kind of thing to a fifteen-year-old girl.

"You know how to swim?"

She blinked. "What's that got to do with anything?"

"Humor me."

"Yeah."

"You afraid of the water?"

"Not particularly."

He nodded. "I used to be. It terrified me. Because I was afraid of drowning, I made myself learn everything there was to know about what a man was capable of in big water. I've got every advanced swimming tag the RC puts out. I know all the strokes, can probably still hold my breath for two minutes, can do five klicks at a stretch. It took years. But now, I'm *comfortable* in the water. No fear."

"Napoleonic compensation," she said.

He looked at her, surprised.

"Some of it sticks," she said. "I'm not stupid."

"I didn't think you were."

The silence between them hung heavy for a time. Finally, she said, "So what happened?"

"Nobody in the world knew my secret fear—except Woody. When we did aquatic training, I pushed hard, got to the top of the scoring stats. The fear was there, but—it didn't show."

She said, "Uh-huh."

"But Woody, my best friend, the only person on the planet I really trusted, *he* knew. And he told Sandy."

Long waited for his surge of anger but it didn't come. He smiled. Still amazing to him that it didn't. It had for so long.

"He figured all was fair in love and war, so he brought that little bit out and presented it. Figured it would make him look better or me worse, I'm not sure which."

"So he fucked you over and got the girl," she said.

"No, he fucked me over, but I got the girl."

She uncrossed her arms, put her hands on her hips. "Is this supposed to be a parable? 'Every cloud has a silver lining'? 'It's an ill wind that blows no good'? Like that?"

"No. Sandy chose me. Maybe she liked it that I was flawed, maybe it didn't have anything to do with that, whatever. We screwed like minks for a week and then we were done. It doesn't really have anything to do with Sandy.

"What it had to with was my best friend who betrayed me. My buddy from when we were kids, a guy I would have laid down my life to save, my one true pal—he betrayed me. Just to get laid. He didn't love her any more than I did. He just wanted to win, at any cost.

"I seriously considered killing him. Because there's nothing worse than being betrayed by somebody you trust, is there?"

She shook her head. Her voice was a whisper. "No. Nothing."

"Yeah, see, you found that out, but that's not the point, either."

She blinked, the tears finally starting. "What *is* the fucking point?"

"Woody and I, we stopped doing shit together, stopped talking. It bothered him but he never understood and I never told him why.

"Come time to pick assignments, I went one way, he went another. End of friendship, end of story, and fuck him.

"Fifteen, eighteen years went by and I still got pissed off every time I thought about him. I knew intellectually we'd both been young and stupid and you make mistakes when you don't know any better, but I never forgave him emotionally. Some crimes earn you a life sentence."

"I hear that."

"It left a big hole in me, his going, me pushing him away, but there wasn't anything I could do about it. I was wounded, he did it. I couldn't let it go. Deep wounds heal the slowest, they bleed a long time."

"So what happened?"

"A couple years ago, he called. He was in town, came across my name somehow. Wanted to get together for a beer."

He finally had her now, her full attention. She leaned forward on the edge of the couch, caught up in his drama.

"We met at a bar. He was fat, bald, worn. He'd been married and divorced a couple of times, unable to father children, had gotten into trouble with the law. He was paying off a heavy tax debt, living alone in a crappy room, working as a night watchman. You know the term 'karma'?"

"Yeah, my mom throws it around pretty good."

"I believe in it," Long said. "I think you get what's coming to you, sooner or later. You put out good, it comes back. You put out bad, that comes back around. I'm not saying that fucking me over was the cause of Woody's miserable life. But he probably did other stuff like it.

"So we drank our beer and while we were doing it, I understood something. Woody never got it. He never came to realize that what you planted was what grew, what you had to choke down. He never learned the lesson.

"As much as I'd wanted to smash his face in at eighteen, that wouldn't have come close to what had happened to him over the years. He had been stretched out and pasted flat by forces a whole lot bigger than I was."

He sighed. Stared into space for a second, then back at her.

"I don't believe in a white-haired old God sitting on a throne throwing lightning bolts," he said. "I don't believe in a fertile fat-breasted goddess spitting out demigod babies, either. But I do believe in karma.

"When I saw Woody sitting there, pounded into submission by life, I stopped being angry with him. He'd paid for what he'd done, paid big time."

"So that's it? You two are like, *friends* again?"

"No. I wouldn't put my hand in the same fire twice. The point of this whole long and boring speech is simple: Sooner or later, your boyfriend will get what's coming to him. It might not be fast enough to suit you, but it'll happen. And when enough time has gone by, you might stop hating him. You might even feel sorry for him."

"I don't think so."

"Come see me in twenty years," Long said. "He hurt you and he'll suffer for it. Sooner or later. Believe it."

He sat on the couch next to her and put his arm around her shoulders. She cried for a while and when she was done, got up and left the room without speaking.

Moon stepped into the room. "Well. Hell of a story."

"Yeah. I've never told it before. Seemed like the right time."

She shook her head. "I don't usually like brave men."

"Brave?"

"Telling her that story took more balls than shooting that gun you carry."

He shrugged.

She said, "You'd make a pretty good father."

He felt his face cloud over. "Yeah. I wish I'd gotten the
chance." He let it go. "Another story, another day."

"Sure. Hey, Hal?"

"Yeah?"

"Thanks."

"You're welcome."

Thou shalt tread upon the lion and adder: the young
lion and the dragon shalt thou trample under feet.

—*Psalms*, 91:13

24

UP ALONE AT home, past midnight, Wentworth cleaned
his pistol.

A lesson his father had taught him, long before he joined
any agency in which guns were required wear. *A clean
weapon in good repair won't let you down*, the old man
used to say. *If your weapon fails because a piece of crud
fouls it, a charging cape buffalo or angry lion isn't going
to stop and politely wait while you clear the jam.*

Wentworth grinned at the memory. The old man had
been a hunter, taken all of the Big Five, even after three of
them—the lion, elephant, and leopard—were illegal. Big
money bought lots of winks and turned backs, especially
in Third World countries where the cost of a good restaurant meal in New York would feed half a tribe for weeks.

Wentworth had the Coonan disassembled. He ran a stainless steel brush soaked in solvent through the barrel,
scrubbed the bore. Nothing else in the world smelled like
this stuff. It always brought back memories.

Yeah, his old man had been quite the sportsman. Wentworth had gone on safari with him a couple of times. Shot the required beasts to prove his manhood, though it had never done much for him. You had all the advantages as a hunter. The brain, the patience, the gun. You drove to where the game was, got out, had a tracker locate your prey, stalked or waited until the animal showed itself. It was hard for an elephant to hide. A high-powered bullet would easily drop him if the shot was placed well, and that was that. *Adios*, Jumbo. No matter how big and powerful, an animal wasn't going to shoot back.

The one time he'd felt a thrill was on a lion shoot on the Bisina Game Ranch by the lake in Uganda. Here the rare animals were stocked for hunters with enough money to afford the kill fees. Without telling his father or his bearer, he removed all the ammunition from his rifle, save one round. If he came upon the lion, he'd have one chance: it would be him or the beast. If he missed, the lion would win. He'd thought that was fair. Unfortunately, he hadn't spotted his quarry soon enough. That canny old black man carrying his weapon—what was his name? Kioo?—had known something was wrong with the rifle, one of Wentworth's father's custom Weatherbys. Not heavy enough, he realized. He checked the action and nearly had a stroke when he realized the gun was almost empty. He raised such a fuss there wasn't any way to download it after that.

Wentworth was sure his old man had figured out what he was doing. He made one remark, that was all, and he never said anything about it again. "What if you had come upon two lions, Ford?"

A good point, one he hadn't even considered at the time.

He took a wire brush to the slide, worried burned powder from the rails, wiped it away with an oily rag. The Coonan, built like the old slab-sided military .45, all straight lines and sharp angles, was a precision instrument. Semiauto pistols didn't much like the standard straight-walled .357 rimmed round. There was a newer cartridge that pinched in at the base where an extractor could grab it, a dedicated self-loading pistol's .357, but it was shorter and not nearly as hot. The ammo he used, jacketed hollow-points that flowered into a star on impact with something the density of human flesh, had a 98 percent stop rate with but a single round. With a double tap, the fight would go out of a man at a rate so close to 100 percent it was statistically insignificant.

He worked a toothbrush soaked in cleaner down the magazine well, poked the rag into the hole and soaked up most of the liquid. The fluid evaporated quickly and left a thin coating of dry lube that protected the surfaces it touched. He could have had somebody do this for him, of course. It took twenty minutes of his more-than-valuable time, but he did the chore himself, liked doing it. There was something about cleaning his own weapon, sharpening his own knife, some . . . Zen kind of thing that appealed to him.

He wiped the parts again. Reassembled the pistol, racked the slide a few times, put in an empty magazine, dropped the hammer. The action was honed, the pull just over a kilogram, smooth and crisp. He carried the piece cocked-and-locked since it was a single-action; all he had to do was thumb the safety off and he was ready to cook. Seven in the magazine, one up the spout. He carried a pair of spare magazines on his shoulder holster's counterbalance, so he had a total of twenty-two rounds on him whenever he went out. The gun didn't have half the capacity of a Glock or Smith 9mm or .40, but it was a classic, a Rolls-Royce compared to a Yugo. Besides, if he couldn't get it done with twenty, it wasn't likely he was going to get it done.

He opened a box of ammo, loaded three magazines with fresh cartridges, chambered a round, thumbed the safety on. Topped off the mag. He slipped the pistol into the holster. Ready to go.

He went to take a shower.

• • • •

Green wouldn't call it a crisis of faith, that wasn't very
likely, but it certainly was troubling.

It was pushing ten P.M. and he was exhausted from the
day's battles, but he couldn't get to sleep. He lay in the
bed staring up into the darkness. Something—he couldn't
quite put his finger on it—something was bothering him.
Some sense of foreboding gripped him, made him fearful.
Not normal worry, fear of failing in his job, but something
deeper, darker, unseen.

Well. He couldn't be *really* fearful, not with the Lord as
his protector. But uneasy, yes, that was certainly true.

*What is it, Lord? Why am I so stirred? What would you
have of me? It's got to do with this temple thing, doesn't
it?*

God didn't choose to answer in any way Green could
interpret.

Long took the smallest room, there was hardly enough
room to walk along one side of the bed that was shoved
into the corner. They had decided to sleep during the day
and travel at night, at least until they were a couple of states
away from Oregon.

A pressed-paper box for hanging clothes sagged at an
angle at the foot of the bed. The box smelled like mothballs
and didn't look as if it would hold a pair of jeans without
giving up the fight against gravity. He took off his shirt
and shoes, unbuckled his pants, but didn't remove them. If
he had to come out of bed in a hurry, he didn't want to do
it naked. Under the sink in the bathroom, somebody had
left a little plastic box of cleaning supplies, a couple of bars
of soap, half a tube of toothpaste, some shampoo, and for
some odd reason, a little plastic can of sewing machine oil.
He should have had that kind of thing packed in his cart, but
somehow had forgotten it. Long used some of the toothpaste on his finger to freshen his mouth. Wiped at his face
and armpits with a wet towel, then took the can of oil and
one of the threadbare gray washcloths into his room. He

sat on the bed, emptied the cylinder of his revolver, and cleaned the weapon.

The gun really wasn't dirty. He had fired it only twice since he'd last changed the barrel and cleaned it, but it gave him something to do. He was too wired to sleep yet.

He used some of the oil on the washrag to wipe the front of the cylinder. He scrubbed at the powder-burn rings on the two fired chambers with the cloth around his pocket-knife until he managed to get the stainless steel clean. He ran one corner of the rag through the same two chambers. It wasn't as good as using a cleaning rod and solvent, but it would have to do. He always cleaned his weapon after shooting it, though a session at the range was usually two boxes of shells and not two shots.

He finished wiping the Smith, reloaded it. He had two speed loaders in his jacket, plus the six in the weapon. Two more boxes of ammo in the trunk of the cart. If he had to shoot, that would be the least of his problems.

He tucked the revolver into the paddle holster and laid it next to his shoes by the bed.

"Hal?"

Alyssa stood in the doorway. She wore a thin nightgown that ended just below her crotch. He looked at her, held back a sigh. She was wounded, lonely, young, and attractive. There was a time when he would have comforted her and taken for himself some comfort doing it. He was tired, tense, and the idea of a warm woman next to him in bed was very appealing. But not a child. She was sexually attractive but what he mostly saw was closer to a daughter than a lover. Mostly.

"Can I come in?"

Her voice was tiny, soft, vulnerable.

"Sure."

She drifted into the room. He scooted back on the bed so his back was to the wall, and she sat on the end by his feet. The gown rode up.

"Thank you for what you said."

"No problem."

"I, uh—"

"Listen, Alyssa, you are a beautiful woman. If I were twenty years younger, I wouldn't let you leave this bed for a week. But I'm old enough to be your father, not just physically, but mentally."

She blinked at him.

"Come here."

She slid across the bed. He wrapped his arms around her and hugged her tight, then used one hand to pet her head. She put her arms around his bare back and clutched at him. After a moment, she tried to pull away, maybe to move onto something else, but he held her, wouldn't let her go. They sat that way for a long time. Finally she relaxed. He released her and she leaned back and smiled through tears at him. "Thanks for the hug," she said. "That's what I really wanted." She hugged him again, then slid off the bed.

She had been right earlier: she wasn't stupid.

"Good night, Hal."

"Good night, Alyssa."

After she was gone, he finally let the sigh out. Man!

He saw Moon appear at the doorway

"Yeah?"

"Just looking for the halo. You're too good to be real. You want to get married?"

Moon padded the short distance back to her room, found Alyssa sitting on her sagging bed.

"Mom? Could I sleep in here with you?"

Moon moved to her daughter. "Sure, sweetie."

The sun was up and the slatted blinds didn't block out all the light, but Moon drifted into sleep with an arm around her daughter. Yes, Alyssa was an adult in the body she wore, but right now she was still Moon's baby. She had never been able to look at her children without that time-telescope effect, seeing them as they were and yet able to see all the way back to when they'd been laughing, gurgling infants she could carry perched on one arm. Probably never get over that, she thought. That was okay.

She drifted off to sleep offering comfort to her daughter, and despite the situation they were all in, feeling better than she had in a long time.

It was nice to be needed.

They say miracles are past.

—Shakespeare, *All's Well That Ends Well*

25

WHEN LONG STRUGGLED up from a troubled sleep, it was daylight—and snowing. He checked his watch. Nearly two in the afternoon.

He rubbed at his whiskered face, walked to the grimy window, and looked out at a world made new and powdery white. Great. Just what they needed.

He put his shoes on, went to the bathroom. He washed his face, used the razor he kept in the cart, attended to his other bodily functions. When he came out, Moon was up. She said, "Girls are still conked out. You want to talk?"

"Yeah. How about out on the porch?"

Long went back to his room. He slipped his jacket on, put his paddle holster into his belt, checked the loads in the Smith, replaced the piece.

Moon waited for him outside on the porch, a synlon jacket over her shirt and jeans. She put her hands in her pockets. Both she and he blew vapor clouds into the cold air.

"So now what?" she asked him.

He thought about it for a second. "Why don't we ask the box?"

She chuckled.

"No, I'm serious. Whatever it is, it's the only advantage we've got. Why don't we use it?"

"You *trust* it?"

"No. But either it's a really advanced computer—maybe even an AI—or the biggest hoax in the world. If it's the first, it knows stuff we don't. If it's the second, we're getting into deep shit for nothing and probably screwed anyhow. Why not see if it can help? We don't have to take its advice."

They watched the snow feather down. The wind picked up a little and the gentle drifting started to flurry, spinning and whirling the flakes in more frantic swirls. A gust of cold washed across the porch and tossed a few stray crystals into Long's face. He blinked them away. Even made the air smell clean, the snow. Looking at all that pristine whiteness, it was hard to believe they were running for their lives.

"Yeah, I guess you're right," Moon said. "Let's go have a talk with the Cassandra box."

At first, they couldn't find it.

"What'd you do with it?" she asked.

"I put it right there in that top drawer."

"Not there now."

"I see that."

"Are you sure?"

"Yeah. Maybe. I was pretty tired. I remember putting it there. The drawer jammed and I had to pull it all the way out and back in again before I could close it."

"Maybe one of the girls . . . ?"

Long continued to look for the box.

He found it on the sink in the bathroom.

"I know I didn't put it there," he said.

"Girls are still asleep and I didn't put it there, either," she said.

Long held the thing in his hand, stared at it. "Oh, well. Somebody did. It didn't just get up and walk there by itself."

"Ask it."

"Good thought. Yo, box. How'd you get into the bathroom?"

On that subject, the box had nothing to say.

"Figures," Long said.

"Try something else. Box, who exactly is it after us?"

"Would you like a complete list of all the players?" the box said. "The current number of people is three hundred and twelve."

"Great. No, skip the lackeys. Who is in charge?" Long put in.

Wentworth emerged from his private bathroom into his office just before five P.M. The outer door was locked and when he checked, his secretary swore nobody had tried to get past her.

But there was a shimmery silver brick on the middle of his desk that wasn't there when he'd left to take a leak.

Green walked to the taco stand around two P.M. and sat at the counter for a late lunch before going back to the office wars. He stared off into nowhere as the counterman worked.

When he looked down, somebody had managed to sneak up without being seen and leave a shining block next to Green's paper plate.

He stared at it. Got a cold flash as he realized what it must be.

How could this be possible?

Yes, the Lord worked in mysterious ways, His wonders to perform, but Walter Green had never actually witnessed a bona fide miracle before. And that's what this had to be. A miracle.

Thank you, Lord.

He reached for the Manifestation.

The world abounds with laws yet teems with crimes.

—Anonymous, *Proceedings Against America*

The weed of crime bears bitter fruit.

—Lamont Cranston

26

"CHRIST," LONG SAID.

"Sounds like He's after us, too," Moon offered. "National Security Agency? United World Council of Churches? Vietnamese gunmen? Big can of worms here. If our little friend can be believed."

Long shook his head. "I can see why the feds want it. But a Baptist minister? A Jesuit priest?"

"They'd want it more than the government," she said. "With the feds, we're talking about power, control, money. Piddly stuff compared to messing with faith. I know so-called Christians who'd push a button to kill everybody on the planet if they believed God wanted them to do it. The bloodiest wars are always religious ones—especially those of male-based religions. If by dying for the cause you're going straight to Paradise to sit at your thundering god's right hand, death doesn't mean a whole lot."

"Are people really that stupid?"

"That's a rhetorical question, right?"

"Yeah, I guess it is."

"So now what?"

"Well. The box is offering us ways to avoid being collected. Unless you've got a better idea, I say we give it a try."

She sighed. "Assuming the box can be trusted, that takes care of the immediate problem. But what then? Eventually, we'll run out of places to hide."

"Yeah, and eventually we all die and the universe will wind down. Let's worry about that later. Now it's one day at a time."

Wentworth was surprised but it didn't take long for him to figure out what he had. "What the hell is this?" he said.

The box told him.

After he got over his shock, he asked it a few more questions.

Christ! It was the thing from the temple! The little device that people had been dying over was here, smack in the middle of his desk.

To be certain, he asked it that: "Are you the thing from the temple in Portland I've been looking for?"

"Not exactly," the box said. It had a low, throaty feminine voice.

"What does that mean?"

"It means I am and am not that which you have been seeking. I am a chronomorph."

"Explain."

"You don't have the mathematics to understand. Think of me as a single item that exists in three places at once. Kind of a triptych in which all three of me are exact mirror images of the others. At the same time, all of us are also the original."

"My physics might be a little rusty but I know something can't exist in more than one place at the same time."

"Your physics is far beyond rust, Mr. Wentworth. Insofar as this matter goes, your knowledge is the oxide dust

under the feet of a tribe of illiterate pygmies, to continue
your own analogy.''

Wentworth stared at the silver ingot. The thing had just
called him stupid. Well, no, ignorant, actually. He didn't
much like it either way. He said, ''But you are the box that
answers questions truthfully?''

''I answer some questions. I am limited in three ways:
One, I do not know the answers to all questions. Two, I
am not allowed to answer certain questions to which I do
know the answers. Three, in my present form my abilities
are reduced by two-thirds' capacity.''

Wentworth picked it up.

''Is each of your other selves thus constrained?''

''Yes.''

''And in order to obtain full operational capacity?''

''I/we must be reunited.''

''Ah. I see.''

He had one-third of the computer. How it happened he
could figure out later. But to make this thing three times as
powerful, he needed the other pieces of it. He was better
off than he was but not as well off as he wanted to be.

''Do you know where the other parts of yourself are?''

''Yes.''

Wentworth smiled.

Green made it back to his room—he dared not risk the
office—and sat on his bed, the silver block next to him. It
refused to tell him where it came from or how it got to the
greasy spoon where he was having lunch. But he knew
what it was. From the Jesuit's description, it could be nothing else. God had delivered it to him.

''How did the courier lose you?''

''He did not. I am still with him.''

''You better explain that.''

The shimmering block did. When it was done, Green
didn't know much more about the thing, but he reckoned
that it was in three parts, all the mumbo-jumbo about being

the same notwithstanding. And while one part was better than nothing, he needed to have the other two pieces of this nasty little puzzle.

He quickly found out the thing was programmed to give less than total truth, though. He asked it about Kyle.

"My boy enjoying himself in Heaven?"

"If by Heaven you mean the Christian concept of perpetual bliss given as a reward for proper faith, no. There is no such place."

Green chuckled. Lying machine. "No Hell, either, huh?"

"Correct."

"And God?"

"Does not exist—if you are inquiring about the Christian image."

Well. In the hands of a slick PR man this thing might be dangerous, but Walter Green wasn't going to throw over a lifetime of faith because some little block of whatever this was said it wasn't so. Still, if it answered truthfully stuff you could verify, you might be apt to give it some credence on the things you couldn't prove outright. That could be a nasty problem. There were people who put more faith into their machines than they did in the Lord, sure enough.

He also realized that with the information he could glean from this device—a creation of the Devil, no doubt—he could locate the others like it, round them all up, put them in a steel case, and bury them where the sun didn't shine. End of problem.

But . . . did the end justify the means? Could he righteously use a toy tainted by the talons of the Lord of the Flies? For *any* reason?

If God had not wished it so, it wouldn't be here, would it?

He reached for his com.

Moon felt out of control, shaped and moved by forces far beyond her. A few days ago, she was a simple priestess, living a measured and calm life, content with her place in the scheme of things. Now . . . now she was a fugitive, running from police and others, cursed with knowledge she did not want to have.

Goddess help me.

But if the damned little box could be believed, the Goddess wasn't going to be leaping in anytime soon. Or ever. Because if the fucking computer or whatever it was wasn't lying through its electronic teeth, there was no Goddess.

In the bedrooms, the girls stirred to wakefulness and Long packed what gear he had. Moon sat and stared at the snow coming down.

On one level, she had always suspected it. Her early faith had been dogmatic, not a thing to be questioned. As a little girl in Butte, she had looked at the stained-glass Jesus in her father's Methodist church—they sprinkled, the Baptists dunked—and felt a certain comfort. That almost-blond, blue-eyed Christ represented by the brightly colored panes was in His Heaven and watching over her. You always had a friend in Jesus, no matter where you went.

Methodists weren't big on hellfire and brimstone.

Later, when she'd gone to Bible college in Loveland, the feeling of warmth hadn't been so strong, but it had been a continuing glow. And if she didn't have the fervent dedication of a newly born-again Christian, at least there was real faith. And she wanted to help other people, so being a minister was as good a path as any.

She'd been Lea Quinn then, not Miranda Moon, and when Martin Steen arrived with his winning smile, good looks, and self-professed dedication to Jesus, she had fallen hard. They married, she got pregnant and dropped out of school to raise the baby. Martin would support them; he had great prospects once he graduated. Life was going to be wonderful.

That hadn't lasted long, the feeling of wedded bliss. Behind the charming facade, the handsome face, Martin was weak. The alcohol and amphetamines drove him, and when he miscalculated the dosages, when he didn't balance the highs and the lows, he started to hit her.

Moon sighed, remembering. Jesus hadn't come to her rescue. Martin was working for Jesus, supposedly. What faith she'd felt in the benevolent Christ began to die the first time Martin slapped her. By the time she left him, that faith was long cold. A male-dominated religion didn't offer much to the women in it, unless they were willing to live as second-class people. The man was the head of the household and whatever he thought proper for his family *was* proper—Martin had preached that at her often enough. He never came right out and said it was right that he get stoned and beat her, but he did say he expected her, as a good Christian wife, to forgive him. Hadn't Jesus said the very same thing? Turn the other cheek? Forgive the sinner? Did not the Bible say, Judge not, lest ye be judged?

Oh, he had been clever with his twists.

So, her faith died, rotted, was gone—but there was a hole left where it had been.

Later, when she came across the Embrace, when she heard women talking about women and love and harmony, the Goddess rushed right in and filled that hollow place in her. It was as much social and psychological as anything, but she tried hard to believe. Now and then, when everything was right, she did believe.

Or had thought so.

But true faith doesn't vanish as fast as hers seemed to when the box told her there was no Goddess, no God, either, not like the Christian one. Yes, there was a . . . *force* that existed, but not one that allowed itself to be anthropomorphized into an image of man—or of woman. Better than nothing, she supposed, but not much better. People were visual creatures, they needed images. "Force" didn't conjure up much. Maybe she should ask the box what it looked like.

"You ready?" Long said.

She turned away from her long stare into the snowy woods. "Yeah. I guess."

"Let's roll. We'll find a place to eat, get on the road in the late afternoon, drive at night."

"Will your cart go in the snow?"

"I've got chains. We'll be okay."

Moon nodded. "If you say so." She went to help the girls load the cart.

And is not time, even as love is, undivided and space-less?

—Kahlil Gibran, *The Prophet*

27

GREEN CALLED GRAY first. Then called the Jesuit. He used his scrambler on both calls.

The Catholic was more than a little excited.

"This is amazing, Walter! I'll be right there—"

"Hold up, Leo. It's not as amazing as you think." Green told the Jesuit about the three pieces. He could almost hear the man frown.

"Well. We have to obtain the other two parts."

"My thoughts exactly," Green said. "But given what I've discovered about this little item, I don't think this is something we can afford to delegate any longer. I believe we must collect these things ourselves."

"Hmm. You're right." There was a pause. "As it happens, I have operatives in the federal bureaucracy who can help with that end. But the courier and the woman . . ."

"They won't be nearly as well-protected," Green said. "And this *thing,* whatever it is, can help us locate them."

"How?"

"I don't know. But it told me it could."

"Fascinating."

"Make no mistake, Leo, this is the Devil's tool, an infernal machine. Once we collect all of it, it must be destroyed."

"Of course."

Green smiled. He didn't need a stress analyzer to detect *that* lie. If the Jesuit got his hands on this monstrous device in any or all of its forms, you wouldn't be able to pry it loose with an atomic bomb. It would disappear into the society and they'd use it—and abuse it—until the sun went cold. He didn't doubt that for a moment. But he also knew he had to keep the Jesuit where he could keep an eye on him. The man was as slick as a boxcar full of axle grease and it would not do to let him get the jump on this. Green already knew the Jesuit had deep-cover operators placed high in the National Security Agency, that was certain, given how fast he managed to collect secret information. It didn't matter who it was, as long as they could convince the man—or woman—to help them nab the third part of this thing when the time came.

Green said, "Meet me at the airfield in an hour. We'll take the council jet. I'm bringing somebody with me."

"Bringing somebody?"

"Gray."

"Gray? The dentist?"

"If he is, that's the least of his talents, don't you think?"

He waited to see if the Jesuit would try to play games. He didn't trust Gray long-term any more than he trusted the Jesuit, but he had to work with the tools he'd been given.

The Jesuit heard the knowledge in his voice. Said, "Yes, well, I suppose that's true. I didn't know you knew Gray."

But I know for certain now that you do. "We've done a little business. And it wasn't cleaning my teeth." As he said it, he wondered if it might not be a mistake, letting the Jesuit know he wasn't a total boob. Sometimes the Alabama darkie persona was very useful. People who underestimated you very often made stupid mistakes. But he was tired of playing spy with a man who was supposedly one of his own people. Besides, it had been the Jesuit who had brought this whole mess to his attention. Although how the box wound up next to him at the lunch counter was certainly none of the Jesuit's doing.

"All right. I'll see you at the airport in an hour. Where are we going?"

"I'd rather not say until we're ready to lift. But bring your hiking boots."

Green sundered the connection.

Wentworth leaned back in his custom chair and said, "I know where they are."

Nguyen's voice from the scrambled speakerphone was polite, if somewhat dubious. "Really?"

Wentworth glanced at the silver block. "Oh, yeah. There's been a slight complication, though. There are *two* parcels we have yet to collect."

Nguyen wasn't slow. "*Yet* to collect?"

Wentworth smiled. "There are three. I have one of them."

The silence stretched for a few seconds. "I see. And where am I to collect the others?"

"One of them, the one the courier has, is in Utah. He'll be stopping to buy food at a general store in the middle of nowhere tomorrow morning. I'll modem the map coordinates. You've got plenty of time to fly in and get ready for him."

"How can you know this?"

"I'm the director."

"What of the other package?"

"It's in the hands of a Baptist preacher named Walter Green, in Los Angeles."

The silence was hard edged this time. "Something wrong?"

''The Green who is the chair of the United World Council of Churches?''

''Ah, you know the man. Good. Save having to zap pix to you. Get the courier's first, then the other one.''

''All right.''

''Take as many agents as you need to do this job, Nguyen. If you need them, I'll send you a company of Marines or Rangers or SEALs.''

''That won't be necessary. I have a debt to pay this courier. The fewer witnesses we can't control, the better.''

Wentworth grinned. Adios, *Long. Nguyen is going to bake you to a golden brown and eat you.*

''Whatever. Just don't screw this up. This is the biggest fish we've ever hooked. If he gets away I will *not* be pleased. Stand by for the map numbers.''

Wentworth touched a control on his desk computer and squirted the information into Nguyen's phone. Signed and sealed and about to be delivered. He shut the phone off.

The box sat on his desk, gleaming in regal silence. ''One down, one to go,'' he said. ''What are the whereabouts in L.A. of our friend Reverend Green, O brilliant box?''

''Walter Green is not in Los Angeles.''

Wentworth rocked his chair forward suddenly. ''What? You said he was!''

''He was but he is not there now.''

''Where is he?''

''On a private jet.''

''Going where?''

''Denver, Colorado.''

Wentworth frowned. ''Why?''

''To collect me from Long.''

''Fuck!''

But when he thought about, he relaxed. Leaned back in his chair. So what if the preacher was going to Denver? The box wasn't going to get that far, now was it? Huey Alphonse Long was going to get ambushed in Utah, hundreds of kilometers short of Denver, Boulder, wherever he was heading. When the preacher went home empty-handed, they'd collect him there. No problem.

But it was interesting to know that the fucking little box played a game of its own. Yeah, it answered questions but you had to get pretty specific about how you asked them because it didn't volunteer anything more than exactly what you put to it. Where is the preacher? Why, on a jet. Where is the jet? In the air? Where is the jet *going*? Finally, the answer you wanted in the first place: Denver. There was truth—and then there was the whole truth.

It was a computer, after all, very literal, even if it was some kind of AI. He'd have to remember that.

"So. How about a list of the men my wife has slept with in the last year?"

"There would be no names on such a list," it said.

"What? You lie. Are you telling me my wife has not had sexual relations with at least four men in the last year, myself not included?"

"No. Merely that she has not *slept* with any of them."

Wentworth nodded. Another imprecise question. His fault. He'd learn.

"All right. How many men has my wife had sexual relationships with in the last year?"

"Six, not counting yourself."

Wentworth sat up. Jesus! Had he missed two men? That was bad.

"The names, please."

Long risked the interstate highway going into Salt Lake City. They'd kept to state and county roads whenever possible, but by the time they got to the heart of Mormon country, traffic was thick and he didn't think anybody would notice him. The roads were full of local commuters.

"How come there are beehives on all the road signs?" Dawn asked from the back. She'd been asleep for hours and just woke up. Long saw Moon grin.

"It's a religious symbol," Moon said. "When the original settlers came here, they called the territory Deseret, a name taken from their holy book. It means 'beehive.' They are an offshoot Christian sect, they use the Bible and several other books particular to their beliefs—''

"Mom, I *really* don't care to know what color their underwear is.''

Moon smiled, and Long enjoyed the expression. Being a parent was a full-time job and whatever joy there was in it was obviously tempered by more than a little irritation. Still . . .

"I have to go pee,'' Alyssa said.

"And I'm hungry,'' Dawn added. "How much longer before we get there?''

Long said, "We'll find a place to stop in the city. Eat, drink, pee, rest. Take off again in the morning.''

"Good,'' the girls said in unison.

"You have to put up with this all the time?'' Long said to Moon.

"Oh, yeah. Makes you wonder why the race hasn't died out, doesn't it?''

They drove through the city, jammed in traffic despite the high-tech computer-operated signal systems supposed to stop that from happening. Every large city had the controls and as far as Long was able to tell, they didn't work in any town with more population than could fill a bus.

To pass the time, Long said, "Why do they call themselves Mormons?''

"Another word from their holy book,'' Moon said.

From the back, Alyssa and Dawn let out theatrical sighs.

"I'm not talking to you,'' Moon said. "Count license plates or something.''

Long smiled.

She continued. "They are officially the Church of Jesus Christ of Latter Day Saints. Sometimes called Latter Day Saints, or just LDS. A man named Joseph Smith founded the church back in 1830. According to the story, God and some of his angels told Smith he was supposed to reestablish the somewhat moribund Christian church. The angels directed him to a field somewhere in which he found buried some thin gold plates inscribed with strange hieroglyphics. Under divine guidance, Smith translated the symbols, which became the Book of Mormon.''

Long lifted a skeptical eyebrow. ''Oh, really?''

She nodded.

''What's the book say?''

''It's been some years since I had to read it,'' she said, ''but the basic story is about a group of people who somehow found their way from from Jerusalem to this country a couple of thousand years ago. One assumes they were terrific sailors. And after Jesus the Christ was cruci-fied, He descended from Heaven into what would become America and showed himself to these immigrants. Laid out the rules, picked some disciples to carry on the work, then ascended back into Heaven.''

''People actually believe this?'' Long said.

''Millions of people.''

''Doesn't sound real likely,'' Long said.

''Faith doesn't have much to do with logic,'' she said. ''Reason doesn't enter into it. You believe it or you don't. You ever read the Bible?''

''Not much. When I was kid. A class in school. My parents weren't into it.''

''Some of those stories are real howlers. And yet I've known doctors, lawyers, otherwise hardheaded scientists who believed, in varying degrees, most of what the book has to say. If you buy the whole package, you can ration-alize away the contradictions. Maybe something got garbled in translation, maybe a particular story isn't supposed to be taken literally but as a parable, maybe you just misunder-stood it. If you take it word for word, there are some bib-lical horror tales equal to anything Poe or King ever did: rape, incest, murder, a vengeful God striking down those who displeased him. Especially the Old Testament.''

Long said, ''That's the problem: when you create a deity

in man's image, it has human failings.''

She shifted in her seat and looked at him. ''You don't believe in gods, do you?''

''Not really. Some kind of creative force like the box said? Maybe, but nothing we can dial up and chat with.''

He watched her nod but she didn't speak to that.

They drove in silence for a time. Then she said, ''The urge to believe we aren't just biological accidents on some minor planet in a minor galaxy is pretty powerful. That we are . . . more, somehow.''

He shrugged. ''Way I figure it, you do the best you can with what you've got, nothing else matters worth a damn. I should have died during the war in Cuba—it's been all gravy since then. One day at a time.''

''The Ram Dass 'Be Here Now' philosophy.''

He swerved to miss a fool white-lining on a fuel-cell motorbike. ''Idiot.'' He glanced at her.

''No past, no future, only the eternal now,'' she said. ''What was is gone, what will be, will be, you shouldn't worry about either, only this moment.''

''Not bad,'' he said.

''Not mine,'' she said. ''And as philosophies go, you could do worse. You can make plans to buy bread tomorrow, as long as you do it with the sense of *nowness*. You can learn from the past but not get so tangled up in it you can't move on. It's kind of the ultimate carpe diem.''

He didn't recognize the term.

'' 'Seize the day.' ''

''Ah. I like it.''

''I figured.''

He drove through the clotted arteries of Salt Lake City, a single blood cell in a giant and sluggish body. ''Be here now,'' huh? Definitely. Given the present set of circumstances, the only way to go.

> To the ignorant, the Self appears to move—yet it moves not. From the ignorant it is far distant—yet it is near. It is within all and it is without all.
>
> —Swami Prabhavananda, his translation of *Isha*

28

THE CART STOPPED and the sudden lack of motion woke Long. Moon was driving and he looked at her, then the road ahead.

Their path was blocked—by a herd of cattle.

Long blinked, thought for a moment he was dreaming.

Three riders, a man and a woman on horses, another man on a three-wheeled electric ATV, guided the cows across the road toward a fenced pasture and an open gate. Even in the winter air there was a smell like an outdoor latrine and reddish clouds of dust shrouded the animal's legs in a cold, dry fog as they moved.

In the back of the cart, Alyssa slept but Dawn stared at the moving beasts, transfixed. ''Wow,'' she said. ''Cows. Real cows.''

Moon said, ''Yep. And much more interesting than computer-generated images.'' She glanced in the rear-view mirror at her daughter. ''Virtual is never quite the same as actual. Genuine people seldom behave like simulations.''

Long caught the quick exchange of looks between the two and wondered what it meant.

Dawn, indignant, said, "You were in my room."

Moon said, "You left the computer on and the door open. Your 'friend' startled me."

Dawn looked away, stared at her lap.

Long felt the discord jangle. Something he maybe didn't want to get into the middle of. He cleared his throat. "On their way to another winter pasture," he said.

"Or McDonald's," Dawn said.

Another minute and most of the herd had crossed the road. Alyssa woke and stared. "Jesus, cows!" she said.

The man on the three-wheeler did lazy figure-eights behind the plodding animals, kicking up more dust, urging them across the road. He wore a baseball cap, brim backward, and had enough dust coating him so that he looked as if he'd been fashioned from the red dirt himself. He smiled and waved at the cart as the last of the beeves ambled across the narrow two-lane road.

"Aren't you glad we took the scenic route?" Long said.

Moon urged the cart forward. Ran over a fresh cow pie. The cart's interior blossomed with the pungent odor.

"Gah," Dawn said. "It stinks!"

"Shit usually does, hairless," Alyssa said.

"That's enough, Alyssa."

Long punched up the computer map and looked at it. No civilization anywhere around, as far as he could tell. "How's the battery?" he asked.

"Down to a quarter charge," Moon responded.

"Hmm."

They drove another forty minutes without seeing a cart or truck or house. Then, on an arrow-straight stretch, they spotted a building. It had to be two klicks ahead of them but it didn't take long to get there.

"Al Patin's General Store," Long read the sign aloud. He pronounced the name "Pot-tan." "Beer, ice, petrol, electric. Rest rooms inside.' "

"I need to go pee," Alyssa said.

Big surprise there. Long pulled his pocket watch out and looked at it. Almost noon. Given the lack of choice, this looked like the place to stop and recharge the batteries, grab a bite to eat, attend to the call of nature.

As they drew nearer, Long checked the compound out. There were three buildings: the store itself was a tall, false-fronted painted wooden structure with a dusty plate glass window on one side. A raised, wooden-railed porch ran along the front, three steps high. To the side facing them was a capped row of quick-charge electrical sockets in a long, silicone-insulated grid, connected to a common meter with LED reads for each socket. There was a water and air station next to these.

Behind the store was a prefab plastic barn, twice the height and width of the store proper, with a big sliding door pulled closed. Probably had some kind of cart or farm machinery repair business in that, to judge from the signs and oil company decals plastered on the pea green siding; that, plus the dark stains in the driveway leading to the door.

The third building, the smallest, was some kind of utility shack. It was in front and slightly farther along, not far from the road. Long saw glyphs for power, petrol, and natural gas stenciled on the shack. The compound was in the middle of a cleared lot covered with gravel.

An old petrol pickup truck and a slightly newer four-wheel-drive electric step van were parked under a scraggly evergreen tree.

Moon pulled the cart off the road. Gravel rattled into the cart's undercarriage as she slewed to a stop next to the electrical grid.

The four of them got out. It was cold, but not as much so as it had been in Idaho in the aftermath of the snow. A brisk breeze blew, though, and the chill factor was enhanced. Long shoved the cart's 220 quadprong into the socket and tapped the quick-charge option. The meter began to flash numbers. The petrol pumps must be on the opposite side. Wise.

The four of them trooped into the store.

It was an anachronism, a market from another century. There were wooden floors, worn to a dull and pitted gleam; a tall ceiling with a slow-twirling fan on it, pushing down heat from a pellet stove in the middle of the floor. The racks were also wood, dirty pine or fir, piled with goods, and there were shelves behind the counter that went all the way up the wall, stacked with blue jeans, work shirts, socks, underwear. Except for the cooler along the back wall and the computer on the counter, this could have been the setting for some cowboy movie in the late 1800s. It was warm, it smelled like dried hay, and it felt homey. Amazing it could still be here this far into the twenty-first century.

The girls went to find the toilet while Long and Moon picked out stuff to eat. He'd pay cash for this stop, no point in leaving any kind of trail, even under his false ID. Somebody might get it into his head to run every Oregon cart plate and charge card in the country and strain them all. The feds had the computer time to spend if they wanted.

The man behind the counter nodded at them. He was Long's age, maybe a little older, and Long walked toward him while Moon collected edibles in a small plastic basket over one arm.

The man seemed nervous, on edge. Maybe being out here all by himself all day did that.

"How's it going?" Long said.

"Fine."

Maybe he thinks we're going to rob him.

Long smiled and tried to look innocuous. The guy had on a sweatshirt with the sleeves cut off and he had a small tattoo on his right forearm. The eagle, anchor, and globe over the words *Semper Fi.*

A jarhead.

"What unit were you in?" Long pointed at the tattoo.

"Fourth Marines. Terrible Teamsters. I drove an APC.

Hauled guys to the beaches in Cuba. When I wasn't shooting babies and raping old grannies, that is.'' He glared at Long as if daring him to say something about it. A lot of people didn't like war or the guys who played it. Long didn't care for war himself but he didn't blame the grunts for it, either. He grinned. Skinned the sleeve of his leather jacket back and showed the guy a corps tattoo that could have been done by the same artist. ''You might have given me a ride. I was there. SCAT unit, rifleman. In '11. Me, I shot at anything that shot at me first, man, woman, baby, or sheep.''

The man's face changed. He smiled. ''Scatman? No kidding?''

''Took one in the leg,'' Long said. ''Hell of a way to get liberty.''

''I hear that. I got a piece of Paco's metalwork still laying on top of my left kidney.''

They shook hands.

''Hal Long.''

''Al Patin.''

For a moment, they were brothers.

Then Al said, ''I don't suppose you murdered anybody recently?''

Long swallowed. His stomach turned to a bowl of liquid oxygen.

''Not that I recall. I shot somebody who needed shooting.''

''Good enough. A leatherneck who got plugged for his country is a man I can believe when he says something.'' He leaned forward. ''You got trouble, pal.''

Shit.

Moon saw Long stiffen at the counter as she piled bread, chips, and assorted cookies into the little basket.

''Moon,'' he said, ''get the girls.''

She heard the worry in his voice. ''What?''

''We got company. Waiting for us outside.'' To the man

behind the counter, he said, "There a back way out?"

"Yeah."

Moon hurried to collect her daughters, fear turning her limbs electric and churning her stomach. She met them coming out of the bathroom. "Come on," she said.

"What?" they said in unison.

"Just come on."

The trio hurried to where Long stood next to the counterman.

"You want me to tie you up?" Long said to the man.

The guy grinned. "Nah. Fuck 'em." He reached under the counter, pulled out a well-worn Beretta 9mm, showed it to Long. "It's all borrowed time anyhow. *Semper Fi*."

Long nodded. "You got that right. I owe you one."

He moved to where Moon and the girls stood. "Okay, here's the deal. There's a guy outside with a rifle, waiting for us. He's probably in the power shed."

"Only one?" Alyssa said.

"That's all Al saw. Could be more but he doesn't think so. The guy arrived in a small flitter. It's stashed in the barn out back. Somehow they figured out where we were going. If you want to stay in here and hunker down, that would be a good idea."

"What are you going to do?" Moon asked. She could see the tightness in him, he was breathing faster, he looked itchy.

"I'm going to go outside, see if I can figure out where he's hiding."

"You could get killed."

"Real possible. I think it's gotten personal with them. If they wanted to capture us, there'd be more than one of them out there. I sure wouldn't go after me by myself." He grinned, a flash of lips that didn't extend to his eyes. He pulled the gun from its holster and started for the back door.

"Long?"

He turned to look at her.

"Be careful. I want you to come back."

He grinned, a little bigger than before. "You and me both, babe."

There was a dog door cut into the bottom of the back exit and it was big enough to let a good-sized mutt in and out. Long dropped to his hands and knees and scooted through. Hoped the dog, if there was one, didn't decide to come in just then. He rolled off the stoop, kept rolling on the hard-packed earth, stopped three meters away from the porch, prone. He was lying with feet toward the house, his Smith pointed at the barn out back. The barn door was closed and he didn't see any movement. Past the barn, way off in the distance, a tendril of smoke rose from something on the ground; the wind blew the dark smoke into a paler gray haze a few hundred meters up.

Long stayed still for thirty seconds. Nothing.

He turned, using his elbows, then crawled on his hands and knees toward the corner of the store. Got there, dropped flat again, edged slowly until he could see the shed out front. The angle was such that somebody would have to be looking right at him to see the top of his head and eyes, all that showed. Most of the barn wouldn't be visible from the power shack, either.

A man hiding in or behind the power shack would be able to see the front entrance real well.

He had to be inside, Long decided. There wasn't a lot of traffic on this road but if anybody happened to sail past, they'd sure see somebody cradling a rifle on the street side of the little building. If the driver was local, he or she would probably wonder about it enough to pull in or at least call Patin and let him know he had a gunner skulking around. Were it Long, he'd be inside the shed, the door cracked just enough to see the store's entrance. When his quarry came out, he could ease the door wider and line the rifle up. It was thirty, thirty-five meters. Not a difficult shot with a decent handgun, real easy with a rifle. He could pop a man in the head at that range, and if the rifle had any punch at all, the guy'd be dead before he hit the ground.

Long moved back slowly. People noticed quick flashes of motion, but with his head at ground level, he doubted the guy would spot him. He'd be focused on the front door. Getting a little sweaty, anticipating his shot, trying to steady his breathing and heart rate.

He scooted back to the back door, went in through the doggy portal again. Moved to where Moon and the girls waited.

"I think he's in the power shack," Long said. "And if he is, he won't be able to see us if we go into the barn out back."

"What good will that do?" Alyssa asked. "Sooner or later, he'll come looking for us, won't he?"

"Yes. But if we take his transportation and haul ass, we can maybe get a big jump on him. If his flitter is one I can operate, we can take to the air. He won't catch us in our cart or Al's truck or van."

"Can't he, like, get us on radar or doppler or something?" Dawn wanted to know.

"We'll treetop it. It'd be tough to track us even if they knew where we were."

"If you can fly it at all," Moon said.

"Yeah."

They all looked at each other. "You could stay here," Long said. "I could draw him away. Once he's gone, you could pulse out in another direction."

Moon looked at her daughters. "They might not be very happy with us, either. If they find us here . . ." She shook her head. "Girls? Stay or go with Long?"

"Go with Long," Alyssa said.

"Dawn?"

"Yeah."

Moon sighed. "Okay. What do we do?"

> Blessed are the forgetful: for they get the better even
> of their blunders.
>
> —Nietzsche, *Beyond Good and Evil*

29

THERE WAS A smaller door set into the plastic next to the large sliding door on the barn and Long eased through it. Gave the flitter parked near the back of the big shed a quick look. A Ford IC six-seater, electric drive motor for the wheels, an alcohol/gasoline engine for the pusher-propeller. A puddle jumper, not more than a couple hundred klicks' range, but he could operate it, and a couple hundred klicks away from here was a lot better than a poke in the eye with a sharp stick.

He turned and stood ready to shoot. Waved Moon over.

She hurried across the ground, mostly dry save for the spots of lube. The gravel made tiny crunching sounds, not likely to be audible past a few meters.

Moon made it to the barn, past Long.

He kept his gaze sweeping back and forth, didn't look at her.

He waved Alyssa across the perilous gap. Come on . . .

She zipped over the gravel and past him, to join her mother.

Two down, one to go.

Where was Dawn? She was supposed to be in the doorway, ready to move right after her sister—

Dawn appeared. A man in a black jumpsuit with a matching jacket was behind her. He had a thin-bladed knife pressed against her throat with his right hand, his left hand on her chest. He had a short rifle with a laser scope slung over his shoulder. He marched the girl through the door and down the steps.

"Dawn!" Moon said.

"Stay behind me. I'll handle it," Long said.

"He's got a knife!"

"I can see that. Stay here and be quiet. She'll be all right. I promise you, she'll be all right. Just let me handle it."

He couldn't spare her a glance, he was focused entirely on the man holding the knife, kissing Dawn's slender neck just under her chin with its hollow-ground edge.

Long moved out of the barn toward the knifeman. He got a better look at him.

It was the Vietnamese, the one who'd been at his house. Figured.

"Let her go," he said. He took slow, careful steps. He had the Smith's sights lined up; the rectangular post perfectly bisected the square notch, a center-hold grid directly over the man's left eye. But it was too far to risk it.

Eighteen meters. Fifteen. Twelve.

The man stopped. So did Long.

"I am Nguyen," he said. "Drop the gun."

"I don't think so." He cheated another half meter. Eleven-five.

"I'll cut her. She'll bleed dry before you can stop it."

"You won't live to see it," Long said.

"*You* won't let her die. You're one of those moral men, a do-gooder, you wouldn't be able to live with yourself if you let me do it. Drop the gun and I'll let her go. I don't care about the woman or the children. It's you I want, Long. The game is over. You lost."

Eleven and a half meters. Still too far for a double-action shot. Right at the limits of what he'd trust the Smith and himself to do single-action. But there was no choice, not really. Given the situation.

Long thumbed the hammer back. The sound was a steel rail thumping a metal drum filled with oil. *Ka-boooom!*

"Don't be stupid, Long. Even if you shoot, I'll slice her on the way down."

Look took a deep breath, let half of it out in a sigh. "Yeah, I guess you're right."

He lowered the gun fifteen centimeters. Saw Nguyen relax a hair, saw him start to smile—

He brought the revolver back up as smoothly as he could. Fired it—

The shot didn't seem as loud as cocking the hammer had.

Dawn screamed, Moon screamed, Alyssa screamed—

Nguyen flew backward in slow motion . . .

Long watched the knife blade . . .

. . . watched the knife blade . . .

. . . the blade . . .

. . . as it moved *away* from Dawn's throat harmlessly.

When the falling man hit the edge of the stair stoop, his arms and legs were straight and stiff. He looked like a cast-plastic doll. Then he went liquid.

Long flashed on a drawing he'd seen in a museum once, a cartoon: "The Boneless Chicken Ranch . . ."

Moon ran past Long to Dawn, who stood frozen.

Long realized he still had the Smith held out in both hands. Good follow-through. He lowered the gun, pointed it at the ground. Took his finger off the trigger.

Moon fussed over her daughter. Alyssa joined her mother and added her own relief to the commotion.

Long moved by the dead man—no doubt about it—and into the store. He raised the gun again, followed it, searched for another agent, any kind of danger. He didn't see any.

He moved to the counter, looked behind it.

Al Patin lay facedown on the floor. He had a knot behind

one ear but he was breathing. Long holstered his piece.
Bent and rolled Patin over, lifted one, then the other eyelid.
The pupils seemed about equal; both were light reactive.
He put the unconscious man down. He would call for emer-
gency medical aid as soon as they were aloft—

Moon came into the store, yelling.

"Son-of-a-*bitch*! How dare you? How fucking *dare*
you!?"

She swung from the shoulder, a wide, sweeping, open-
handed roundhouse. He saw it coming a klick away, but he
didn't block and he didn't duck. He let it come. He didn't
blame her.

She slapped him hard, just above his left ear, then jerked
her hand back and shook it, grabbed it with her left hand.
"Ow!"

"You okay?"

"Am I okay? You just risked my daughter's life and you
have the fucking nerve to ask me—"

"I didn't risk it."

"What?"

"There was a little danger, not much. I'd have done the
same thing if she'd been my daughter. I'd have wanted
somebody to do it if it had been me in her place."

Moon was still hot, but she backed off a little. "What
the hell are you talking about?"

"If it had been a gun I wouldn't have tried it, but it was
a knife."

"People kill each other with knives every day!"

"Not when they've been shot in the brain with a .357.
That kind of trauma usually causes a major muscle spasm.
The whole body contracts at once."

"He could have taken her head off!"

"No. I knew he'd straighten out his arms and pull the
blade away from her neck. Triceps are much stronger than
biceps. Even if they were equal, then the spasm would have
just locked his arms solid, but the bullet to the brain kicked
all his muscles into overdrive. The stronger muscles win.

He had to straighten his arm *away* from her, not curl it toward her."

"How do you know that?"

"I've seen it before. Even an expert can't control an involuntary spasm. Certainly not when his brain is shattered."

She didn't say anything for a moment. He didn't tell her that he'd been only eighty percent sure it would happen the way it did. Because it happened that way only eighty percent of the time. But an eight-in-ten chance was a lot better than the odds that the dead man would have left any of them alive after he gunned Long down. Nguyen probably would have shot his knees out, then let him squirm in pain for as long as it took to let his revenge steep before killing him. Even a nasty cut on Dawn's neck would have been worth all four of their lives, plus the life of the zonked man on the floor next to his feet.

He said, "He would have killed us all. He would have had to."

He saw her absorb it. She shook her head. Didn't speak. "Come on. We've got to get moving."

Long started the electrics and taxied the little flitter out of the barn. He stopped at the fuel pumps and topped the tank off. The flitter had the standard vertical box-wings of land/air cars and a big pusher-prop enclosed in a wire cage. Once he was on the road, he lit the pusher engine and zipped down the bumpy path until he got enough ground speed to lift. On the ground it drove like a truck with manual steering, and it flew pretty much the same way, but anybody with half a brain could manage it.

He'd set the timer on Patin's computer to call for medical help in five minutes, which ought to give them enough time to get a few klicks away before an ambulance copter arrived. He'd probably be okay. And there wasn't anything Long could have done for him anyhow.

He kept the flitter at forty meters and a hundred eighty

kph and headed due north. If somebody spotted him—and
anybody out in their yard or driving along surely would—
they'd point followers in the wrong direction, if they felt
disposed to say anything. In another twenty minutes he intended to climb to standard passenger cruising lanes and
head south again. Another hour or so of that, and he could
turn back to his original direction: east.

In truth, he didn't think it was likely anybody was going
to spot them. Nguyen, the dead man, had done this on his
own, Long was pretty sure of that.

Though how the man had found them at the store, that
was was more than a little puzzling.

He decided to ask the box. He pulled it from his pocket.
"How did Nguyen find us?"

"I told his master where we were," the box said.

"Huh? Explain."

The damned box did just that.

Moon watched Long drive for fifteen minutes before she
had calmed herself enough to speak to him. "I'm sorry,"
she said.

"For what?"

"Slapping you. I lost my temper. That doesn't happen
often. I feel sick about it."

"Forget it. I understand how you feel."

"Yes." *You would know. Your daughter died.*

They didn't say anything else about it. Meanwhile Moon
was intrigued by what the box spilled regarding how the
thug had found them. This whole affair was getting twistier
and twistier. She'd gone way beyond scared; now she was
terrified. She turned her attention to Dawn.

Wentworth discommed and stared at his desk, stunned.
Nguyen was dead. Dead! How could that be?

Well, he knew exactly how it could be. That damned
pride of his, that I'm-numbah-one-dog attitude, had done

it. He'd gone after Long and the woman and children all alone. Stupid!

He pulled his Coonan from the desk drawer, went through his ritual of ammo-swapping, shrugged the shoulder holster on.

Even so, Nguyen had been the best. He had been an adder: deadly, fast, and he'd had the advantage. He should have been able to crumple the target, no sweat. That Long was still alive and Nguyen was dead was something to be worried about. Either this courier was very good or the luckiest man in the country. Maybe both. It didn't really matter; what mattered was he had taken out Nguyen, who, if he wasn't exactly his protégé, had been Wentworth's man, body and soul. He'd put a lot of work into Nguyen, brought him along slowly and carefully, and now this West Coast razoo had killed him. If the little silver computer didn't even exist, Long had to die for what he'd done.

Wentworth was going to take care of that personally.

"Cancel the rest of the day," he said into his com. "Call the airport, get my jet ready. I want to be in the air in an hour."

It had been a long time since he'd walked in the field, but he was still sharp, he still had the moves. He would go and find this fool who had dared cross him and he would flatten him like a steamroller.

> But why are the people ignorant? Because it is good
> for them. Ignorance is the guardian of Virtue.
>
> —Victor Hugo, *The Man Who Laughs*

30

GREEN LEANED BACK into the chartered jet's too-soft
seat cushion and watched the Jesuit across the aisle. The
man spoke into his com. His voice was quiet but he talked
rapidly and waved one-handed, as if casting his bread upon
the waters. Or shooing flies.

Gray was five rows back, sprawled across two seats,
asleep. He snored.

When the Jesuit broke the connection, he dropped the
com onto the seat next to him and shook his head.

"Bad news?" Green ventured.

"My agent with the National Security Agency has been
killed. The courier got him."

Green shook his head, too. "The man is a walking death
machine."

"From what I understand, it was my agent's own fault.
But it does complicate things somewhat."

Green patted his pocket. "Well, we still have our chatty
little disembodied friend here."

"True. And muscle comes much cheaper than brains."

"I believe I'll visit the facilities," Green said. "Be right back."

Once inside the little cubicle at the rear of the jet's passenger cabin, Green pulled the silver block from his jacket pocket and looked at it. Said, "Who was the agent Leo was referring to a moment ago?"

"Minh Nguyen, age twenty-five, born Saigon, Vietnam, December fourteenth, 2004."

"Whom did he work for?"

"Ford Kennedy Wentworth, operational head of the President's Special Section of the National Security Agency."

Hmm. Green glanced at himself in the mirror above the plastic sink. He had to grin. Here he was in the toilet of a jet zipping toward Denver, talking to a little box, as if he had good sense. Wasn't life funny?

"Well, let me ask you a couple of other questions. . . ."

Long put the flitter down in western Colorado, near a smallish town, and rolled to a refueling station. He paid cash for the octane and electric, while Moon and the girls bought something to eat. He made a quick visit to the fresher. They'd have to get where they were going and ditch the flitter soon. It didn't appear to be government issue, it looked like a rental, but as soon as somebody found the dead Vietnamese agent, they would probably start backtracking him. He didn't think there'd be a GPS locator installed—the big rental agencies were too cheap to put those in all their vehicles—but the flitter would link them to the dead agent and it wouldn't be long before somebody came up with Nguyen's mode of transportation. The cart they'd left at the store in Utah might throw them for a little while, but it was a short delay at best. And the name of the person the cart was registered under was dead, too.

Long and Moon walked around the back of the fuel station, stretching their legs, eating as they walked. There wasn't any snow on the ground here but it shrouded the mountains they could see, and it was cold enough for breath fog. Least of his worries, that.

Moon said, "This doesn't feel good, Hal. This is the federal government chasing us. They'll get us sooner or later."

Long took a bite of an apple she'd given him. It was tart, crisp, good. He chewed and swallowed the bite, relished the taste. He thought about her question for a moment as a sudden frigid breeze stroked them with icy fingers.

He said, "When I was a kid, my parents took me to a reptile farm just outside a town called Thibodeaux, a couple of hours from where we lived in Louisiana. It was supposedly the world's largest alligator station, more than fifty thousand of the animals altogether.

"They raised the gators for the leather, for some kind of pharmaceutical component they got from the glands, to attract paying visitors—and whatever other reasons they didn't tell us about.

"They put on quite a show. Guys would wrestle with big ones, put their heads inside the jaws of specially trained gators who could kill them with one bite. Feeding time at the show ponds was pretty impressive. The water roiled, bloody raw meat got shredded, sometimes the larger gators would chomp smaller ones who got in their way when dinner was served. All pretty dramatic."

He took another bite of the apple, chewed it thoughtfully. Watched her. "That's what the tourists saw and remembered. But my father was a state cop, and one of the managers of the place had been a state cop, so we got the backstage tour.

"A few of the animals were in ponds where the tourists could see them but most of them were in little concrete pens, topless boxes just big enough to hold one about this size."

He spread his hands about a meter.

"Guys stood around with hoses, washing the critters and their concrete pens down—they had drains in the middle—

or feeding the things something that looked like dog kibble. The place stank of swamp and fresh reptile dung, and it was an overpowering stench. And they made noises, too, squeaks, squeals, grunts.

"My father said to his buddy, 'Those pens are kind of short, aren't they? Don't some of them get out?' And the guy answered, 'Nah, they can't climb.'

"His timing was perfect, because right then, one of the gators not more than ten meters away from where we stood somehow levered itself up on its tail and crawled over the edge of the wall surrounding it and into the next pen.

"My father laughed. 'I guess they don't know they ain't supposed to be able to do that, huh?'

"His friend said, 'So what did it get him? Now he's got a roommate, half as much space and food. Plus, he pissed me off, so I might just have him harvested a little early for his trouble. It's not a survival characteristic.' "

Long glanced at the remaining section of apple. Took another bite.

"My father said, 'Yeah, but if he'd gone the other way, he'd have made it outside the pens and onto that catwalk. If he'd gotten some speed up, you'd have played hell catching him there.' "

" 'But where would he go? It's all alligator farm as far as he can crawl before he runs out of steam. Sooner or later, we'd get him.' "

"And my father, a man I never thought of as a real deep thinker, even as a kid, said, 'Sooner or later we're all dead, old son. Isn't the point to put it off for as long and as interesting a time as you can?' "

Long finished the apple, ate the core, seeds and all. Gave her a thin smile.

Moon said, "You missed your calling, Long. You should have been a storyteller."

"I'm open to any useful suggestions," he said.

Now she smiled. "If I had any, I'd be throwing them at you. Come on, let's get the girls. It's getting cold out here."

Yes. It was getting very cold out here.

Then she reached out and took his hand, as easily and naturally as if they'd been doing it for years. It surprised him.

The cold suddenly seemed less biting than it had been.

On his private jet, Wentworth was getting frustrated. The talking box not only had limits, it seemed to be reaching them more and more often. Half his questions went unanswered; either there was no comment at all or it said it wasn't allowed to respond. He didn't know what that meant but he didn't like it.

"Denver in about two hours," the pilot called back over the com.

"Good. Have the field office AIC meet me at the airport. Tell him to line up a couple of helicopters and eight of his best shooters."

"Her," the pilot said. "The AIC in Denver is a woman."

"Who gives a rat's ass? Just make sure it's done."

"Copy, Chief."

Wentworth held the box up in one hand. "Okay, pal. Where are they going? The courier Long and his girlfriend and kids?"

"Boulder," it said.

"Yeah, you told me that already. Be a little more specific. It's a whole city. *Where* in Boulder?"

The box was silent. Wentworth had a sudden urge to slam it against the side of the jet. "Come on, where?"

Nothing.

"You piece of shit!"

Apparently it didn't care if you insulted it, either.

"Goddammit!"

Moon had shocked herself when she reached out and took Long's hand. His hand was warmer than hers, strong, though he gripped her gently, as if he were holding a raw eggshell.

This was not a good idea, she told herself.

Then again, given the circumstances, not much of anything seemed to be a real good idea lately. They might be killed or shoved into a cell forever and ever any minute now, so what the hell. She'd never been big on that be-here-now stuff, never got up in the morning figuring that day would be her last, she should live each moment to the fullest. You couldn't function that way, you'd burn out. She'd known women in the Embrace who'd tried that, never said good-bye but that it might be forever, never went to bed with important business undone. It wasn't something you could maintain; you needed the past to ground you, the future to give you hope, even though you couldn't live in either place.

When the girls saw her and Long coming, Dawn flashed them a radiant grin. Alyssa frowned, but hid it quickly.

As Moon climbed into the stolen flitter, Long still outside and checking the fuel tank lock, Dawn leaned close and said, "Way to go, Mom."

"We were just holding hands, brat."

"Yeah, uh-huh." She grinned.

Alyssa didn't say anything, just sat in the back, her arms crossed.

Long slid into the driver's seat, closed his door, cranked the flitter's heater up. Taxied to a takeoff strip behind the station.

If looks could have killed, Long would have been a dead man and Alyssa would have been a murderer.

Sweet Goddess, Moon thought.

The erotic instinct is something questionable, and will always be so whatever a future set of laws may have to say on the matter.

—Carl Jung, *The Psychology of the Unconscious*

31

FROM THE AIR, Sugar Loaf Hill looked pretty much like Long imagined it would look. Never having seen sugar in solid form other than in cubes, he couldn't be sure. It was covered with snow and did somewhat resemble a loaf of bread.

"*That's* where we're going?" Dawn said.

"Yes," Long said.

"I hope this buddy of yours has a heater installed in his cabin," Dawn said.

"Me, too," Long said.

From the air, the hill looked more or less deserted. Long didn't see any snow machine tracks around the few cabins sprinkled among the wooded patches; there didn't seem to be any smoke rising from chimneys, no cross-country or downhill skiers out and about.

It looked like a good place to go to ground, and it would be—it was Marvin's bolt hole, and the old topkick would not have picked a place unless he had scoped it out.

Anytime you need a place to hide, kid, be my guest. Only

a couple of ski nuts go there in the winter that I know of, and the summer crowd—all nineteen of 'em—is real tolerant, long as you don't blow nothin' up. Can't get there by road once it starts snowin'.

Marvin's cabin was the highest on the small mountain, with a copse of aspen or ash or some such forming a semicircle on the downhill side and a small upthrust of boulders and dirt on the upside. Very private, and far enough away from the other summer homes that nobody tended to wander over just to visit unless they were fairly athletic, Marvin had said. The cabin was stocked with supplies to last one man six or eight months, rigged with a good security system, and had barred windows and a reinforced roof and doors. No vagrant was going to happen by and get in, not unless he was a very adept lockslipper.

Long put the flitter down twenty meters from the cabin, on what he hoped was a landing pad. Couldn't be sure for all the snow, but there were orange plastic flexipoles with little red flags on the tips, stuck up in a ten-by-ten-meter square that should mean it was a landing pad.

The dry, powdery snow blew up like talcum dust, and fogged the air around the vehicle in a white-out until the prop wash and VTOL fans died. When the crystal dust finally settled, Long said, "Here we are."

"How are we supposed to get to the cabin?" Dawn said. "There must be a meter of snow on the ground."

"We'll manage," Moon said.

Probably were snowshoes in the cabin, and if they had to go out later, that would be useful. For now, though, the slog through the fluffy-looking stuff was cold and quickly wet as it melted against them. Long went first and tried to clear as much of a trail as possible, but by the time they made it to the cabin, they were all breathing hard and quite damp.

The front of the cabin had a narrow porch under an overhanging roof, braced by stained wooden posts, each as big around as Long's leg. As he neared the two posts bracketing the door, he stopped. Squatted and looked closely. Smiled.

"You want to hurry it up? We're standing ass deep in the fucking snow here," Alyssa said.

"There's a trip wire between these two posts," he said. "About as thick as a hair and matching the wood under it. Right about ankle level. Be sure you step over it."

Once they were on the porch, Long pressed his right thumb against the lock plate. The red diode under the plate blinked out and a green light lit. The door silently swung inward.

Lights went on automatically.

A feminine voice said, "The house alarm system is armed. You have thirty seconds to disarm it before it triggers."

Long moved to the alarm console mounted on the wall just inside the door. He thumbed the reader plate, then tapped a twelve-letter code on the button pad next to the plate. The code word was "motherfucker." Marvin said it was easy to remember and probably what a thief would be thinking if he got this far, though he'd never figure that was the right code. That amused Marvin.

"The house alarm system is now disarmed," the femvox chip said. "Welcome, M. Long."

Moon said, "He knew you were coming?"

"No. Just programmed the system to recognize me in case I ever did."

Dawn looked at the console. "Pretty high-tech hard- and software for a cabin. With all this, how come the wire outside?"

Long said, "Marvin is a cautious man. Sometimes the little things work when the big ones don't. The power here is battery, solar charged, so the systems are off the grid, but somebody with a heavy-duty EMP generator might take the electronics off-line. The security computer is pretty good but the wire is a simple mechanical trigger. A lot of people wouldn't even think of looking for something so simple.''

"Chinese earthquake detector,'' Alyssa said.

Long looked at her. "Excuse me?''

She said, "Some Chinese guy, Zhang, Wang, Heng, something like that, he made this big copper urn, like in the year one. On the outside were these little dragon heads stuck to it all the way around, six or eight of them. Each dragon had a little bronze ball balanced in its mouth. Underneath each dragon was, like, a little toad or frog statue with its mouth open. Inside the urn was a pendulum. When the ground shook, the pendulum would swing and hit one of the little dragons in the butt or something and knock the little ball out of its teeth. When it fell into the toad's mouth, it made a clang! and warned people of a quake. And you could tell which direction the quake was coming from by which ball fell into which toad's mouth.''

Moon stared at her daughter.

"I have to go to school, I might as well learn something,'' Alyssa said. "Thing was, anything that shook the ground would set it off. Tree falling, somebody with big feet. Supposedly the emperor once triggered it while fuc—while . . . making love to one of his concubines.'' She looked at Long. Smiled. She was showing him how bright she was. Bright and beautiful and maybe a little jealous of her mother? A dangerous combination.

Long stepped back outside, turned the button lock on the post and unhooked the trip wire. Somebody would surely hit it otherwise. He came back inside,

Moon moved to a radiator and dialed the heat up. It wasn't freezing in the cabin—the radiator was set higher than that—but it was a little too cold for uncovered comfort. It took about fifteen minutes for the place to warm up and by that time, they had explored the inside somewhat.

There were four rooms: a kitchen/living area, a bathroom, and two bedrooms. The bedrooms each had two twin beds. The couch in the living room pulled out to a double bed. At one end of the room, a wooden console held a holoproj set, a home computer, and a built-in com unit. At another end of the room, there was a stone fireplace with a glass-fronted insert; to the side of the fireplace stood a pine case of hard-copy paperback books and a stack of CD-ROM books on disc.

The cabin's water supply came from a 300-liter tank mounted on an exterior wall and automatically fed by snow melted from a heated section of the roof. An inside water heater in a bathroom cabinet held about forty liters. They wouldn't be taking any long, hot showers, but there was enough to probably fill the bathtub with fairly warm water.

A trapdoor in the kitchen floor led down a short flight of steps to a basement, which was stacked with canned and dried food, a propane tank that fed the stove and water heater, and a bank of rechargeable rubberized-lithium batteries inside a big vented plastic case. There was also an electric water pump, apparently for when there wasn't any snow to melt. A catch-all trunk held a pair of plastic snowshoes, some tools, flashlights, a short-barreled 12-gauge pump shotgun, and three boxes of buckshot.

Over in the corner was a big machine and two large bins. Dawn said, "What's that?"

Long explained. "That's a fabricator—a fabber. Say a part falls off your cart. You have the specs in your computer. You log them into the fabber and it uses a couple of laser beams to make you a copy of the missing part. Those bins have either plastic or metal polymer dust in them, they harden when you shine a laser on them. Pile a heap of it on the fabber's platform and it builds the object one layer at a time, kind of like a laser printer. Go upstairs, make yourself a pot of coffee and have a cup, and when you get back, you have a nice shiny new bolt or nut or whatever waiting for you. Not quite the tensile strength of the original if it was steel or carboflex, but usually sufficient."

"Must cost a lot," Dawn said.

"They're not cheap. Mostly you find them in industry."

Pretty self-sufficient of old Marvin to have one, though.

When they went back upstairs, Long noticed that the message light on the com was blinking. He thought about it for a second, then tapped the play command.

It was Marvin's voice. "Hey there, Long. If you're here, you must be in trouble and I hope you weren't so stupid as to leave a trail on your way in. I'd purely hate to have my cabin all bloodied up. If you need help, you know how to get a hold of me. Take care, boy."

"He sounds like a nice man," Moon said.

Long nodded. "You know the definition of a true friend?"

It was a rhetorical question and she waited for him to tell her.

"A person who, if you call in the middle of the night and tell them you've just killed somebody, will come over and help you bury the body, no questions asked. That's Marvin."

She nodded. "Wish I had a few friends like that."

Long said, "Maybe you've got one."

They looked at each other. Smiled. He felt her pull as if she were holding his shoulders with her hands and urging him to her. Man.

"Why don't you just rip each other's clothes off and do it right here on the floor?" Alyssa said. She turned and stomped off to one of the bedrooms. Slammed the door behind her.

"I think maybe she's upset," Dawn said.

"Thank, you, dear," Moon said. "I'll go talk to her."

Moon moved toward the closed bedroom door.

Dawn said to him, "Boy, I hope we don't have to stay cooped up in here too long. Could get real ugly. Either way."

Long grinned.

Green stood on the concrete outside the rental jet, a cold wind cutting through his thin jacket. Problem with being able to fly so far so quickly, he thought. You changed geography and climate and your body and brain couldn't quite figure out what you'd done to them.

Next to him, the Jesuit shivered. "Lord, it's cold. Let's get inside."

Gray, if he was affected by the sub-freezing wind, didn't show it. He got around a lot more than Green or the Jesuit, though. Old hat to him.

Inside, the Jesuit said, "Do you know where we're going, Walter?"

"Not exactly. I know the courier is in Boulder. Other than that, it won't be more specific." And the "it" in this case was the box.

"I don't suppose you want to let me play with that thing a little?"

Green smiled. "In good time, Leo. Let's wait until we get all the pieces, okay?"

It wasn't okay, but what could he say? If God had wanted the Jesuit to have the thing, he would have given it to him, wouldn't he?

They moved toward the car rental counters.

The clouds began to thicken in the late afternoon, the sky went pewter, and snow started to fall. It came down as fat and slow flakes at first, then in harder flurries as the wind shifted, swirling and driving.

Moon sat in front of the thick window—bullet-resistant plastic, Long had said—and watched the roiling snow. She'd talked to Alyssa, tried to make peace, but it was hard to tell what was going on in her daughter's mind. Kids grew up so fast these days. Alyssa had a woman's body and a woman's desires; she was bright, but at fifteen, she hadn't had time to accumulate any wisdom. Experience, yes, too much, but only time would wear off her sharp edges. It was still easy for her to cut herself if she moved suddenly.

Long was in the tub, soaking in the hot water. Dawn had perched in front of the holoproj and was watching one of her soap operas, as if none of the past few days had happened.

Alyssa drifted from the bedroom and came to stand next to Moon. The two of them stared through the window as the snowy day wound its way toward night.

Finally, Alyssa said, "I'm sorry. It's just that Long, he's so, so—"

"Nice?"

"Yeah. I guess that's it. Most of the men I've been with only want one thing, and once they get it, they don't seem so interested in you anymore. Or all that interesting themselves. They all look alike in the dark."

Moon nodded. "The good ones are out there but you have to work for them. The bad ones are easy to find."

Neither of them said anything for a time.

Then Moon said, "I have to tell you, I like him. I find him attractive the same way you do. But if it is going to be a problem between us, nothing will happen with him and me."

Alyssa gave her a small grin. "Thanks, Mom. That means a lot to me. But if he'd wanted me that way, he could have had me already."

"He likes you, baby. A lot."

"But more as a friend. Or a daughter," Alyssa said. "But you know, that's better than nothing. I never actually had a man friend before, one who didn't want to get me shucked and fucked as fast as he could. I could maybe get used to it." She paused and it seemed like a long time. "Okay. He's yours if you want him, Mom."

Moon didn't know whether to laugh or to cry. She was being given something her daughter had no right to give, but she understood the sentiment. She compromised with a teary smile. "Thank you," she said. She kept her voice grave.

They hugged and for that moment, at least, they were not just mother and child but also sisters.

Not a baby anymore, she thought. Then she did cry.

Too much of the animal disfigures the civilized human being, too much culture makes a sick animal.

—Carl Jung, *The Psychology of the Unconscious*

32

MOON GOT ONE of the bedrooms, Dawn and Alyssa shared the other one. Long pulled the couch bed out. He undressed, put his gun on the floor next to the bed, crawled under the covers. The air was a little chilly but with the heavy wool blanket over a cotton sheet, it didn't take long to warm up.

The snow continued to fall. There was a quarter meter of the fresh blanket on top of the older stuff and, viewed from the air, the flitter they'd arrived in had to be no more than a white lump, their tracks from it to the cabin mostly filled in. As much as he would have liked to crank the fireplace up for the cheery glow and crackle of burning wood, Long knew it was better to let the place look empty from outside. Lights were no problem, they could be automatic, but smoke coming from a chimney would be a sure sign somebody was home. He guessed that Marvin had bought this place under a pseudonym. And it would be a stretch to make the connection between him and Marvin, but if the fed had an idea, whatever computer time necessary to run it down would sure as hell be available. They could crunch Long's life and cross-reference everybody he had ever known without raising a light sweat. Checking it all out might take a little longer, but if they wanted him bad enough, they had the people power, too.

He wished he had some idea of what he was going to do about all this. Getting here had been the goal and now that they had made it, the next step was in question. He could ask the box, but he didn't trust it, given that its siblings or some impossible subdivision of it now lay in the bad guys' hands. Plus, it might give him another "Run away" answer, and he didn't need that.

He considered again where the box might have come from. If it was what it seemed to be, current technology couldn't have made it, at least not as he understood the limits of science. Therefore it was either alien, which didn't seem likely; magic, even less likely; or from the future. Or maybe some alternate universe. Time travel and other planes of existence were something beyond his ability to relate to, that was for sure.

He rolled over onto his side.

Saw Moon standing in the doorway to her bedroom.

She had on one of Marvin's T-shirts, borrowed from a closet, and nothing else.

His heart speeded up. He watched her walk toward him and it was as surreal as any of the rest of this whole adventure. He sat up as she sat down on the end of the foldout bed.

"Hi," she said.

"Hi."

"I couldn't sleep."

"Me, neither."

She clutched the hem of the shirt, twisted it, worked it back and forth. She was nervous. Very.

He knew how she felt. His breathing was trying to catch up with his pulse and his mouth suddenly seemed as dry as thousand-year-old paint. It was a big nasty world out

there and it seemed as if half of it was out to get them.
There were a couple of times when he'd wanted to grab
his hair and pull it out. Or run screaming into the nearest
patch of woods and look for a hollow tree to hide in. Some
comfort would be nice, but . . . was this a good idea? Did
he want to risk screwing up what little connection he had
with this woman? He'd liked holding her hand, feeling connected without the complications that sex would add. Right
now, they were maybe friends. That was a lot by itself. She
was an attractive woman, bright, and he was more than a
little lonely. She'd raised a couple of good kids on her own,
that counted for a lot. She had a sense of humor. They were
in the same leaky boat and the storm was howling around
them. Was it worth the risk to push it?

"Hal, I—"

Hell with it. Thinking too much would probably get him
in more trouble anyway, right? He reached out, enfolded
her in his arms.

Her lips were hot on his, her tongue soft but probing.
He lay back and she lay on top of him and for a long time,
all they did was kiss. He felt his desire growing—and it
manifested in growth elsewhere—but he was content just
to feel her warm skin against his own, her weight pressed
on him, the smell of her hair, the taste of her. She felt so
good. So . . . right.

It had been too many years since he'd been with
somebody he actually liked.

She dropped her hand to his thigh, moved her fingers
slowly to his groin.

"My. Look what I found."

They both chuckled, but quietly. He was very much
aware of the two girls in the bedroom.

She read his mind. "Nobody will be getting up to go
pee or get a glass of water for a while," she whispered.
She squeezed him.

He groaned softly. "It's been a long time," he said. "I'll
be too quick."

"Take your edge off," she said. "Then we'll get down to some serious work."

She was at least as ready as he was, if wetness was any indication. She slid onto him, surrounding him in tight liquid heat. He tried to hold still, couldn't. He thrust, she met it. They rode each other and he was right: it was a sprint, a dash, it lasted only a few seconds.

He didn't think he was ever going to stop coming. It was so intense it was painful. He felt like a puppet whose strings had all been cut when it finally ended for him.

"We're going to need a towel," he said, smiling into the side of her face. "A beach towel. Maybe a mop and bucket, too."

She sat up. He was still erect inside her, the move caused him to throb again. She pulled the T-shirt off, wadded it up, stuffed it between their crotches. "If Marvin is as good a friend as you say, he won't mind."

They laughed together. He liked it a lot.

With the help of the T-shirt, they were able to separate and lie side by side. He cupped her pubis, stroked her with his fingertips. When she spread her legs wider and lifted her hips a little, he slid down her body, trailing kisses along her neck, breasts, belly, and hips. She'd borne children, there were some sags, some little stretch marks, but they weren't imperfections, they were badges of her experience. When he reached her mons, he burrowed through the curly public hair and settled in for a long and slow tease with his lips and tongue. He wanted to bring her to the edge and hold her on it, to let her feel deliciously good for hours, days, weeks, eons before she sailed over it into her orgasm. . . .

It didn't happen that way. She lasted about as long as he had.

As she throbbed and pressed herself into his lips, he smiled again. It had been a long time since he'd been so comfortable with a woman. Not since Sienna.

He said, "My. Neither one of us was ready, were we?"

She twined her fingers in his hair, urged him up. "Not going to be a lot of friction there now," she said. "But you need to come back in."

"I'm not in a hurry," he said.

On top, he slid into her. Moved slowly. The hundred-meter dash was over, now it was time for the marathon.

Now they danced the dance, now they rocked slowly in the most primal of human rhythms.

In the moment. I, you, us . . .

One.

"Motherfucker," Wentworth said. He held the box in one hand and whacked it with the other hand. "You have to do better than that. I need a fucking location, something closer than a goddamned city."

The box did not respond.

He turned to the AIC, a short and muscular woman who looked as if she lifted weights. Probably had black belts in all kinds of deadly stuff, too. "All right," he said. "Get the local police in on it. Tell them it's national security, don't give them anything other than a description, the vehicle ID. Keep them in the dark."

The AIC made a noise halfway between a snort and a laugh. "That won't be too hard, given how dark it is where I'm standing."

"It's need-to-know only," Wentworth said. "Sorry."

"You're the man."

She moved off, a tight and powerful roll to her walk.

That was right. He was. And he didn't need sass from some hick AIC in Denver fucking Colorado.

Easy, boy. Don't get upset. When this all shakes out, you'll be sitting a lot prettier than just about anybody in history ever sat. Just take it easy and get there, that's the important thing.

Yeah.

•   •   •

Green sat in his room, alone. He put in a com to Loretta. Somebody had freshened the air with something that smelled like pine cleaner. It didn't go with the snow falling past the window in the night. Smell like that went with the toilet in an Alabama bar in the hot summer. Been forty years since he'd been in one of those places but you never forget that pee-tobacco–pine cleaner smell.

"Hey, hon. How you doin'?"

"Okay. We're in Denver, be catching a shuttle to Boulder in a little while."

"You know where you goin'?"

"Not yet. But I know they're close, I can feel it. And that the feds are here, too. National Security Agency, the President's Special Section, top man himself."

"Box told you that?"

"Yes."

"You be careful, Walter. It's the Devil's Tinker Toy you fooling with. Don't let it lead you astray."

"I know it. Don't worry about me, I'm going to be real careful."

There came a knock at the door. "Got to go, babe, we're about to take off."

"I love you. Trust in the Lord, Walter."

"I love you, too, and I always do. Bye-bye."

He cut the connection.

Gray was at the door. "Got us a copter, Rev. You ready?"

"Yes. Let's go."

Moon had not felt so relaxed in a long time, not since the early days with Martin, before the children, back in Loveland. Here she was, a priestess of the Goddess, lying on a lumpy foldout bed next to this big, scarred, smiling man. A gunfighter, a violent and deadly human being, and yet, compared to her minister ex-husband, he felt gentle. You could learn a lot about a man while making love, from the little things. If he supported his weight on his hands or elbows to keep from pressing too hard on you, if he looked to see that you were *there* with him, if he laughed, those things meant something. Maybe it wasn't right to extrapolate from that; but when that man's mind was mostly shut down as he pumped frantically toward an orgasm and he *still* took the time to make sure he wasn't squashing you, she figured that *had* to mean something. What was the quote? "From one thing, know ten thousand things"?

She put one hand on his neck, played with the short hair there. He smiled at her.

He didn't have to be here. He could have walked away, left her and the girls alone to deal with the Cassandra box and its consequences. She wouldn't have blamed him. But here he was.

"You're like an old pair of shoes, you know?"

He raised an eyebrow. "I don't think anybody has ever said that to me before. Should I be crestfallen?"

She smiled, tugged on his hair a little. "No. I just meant that it's way too comfortable being here with you. Like I've known you for years. Like I don't have to do anything, be anything, I can just lie here and relax."

"I hear that. Me, too."

He leaned over, kissed her lightly on her nipple.

"Are you two goats *done* out there yet?" Alyssa yelled from behind the bedroom's closed door. "I have to go pee!"

Moon and Long both laughed. She pulled the covers up a little. "Clear!" She yelled back.

Alyssa emerged from the bedroom wrapped in another of Marvin's shirts, gave her mother and Long a grin. "So, how was it?"

"How was what?" Moon said.

"It was great," Hal said.

"Welcome to the family, Hal," Alyssa said. She turned and headed toward the bathroom.

After she was gone, Moon turned back to face Long. "Yes," she said softly. "Welcome to the family."

• • •

Wentworth sat on the bed in his rented room, staring at the box, trying to figure out a way to get it to tell him what he wanted to know. Finally, he said, "Okay, box. Is there any way to get you to tell me how to find the courier?"

"Yes," the sexy voice said.

"About fucking time. How?"

"Lose the company."

"Excuse me?"

"I will direct you to the courier's location but you must go alone."

"What? Why?"

The box didn't answer.

He tried it again but got the same lack of response.

"Is this some kind of trap?"

"No."

So much for that.

He thought about it. He knew it was better to be lucky than good but he also figured Long's luck couldn't hold forever. He'd dodged and slipped and slid, managed to stay free—*and* take out Nguyen, but Ford Wentworth was no Third World orphan with a fast gun and too much machismo. He was a pro, and he hadn't gotten to the top of the heap by accident. If he had to go and brace Long alone, so be it. He owed the man, anyway, and like Nguyen had intended, it was better that there weren't too many witnesses to see what happened when Long got paid his due. Unlike Nguyen, he didn't intend to make any stupid moves and lose.

"Fine," he said. "I'll go alone."

But not tonight, in the middle of a snowstorm. In the morning.

> To those certain they are in control of everything in
> their lives, God sends dreams.
>
> —John Lotz, *Life Asleep*

33

LONG SAT ON the deck, drinking beer from a tall cold
bottle, watching the sun settle slowly through the thick hu-
mid air into the cypress swamp in the distance. Mosquitoes
too stupid to know they should be attracted to the ultravi-
olet lamp and zapped by the bug killer's electrical grid
buzzed and hummed around his head. In a few minutes,
he'd have to go inside, the insects would be too pesky to
let him enjoy the warm night even if he slathered himself
in repellent. The summer shower had been gone two hours
but the air carried the rain's leftover scent, something between wet hay and mushrooms.

From the house, fixing her part of the supper—he'd done
the salad and baked beans, she was doing the chicken—a
very pregnant Sienna said, "I like her."

Long sipped his beer. "Who?"

"Miranda."

"Who?"

She walked out onto the deck. "Moon, silly. The woman
you're sleeping with right now. This is a dream, you know.

That's not my butt you're pressed against, it's hers.''

He hadn't known. And what she was saying didn't really make any sense, but he nodded. "Okay."

"You need somebody," she said. "Somebody nice. Somebody who will love you and take care of you. She won't do as good a job as I would have, maybe, but she's okay. Okay kids, too, her girls." She patted her belly. "So you have my blessing."

Long shook his head. What *was* she talking about?

"I'm going to go finish the chicken now," she said. "You remember what I said when you wake up."

Green sat in the front pew, right in front of the pulpit. The church was full, a big congregation. There was a tall man behind the stand, reading from a big, white, leather-bound Bible with gold-edged pages. He couldn't see the man's face, he just got an impression of it and it was vague, but the man spoke with his father's voice.

Green recognized the verses—there were few verses in the Bible he did not recognize after more than fifty years of study—and they were from the twentieth and twenty-first chapters of Revelations, concerning the Resurrection and God's judgment of the dead, from the Book of Life. Here were they judged; every man given up by the sea and hell and according to their works, and those not found written in the Book of Life were cast away. There they went, the fearful and unbelieving and the abominable, the murderers and whoremongers and sorcerers and idolaters and the liars, splashing all into the lake of fire.

Green could see it, for of a moment, he stood on the shore of the fiery lake, felt the heat coming off the molten brimstone, smelled the rotten-egg stench, heard the pitiful cries of the wicked as they cooked in the second and final death. All they'd had to do was give themselves to the Lord, but they had not—and this was their just punishment. This was how it ought to be. This was the promise.

Then he was back in the church, and instead of the white

Bible and the gold-edged pages, there now sat upon the dais in front of the speaker the silver block, and from it came the voice of Green's father, saying, "I am the Book of Life."

Blasphemy! Satan's handiwork sought to present itself as that wrought by God!

Long started forward, intending to smash the thing before it could further corrupt the congregation. But he was mired in thick air, his feet could hardly move against the slowness that fought him.

"I am the Alpha and Omega," the block said. "The beginning and the end. . . ."

No! Green tried to yell, but he had not any voice; no speech and not a sound could he utter in protest. He had been struck dumb, forced to watch and listen as the congregation was led down the garden path.

"Amen," intoned the congregation.

No . . . !

Moon was at home, watching her uncle, the deputy. He had his gun out. It sat with the wire brushes and the bottles of oil and cleaning fluid and bullets on an unfolded newspaper on the kitchen table. He wiped at the blued metal with a rag, smiled at her, then held the gun up to the light and looked through the chambers.

"You ever shoot anybody, Uncle Larry?"

"No, honey, I never have. Hope I never have to."

"Can I see it?"

"Sure." He wiped the gun with the rag, handed it to her. "Just remember: a gun is *always* loaded unless you just unloaded it yourself. Never trust anybody on that, and never point a loaded gun at anybody you don't want to shoot."

It was heavy, the gun, and then it was somehow alive. It twisted in her hands and when she tried to rearrange it, she looked up and saw it was pointing at Martin. It didn't seem strange that he would be here, in her uncle's house.

He smiled at her. "Give it to me," he said. Then his face got ugly. "Now, bitch!"

She didn't mean to do it. It just went off.

Martin fell. For a long time, she just stood there. Then she saw that the gun had vanished, and her house had changed. It was the apartment on Ritterman Street, and Martin was on the floor, but now he was getting up and there wasn't any blood, he wasn't hurt, he was just mad. He came at her.

"If you hit me, I'll leave!"

But he kept grinning because he knew she wouldn't leave him.

She never did.

The raghead slammed the door open behind them, calling Jimmy and Ford bastards and threatening to spit on their mothers. Ford was halfway across the ladder when he missed a step and fell. He hit the floor of the alley and died. But he was a ghost or something because he was still inside his shattered body. He heard Jimmy screaming as he wrestled with the guard, and Ford was somehow able to . . . leave his body and float upward, like a half-filled helium balloon, until he was level with the roof again. He watched the dark-skinned guard beat the shit out of Jimmy, cuffing him, slapping his face, screaming at him in a language Ford didn't understand. And when he looked down, he saw his own body lying on the alley floor.

Definitely dead, the way the head was all mushed up like that.

It was an interesting situation.

He floated over to where the guard was continuing to slap Jimmy around. He thought he was invisible, but the raghead saw him and screamed louder.

It was easy for Ford to float over and shove the bastard off the roof, so he did it.

Jimmy couldn't see him. He stared over the edge of the building.

Then he was somehow in Africa, watching his father inside his private tent. His father lay on his cot, but he wasn't alone. There was a native girl under him and he was pumping away at her, the woman muttering in Swahili or something and his father moaning.

Then Wentworth found himself on the veldt and a charging lioness was coming right at him. He snapped his rifle up smoothly, overlaid the front sight squarely on the big cat's head, squeezed the trigger.

There was a click, but no boom.

Misfire!

The lion leaped and he had time to feel the fear and know he was about to be eaten before she hit him.

Next to him on the ground, a small silvery box laughed loudly as the lion bit into Wentworth's throat and killed him for the second time.

The opening and middle game are vital but a player up two pieces might have a heart attack and have to forfeit. The end game is what counts.

—Pablo Pedro Gomez, *Zen Chess Handbook*

34

GREEN SAT ON the edge of the bed, tired from the dream. A satanic sending, surely.

He got up, moved stiffly to the bathroom, relieved himself. Stood under a hot shower for five minutes, toweled off, felt a little better. He called room service and ordered coffee and a sweet roll. Got dressed in warm clothes. The snow had stopped but it looked frigid past the thermal panes of the hotel's window, and the glass was cold to the touch, even through the triple layers. The sky was crystal blue and no hint of wind stirred the fresh snow. What his father would have called a ball-chiller out there.

His breakfast came, if you could call it that, and Green tipped the bellboy, closed the door, then sat in the chair next to the window, staring out as he sipped his coffee. Nasty stuff, this hotel brew. Nothing like he'd be drinking at home. Lorrie knew how to make coffee.

Right at this moment, all he wanted to do was climb onto a fast jet and go home. Forget all this spy business and crawl into bed with Lorrie, sleep all day, putter around in his bathrobe until spring. Preach a nice sermon twice every Sunday, smile on his flock. It was a nice fantasy and he took comfort from it. Here lately he was wanting it more and more. Shuck all the responsibility and just spin a nice, thick cocoon and stay in it until the Final Judgment. Maybe grow a few vegetables along the way, that was it.

He sipped the vile coffee and stared at the white world outside the hotel. No, that was not his lot. The Lord had given him a hard row, fine, he would hoe it as best he could. He knew his duty, knew he would do whatever had to be done. It was tough sometimes and he was often full of doubt as to how exactly to proceed but he would muddle through. Somehow.

He turned and looked at the box on the table.

"I don't much like using you," he said. "I know there are times when the end justifies the means and any tool in the service of the Lord is holy, but I purely do not trust you. You brought us here and now you playin' with us. We might as well be a million kilometers away. How are we supposed to find our way to the goal now?"

The box, in a voice that sounded too much like Green's father's, told him.

Somebody had shoveled a path to the copter but they had done a crappy job and left a thin layer of tromped snow that had gone to ice on the pad across the helipad. Twice Wentworth slipped and almost fell. His balance wasn't helped by the thick parka, heavy gloves, and new boots he wore. Normally in this kind of weather he'd be wearing electrics or chempacks, but his thermoflex body suit had a short in it and he didn't have time to fuck with it now. He hoped he wouldn't be outside long enough for the subzero weather to bother him through the unheated clothes. At least the wind wasn't blowing.

He'd had the pilot warm the copter's interior and preheat the engines, though the rotors were still unmoving. He shoved the sliding door open and hopped in.

"Morning," the pilot said.

Wentworth gestured with his thumb. "Morning. Out, please."

"Excuse me?"

"Go back to bed, eat breakfast, get laid, whatever. You've got the day off."

"You can fly?"

Wentworth shook his head. What kind of idiot would make such a remark? Did the man thing he was just going to sit here on the pad all day and play with himself?

"Good-bye," he said. "Don't fall and break your leg."

When the pilot was five meters away, Wentworth put the rotors on-line. The prop wash blasted the powdery up in a haze of white, blew the retreating pilot's hat off. Maybe the cold wind would do the man's brain some good, Wentworth thought as he urged the copter into the icy morning air.

The hunter was up and prowling. Time to go and bag himself a lion.

Long awoke suddenly, spooked. He looked around. Moon lay next to him, her face slack in deep sleep. The alarm light blinked green. The door to the girls' bedroom was closed. It was early morning, from the yellow sunlight slanting through tiny gaps in the curtains. What—?

In the distance there was the drone of an aircraft engine. The rumble grew louder. Long lay there, listening. Copter, from the sound of it. It neared the cabin but did not pass directly overhead. After a moment, the craft dopplered away. Flew straight past, didn't slow, no looping around in a circle. It faded to silence after another few moments.

Long sighed. Was this how it was going to be? Fear every moment from now on? How long could you live that way, always looking over your shoulder? Not a bright future, even with Moon in it. Especially with her in it. He didn't want anything to happen to her or her girls. Maybe he could work something out. Maybe he could figure out a way to get the feds off his back.

Maybe he could learn to walk on water while he was at it.

He sighed again. He needed to go pee, but not so bad he wanted to disturb Moon by getting up. He allowed himself to drift back to sleep. Just before he faded, he remembered his dream.

Thank you, Sienna.

Gray was not happy but the Jesuit was beside himself.

"No, you can't!"

Green held the box up on his outstretched palm. "Ask it yourself."

"I will." He glared at the box. "Is this the only way you'll lead us to the other component parts of yourself? For Father Green to go there alone?"

"It is," the box said.

Were it at all possible, Green thought the Jesuit surely would have burst into flames at the box's reply.

Green looked at the other two men. "But you don't know how to pilot a chopper," the Jesuit tried.

"No. But I can fly a flitter."

"It won't be as easy to land in this weather."

"I'll have to manage, Leo. We don't have any choice."

"He's right," Gray said.

The Jesuit shook his head. "What is he going to do when he gets there?"

Gray shrugged.

The Jesuit could hardly be out of arguments but there wasn't any point in more of the same. The decision was already made. God would see to him. He always had.

Wentworth kept a pair of binoculars trained on the cabin while the autopilot flew the copter past the place at a reasonable distance. No signs of life, everything was buried in the snow, but unless the box had taken to outright lying, that was the place. He punched up a title registration on the

NSA net comp but the name Johannes Smythe was probably some kind of lame joke. John Smith, indeed.

Didn't matter. What mattered was that his quarry was inside that cabin. Now, the trick was going to be how to get there without being spotted. If he dropped the copter right next to the place they would sure as hell notice that. He wore a spidersilk vest under his clothes, it would stop just about any handgun round Long could launch at his torso, but the man had shot two of his agents in the head and he couldn't assume Long's aim—or his nerve—had gone bad since. If Wentworth tried slogging through the snow in full ceramic body armor—gauntlets, helmet, face shield, boots—he'd probably sink into the snow up to his eyeballs, snowshoes or not.

He could call in the Marines—or better, the SEALs—and flatten the cabin and everybody in it, but that wasn't how it was going to go. The box might be damaged. Plus he wanted Long to himself. A hammer would work but what he wanted was to put a needle into the man's eye. Repeatedly.

No, he'd have to park the copter someplace out of earshot and figure a way to get there without being seen. Which meant using a shiftsuit or, at the very least, some white camo. Since he didn't have either, *that* meant going back to town and getting the gear or parking somewhere and waiting until dark. He didn't want to wait. Shiftsuits were very rare and very expensive, and by the time he pulled in some big favors, had one flown in from one of the military or CIA bases that had them, it would probably be dark anyhow. Prying hardware loose from the military was harder than stealing gold from Fort Knox. He could do it, of course, but by the time he finished filling out the forms, Long might be dead of old age. And he didn't much feel like zipping back to town to hunt up a white suit, either.

Maybe there was another way. There were cabins farther down the hill that were probably empty. Surely they must have bedsheets?

Wentworth grinned at the thought. The simplest of costumes. Poke two holes for the eyes and presto! A ghost. The idea of centimetering his way up the hill as a spook was really quite funny, given his business. And not really that farfetched. You were in the field, you had to make do with what you had.

He swung the copter around.

Moon awoke and was aware that Long was awake from his breathing. "Hi," she said.

"Hi, yourself."

"Sleep okay?"

"Pretty much. Dreamed a lot."

"Me, too."

"Much as I hate to sound like my daughters—"

"Go ahead," he said. "I'll go when you get back."

They smiled at each other. He was warm and cuddly and if she hadn't needed to go pee so bad, she wouldn't have gotten up. It was like leaving a womb, but she managed it. The wooden floor was warm under her feet, though. Must be heat-threaded.

She finished, splashed a little water on her face—now *that* was cold—ran a comb through her hair, rinsed her mouth out with some alcoholic minty blue stuff from the mirror cabinet. Tried a smile. Best she could do.

He had moved over to her side of the mattress and she understood that he had done it so that it would be warm for her when she crawled back under the covers.

Where *was* that halo?

"Back in a minute," he said.

She watched his bare backside as he left the room. He probably threw his underwear on the floor or belched in public or something. He had to have flaws.

She knew she was in real trouble when she realized she was looking forward to finding out what those flaws might be. And that there would have to be a lot of them to dampen the glow she felt right now.

Damn.

• • •

Green flew the little car artlessly but well enough to keep it from falling and plowing a big furrow in the deep snow. As he followed the box's directions, he wondered again exactly what it was he intended to do when he got wherever he was going. Walk up to a man who had shot people left and right and demand that he turn over his third of the cursed little puzzle? Somehow he didn't think this Long person would be a God-fearing soul. Waving a Bible at him and demanding anything might not be a good idea. He would have to think of something. Appeal to something in the man.

"How much farther?" he said aloud.

"Nineteen kilometers."

"Is there a place to land this thing anywhere close?"

"Define 'close.' "

"A kilometer or less."

"No."

"How far away from my destination is the closest place that I can land this craft safely?" Best you keep it real specific with this thing.

"One point one kilometers."

Hairsplitting little sucker. One point *one* kilometers.

"That's not so bad," Green observed. "I can walk a klick in snowshoes. Flat ground?"

"Uphill," the box said.

Figured. "Any other obstacles I should know about?"

"Aside from Ford Wentworth, no. No burning bushes in the way."

Green stared sharply at the box. The Devil's tool, no doubt about it, to be making fun of him like that.

Long pulled his pants on, his shirt, tucked it in. Went to the kitchen.

"Don't tell me you cook," Moon said.

"Not much to work with here, lot of canned and freeze-dried stuff, but I can probably make an edible breakfast," he said.

"Jesus. You aren't going to take the trash out, are you?"

"What?"

"Nothing. Private joke. Coffee?"

"Yeah."

She nodded. "I can get that."

Wentworth found the cabin's com dish and clipped the input wire. Most people didn't know that basic home alarm systems were useless if the phones were out. Might be an audible inside but if it screamed, nobody was likely to hear it, and as long as it didn't call out for help, he could live with a little noise.

He kicked the door, shattered the locking board, and walked into the cabin. Sure enough a little siren squalled at him. Nobody home.

The siren was behind a thin grate over a heater vent. He found a broom, jabbed the handle through the plastic, and battered the siren until he hit something breakable. The alarm shut up.

The owners had a nice supply of sheets; unfortunately, most of them were red-and-white candy-striped flannel. Fortunately, there was a plain white set on the foldout couch bed and he pulled these off. He draped the top sheet over himself, marked it, cut a slot for his eyes wide enough to allow peripheral vision. Presto.

Somebody might notice the copter if he left it here but that didn't matter. A strange copter parked in somebody's landing pad wouldn't be a high-priority item in the aftermath of a big snowstorm. Time the local sheriff got somebody out to check it, likely his business would be done. Besides, even if he wasn't finished, he wouldn't be here, he'd be a few klicks away and up the hill.

Wentworth grinned and nodded to himself. Took his camouflage and went outside. Months early for Halloween, but what the hell?

Trick or treat, neighbors.

Great things are never easy.

—Adeimantus, *Glaucon's Case for Injustice*

35

SIX HUNDRED METERS from the target cabin, Wentworth squatted and tried to catch his breath. He needed to spend more time in the gym if he was going to be climbing hills in deep snow. He needn't have worried about the cold, though. The sheet over his heavy clothes kept him warm enough. He could feel the heat waft past his eyes as it escaped through the slot he'd cut. Hell, this was *work*.

He checked the position of the sun. Even though he was in white, he would throw a shadow, plus his tracks would also show up, so he wanted to use what trees and rocks he could for cover. You want to be real careful when you're sneaking up on a man who has a gun and isn't afraid to use it. Yeah, he was pissed at Long for taking out Nguyen and his other ops, not to mention screwing up what should have been a simple fetch, but Wentworth wasn't going to be the next notch on the bastard's weapon.

No way.

He took a couple of deep breaths, waited for his heart to slow a little, then angled slightly downhill and away from the cabin, toward a pile of somewhat bare rocks poking up above the snow. Easy does it. He'd feel pretty stupid if he croaked from a heart attack on the way up the hill.

The girls were still asleep as Long and Moon ate. Reconstituted eggs never were as good as fresh, but there was a whole cabinet of spices. Marvin's tastes had gone Louisiana, where every other meal was fried or peppered or soaked in Tabasco sauce—or sometimes all three. Frozen bread toasted just fine, and there were even some dried peaches that plumped up nicely in water. Jam, but no butter or even any of the fake yellow stuff in a squeeze bottle.

"Good," Moon said around a mouthful of eggs.

"Thanks. I always liked to cook. I never learned to bake very well, but barbecue and pan frying, those I can manage."

"I can bake a decent pie or cake, but I always burn fried food," she said. "We make a good team."

"Yeah, I noticed that." He grinned.

She blushed.

He was charmed.

Green didn't have much experience walking in snow, they didn't get a lot of that down South. Usually an inch or so every ten or twelve years during a bad cold snap. Hardly more than a dusting, really, and when it happened, everything shut down. Everybody went out into their yards and rolled it all up into snowmen or giant misshapen balls filled with brown pine needles and dead St. Augustine grass. It was kind of funny to look at, all the yards bare with big blocks of dirty snow in them.

They didn't have that problem here. Weren't for these plastic webbed things on his shoes, he'd be up to his nose in the cold stuff, probably freeze to death. And even with the snowshoes, it was tough going. You had to lift your foot real careful and put it down easy, but firmly. Not real high. You tried to shuffle along too fast, you just kicked up a bunch of the white powdery stuff, so cold it seemed like dust.

He could see where he was going, up that little hill. At least it had looked little when he got started. Now it looked more like it was straight up and a thousand meters tall.

Oh, well. He needed to exercise, he kept telling himself that.

He took a couple of breaths and trudged on.

Man that is born of a woman is of few days, and full of trouble. He cometh forth like a flower and is cut down: he fleeth also like a shadow and continueth not.

—Job, 14:1–2

36

THE GIRLS GOT up. Dawn came into the little kitchen first, Alyssa not far behind her. Both wore more of Marvin's T-shirts. If they survived this, they were going to have to buy him some new ones.

"Wow. Real food," Dawn said.

"Have a seat," Long said. "I'll get you some."

"You cooked it?" Dawn said.

"He must have," Alyssa put in. "Mom would've burned it black."

"Ho, ho, ho," Moon said. But she was smiling. If they weren't being chased by half the planet, this would be fun. Truth was, it was fun anyway. She couldn't remember when she'd felt so comfortable.

There came a knock at the door.

Moon and the girls flinched, but Long just turned and looked at the door. He said, "I'd like you to go to the basement, please. You know how to load and use that shotgun, don't you?"

Moon nodded. "Yes."

"Do that. If anybody but me comes through the basement door, you might want to consider pointing the gun at them and telling them to stop. If they don't—"

"I couldn't shoot anybody," she cut in.

"They don't have to know that."

The knock came again. It wasn't loud or insistent.

Long got up, pulled his gun from the holster on his belt. Smiled at Moon. "If it was the bad guys, probably they wouldn't be so polite," he said. "Could just be a neighbor."

"Hal . . ."

"Go ahead. I'll handle it. This is what I do."

Moon nodded, her mouth dry. A moment ago she was happy. Now she was terrified.

"Better grab some more clothes, it's probably cold down there."

Green rapped on the door a third time. He knew they were in there, the place felt occupied, though he didn't stoop to peek into the window to check.

The door opened a little. A man stood there, a hard-looking man.

"Yes?"

This was Long, had to be.

"I'm Walter Green. Could I come in and talk to you for a minute?"

"Ah. You alone?"

"Yessir, I am."

"Well, don't stand out in the cold, Reverend."

So, Long knew who he was. Of course. He had a third of the box and no doubt he'd been asking it a whole lot of questions.

The man opened the door and Green saw the gun in his hand. Shiny thing, white handle. Pretty to be so deadly. He looked past Green, his gaze sweeping back and forth like a hunter seeking a target. If he saw anything, it didn't show on his face.

"Thank you," Green said.

• • •

Wentworth couldn't believe his luck. He had the binoculars trained on the two men, and that was the preacher Green that Long had just admitted. Long had taken a good look around behind the old man but Wentworth stayed very still.

Didn't see me. No way.

The cold must have affected the parabolic circuit on the scope, he couldn't hear anything but a staticky drone, but he was pretty sure there couldn't be another tall, black old man wandering around in the snow. How he had gotten here wasn't important, now he could kill two birds with one stone.

He should have brought a rifle, he thought for the tenth time, regretting it. Then again, he didn't really want to kill anybody until he was sure he could collect the prize. For that, he needed to be close enough for a handgun anyhow.

Both prizes now. Surely the old man had his box in one of that parka's big pockets?

Well. Long was occupied with Green and the time might not ever get any better to take him.

Wentworth moved toward the cabin in a shuffling crouch.

Damn, but this was hard work.

Long watched Green shuck his coat and hat, peel the snowshoes off. He might have a gun hidden under his sweater but Long didn't think so. He holstered his own revolver. Walked to the trapdoor to the basement. "Moon, you can come on back up."

After a moment, Moon, shotgun in hand, came up the stairs. Saw Green and Long.

"This is Reverend Green. And as you probably know, this is Miranda Moon."

She nodded and put the shotgun in a corner.

The tall black man nodded in return, gave her a small smile. "Miz Moon. Your daughters are with you?"

"Yes." She looked at Long.

Long said, "Care for some coffee, Reverend?"

"Please. And call me Walter."

Long fetched a cup, gave it to Green. The older man sipped the brew. "Ah. Good coffee. Much better than the hotel stuff I usually wind up drinking."

Long said, "I guess I don't have to ask you what you're doing here."

"Could we sit down, son? I'm not as strong as I once was. I had a long hike in the snow."

"Living room? Or here in the kitchen?"

"Kitchen is fine. I always like being in the kitchen when Loretta—that's my wife—cooks."

"Have a chair."

He sat, obviously relieved to be off his feet. Sipped at the coffee again.

"I'll get right to the point, son. I want you to give me that box you got."

Long flashed a tiny grin, small but high wattage. "The one everybody and his kid brother has been shooting at me for?"

"I understand you shoot pretty well yourself," Green said. "I'm sorry it got to that."

"So am I. Why should I give it to you? Why don't you give me yours?"

Green stared into the coffee cup as if seeing to the center of the universe. "If I thought you would put them in a hole and bury them until the end of time, I would. These things are dangerous."

"I know they are dangerous to me," Long said. "Considering how I have been nearly killed several times. But that's not what you mean, is it?"

"They're dangerous to his faith," Moon said.

Green smiled at her. "No, ma'am, that's not true. Not dangerous to *my* faith. To my church, maybe. To any church. I don't believe these . . . things are telling the truth, but the world is full of gullible people."

"Many of whom have been suckered into your mean-spirited religion," Moon said, her voice bitter. "You wouldn't want the sheep to take off on another exodus, right?"

"Miz Moon—" he began.

She cut him off. "I know the house you live in, preacher. It's a place for the elite. If you aren't a member of the club, you lose the big prize. Your religion is exclusionist, sexist, racist, and ugly."

"You confuse the practice with the practitioners, Miz Moon. Men can only strive for perfection, not achieve it."

She blew out a disgusted sigh, shook her head.

"I'm not here to argue theology with you," he said. "You have valid points about some people who pass themselves off as Christians, I won't dispute that. But this *thing* you have is evil. In the wrong hands, it could cause no end of problems. If it says a thousand things and you can prove that nine hundred and ninety-nine of them are true, people might believe the Big Lie that is the last one. Don't you believe in a God? Or in your case, a Goddess?"

Long looked at her.

Moon didn't speak for what seemed like years. Then she said, "Not anymore. Not like I once did."

"Sweet Jesus, woman, was your faith so weak a *machine* could break it?"

"Yes. I guess it was. I wanted to believe, I convinced myself that I thought I did, but in the end, I guess I never really bought into it."

Green shook his head. "You see? You were a good woman, a moral woman, you might have been on the wrong road, we could argue about that, but you were trying. Now? Now you've fallen from the path. And it is this"—he pulled from his pocket a shimmery rectangle that was twin to the one they had—"this *abomination* that has done it to you. Don't you see? There is wickedness in the world, the Devil can cloak himself in any form he chooses."

"You think this is a satanic plot to destroy religion?" she asked. She and Long exchanged glances.

Green didn't need to answer.

Long took it up: "God threw his children out of the Garden because they chose knowledge over ignorance. That's at the heart of your religion. I can understand how you feel that way. But bowing to dogma is not the path to enlightenment, and ignorance is not bliss, not for me.

"And what if you are wrong? What if the box is right? You just want to bury that, no questions?"

"It can't be right, son. Life would be meaningless if it was."

"I'm sorry, I don't buy that. Never have."

The trio stared at each other.

Wentworth made it to the porch. Free of the snow, he tossed the sheet off and unzipped his jacket. Drew his pistol.

And, as he had done hundreds of times before, so many times it was unthinking and automatic, he popped the magazine out and ejected the round in the chamber for his ammo swap.

The ejected .357 cartridge fell in slow motion but he couldn't catch it.

It hit the wooden floor of the porch. *Clunk!*
Shit!

It wasn't that loud, couldn't be. But he shoved the magazine back in, racked the slide, and flattened himself against the wall. Dammit!

Nobody heard it. No way.

"What was that?" Moon said.

"I don't know." Long pulled his Smith. "You sure you didn't bring company?"

"I flew here alone. My flitter is more than a klick away," Green said.

"Better get down to the basement with Moon and the girls while I check. There are other players in this game."

Green nodded. Moon picked up the shotgun again.

Long moved toward the front door.

Evenly matched opponents generally killed each
other, but few gunfights took place between experts.

—Joseph G. Rosa, *The Gunfighter: Man or Myth?*

37

LONG BYPASSED THE door and moved to the window.
He held the Smith tightly in both hands, and used the barrel
to nudge the curtain a hair to one side. Slowly.

He didn't see anybody standing at the door.

Could that small noise have been something natural?
Some creak of the wood in the cold? Maybe a small animal,
a squirrel or rat or something looking for an easier meal in
the dead of winter?

Maybe.

But getting spooked over settling wood or a squirrel
would be embarrassing at worst. Ignoring somebody with
a gun could be fatal.

Long shifted his position and moved the curtain again,
looked out at the hillside.

He didn't see any vehicles. He did see two sets of tracks.
One set would belong to Green. The other line of trod-upon
snow was more serpentine; it wound away from the porch
and out of sight toward the aspen trees down the hill.

So. Another visitor. With Green or not?

It didn't matter. He had to assume they were hostile, whoever they were.

Somebody moved the edge of the curtain in the window. Wentworth stopped breathing. They couldn't see him from this angle, but if they moved to the opposite end, they could spot him.

He avoided the temptation to put a couple of rounds through the glass. They'd go down, but if it was anybody but Long, he'd lose whatever advantage he still had. They couldn't be sure he was out here, they were being careful, but if he started blasting, Long would know exactly where he was. So he stayed very still. And waited.

In the basement, Moon clutched at the shotgun's plastic stock, her hands sweaty.

Dawn spoke. "Mom?"

"I don't know, baby. I don't know."

She looked at the preacher. He didn't seem like an evil man. He had a kind face, a lot of smile wrinkles, but he was part of the problem and definitely not part of the solution to this whole crappy mess. He didn't look scared, either. Whatever else it was, faith was sustaining—if you had enough of it. If it was strong enough.

Moon strained her ears to hear any sound from above. Please be careful, Hal, she thought. I don't want to lose you.

A drone in the distance grew louder. Long saw a dark dot moving up the hill toward the cabin. As the sound increased, he realized its cause was a snow machine, and it looked like two passengers on it, roaring directly at him.

Who the hell was this?

Wentworth stared at the approaching snowmobile. No doubt it was coming this way, and if he could make out the two guys on it, they could see him. Who were they? Were they with Long? Or Green?

What did they want?

What were they going to do?

Long felt the bullet hit the wall of the cabin before he heard the sound of the projectile as it broke the sound barrier. He saw the hole appear in the wall, heard the hammer-against-wood *thump!* as it punched through the thick wall without leaving splinters. Plasma rifle, probably, talking very high velocity. The impact was high, a good two meters from the floor.

Kind of hard to shoot from the back of a snow machine going full out.

Question was, who were they shooting at? It didn't make any sense to blast the cabin. Maybe they were potting at somebody on the porch?

Long dropped to the floor and did a fast crawl toward the back door. He thought about going to collect his jacket, for the warmth and the speedloader of extra ammo, but things were happening too fast. Time to go out and see what he could see.

Wentworth dropped into a crouch, both hands extended, with his pistol toward the oncoming snowmobile. Fuck! The cocksuckers were shooting at him! It didn't matter who the hell they were, that had to be stopped, right now!

They were past the little stand of aspen and the driver was now weaving back and forth a little. The passenger had the rifle and he let off another round. Wentworth heard it thwack into the cabin three meters to his left before the noise of the bullet got there. High-powered weapon, sniper's rifle or maybe a plasma carbine.

He held high, aiming at the driver's head—they were still seventy or eighty meters out—and fired the Coonan. Let the recoil shove his stiff arms back a little, brought the piece back into battery and fired another one.

The snowmobile swerved, threw up a sheet of white as it slewed around broadside.

Wentworth fired again. Saw a spark, heard the *clang!* as the AP round hit something on the snowmobile. The engine coughed, stuttered a couple of times, then stopped. The machine slowed, skidded to a halt.

Wentworth grinned. Fifty, fifty-five meters. He could make that shot on a stationary, man-sized target all day. He had ejected a round accidentally, fired three, that left three in the pistol. One more than he needed—

They didn't give him the shot. The two on the snowmobile bailed, hit the soft and deep powder, and just . . . disappeared.

Well, shit!

Wentworth flicked his gaze to the sides. Those two were out of the picture, at least for the time being. But even if Long was asleep in the cabin, those two rifle slugs passing through must have woken him up.

What would I do if I were inside and heard all the ruckus?

Burrow down and wait or come out to see?

Whatever else he knew, Wentworth didn't think Long was a burrower. Which way would he be coming? Not through a front door that had just been bracketed by fire. Through a window or the back door.

He did a tactical reload, ejected the partially used magazine, shoved the spare into place. Seven again. He put the old magazine into his pocket.

He hurried toward the east of the cabin.

Long shoved the back door open, dived out low, did a shoulder roll, and came up on one knee, scanning fast for a target.

Nothing. Big rocks up the hill, a few scraggly trees. He knew it was cold, he saw his breath fog, but he didn't feel it much. He did a crouching, sideways duckwalk to his left, to the west side of the cabin, kept his back to the building.

He glanced at the east corner just as he made it to the western edge.

Saw a puff of vapor drift into sight.

Somebody was there, breathing heavily.

Long dropped, dived, got the cabin between him and whoever it was circling around the other way. Twisted around and dropped prone, facing back the way he had come. He held his revolver by his ear and centimetered forward, his nose almost touching the ground. The roof overhang had kept most of the snow off but there were little drifts piled up against the cabin's base. Long slid through the one on the corner and slowly peeped around it.

At the other end of the cabin a man stuck his head around the edge quickly then jerked it back. He didn't see Long, because a second later, he came out, into plain sight. He had a pistol in a two-handed grip.

Long took a deep breath, let part of it out, gathered himself to edge forward enough for a shot—

Heard the squeaky *scritch-scritch-scritch* of somebody trying to run through deep and very cold snow behind him—

Rolled over onto his back, saw a man coming, a rifle held halfway up, continuing into position for a shot—

Long snapped the Smith down, arms extended, the weapon right over his crotch—

Fired, once, twice, three times. Felt the blast from the cylinder gap slap hot bits into his groin—one, two, three!— saw a big hunk of snow break off from the roof and fall as the booms thumped it, saw the charging man go limp, fall, hit his face, and skid to a halt, his head buried in one of the drifts. The rifle sailed in slow motion like a fat and dull javelin. Landed barrel down and stuck up in the snow, banked against a thin evergreen tree.

Man!

No time, no time! The guy behind the cabin! Get him!

Long rolled up, scrambled to the corner.

• • •

Wentworth heard the shots—three of them, from a hand-gun—and he skidded to a stop on the slick porch next to the back door. Around the corner, somebody was blasting—

He shoved his pistol out, aimed at chest level—

A man in a T-shirt and jeans appeared, but prone, and with a gun pointed at him.

Long!

Wentworth fired, knew he was high, tried to bring the piece down even during the recoil—

The bullets hit him in the chest, one, two! Ow, shit! It hurt! One of them missed the fucking trauma plate but the vest held. It must have held or he'd be down, right? He was okay, he had to be okay! He squeezed the trigger wildly, fired three or four times.

Long vanished.

Did he hit him?

Wentworth was confused. He saw the door next to him and he grabbed the handle and twisted as he threw himself against it. The door opened and he fell into the cabin.

He got up, waved his gun back and forth. Nobody.

Cut through the cabin, get to the front door! he thought.

He was running toward the door in a half crouch when he snagged his foot on something and fell. He hit a couch and shoved it half a meter. A leather jacket on the couch fell onto the floor.

A speedloader rolled out of the pocket.

Wentworth stopped, bent, picked up the speedloader. Six rounds, .357 jacketed in it.

He had a sudden realization.

Long was out there in a T-shirt, no coat.

The man didn't have any extra ammunition for his gun.

Wentworth took several deep breaths. He had a terrific urge to take a dump, to pee, to throw up. How many times had Long fired? Three rounds at something, then two more at him. Five. From a six-shooter. To reassure himself that he was okay, Wentworth pulled open the closures on his coat and looked at the vest. Holes in the sheath, but the underweave stopped them short of his skin. He reached inside the vest, felt the slugs trapped in the thick fabric. Felt a great sense of relief. He'd have a couple of nasty bruises from the impact but that was all.

Long had one round left in his weapon. And his jacket, with its spidersilk armor, was here in the cabin.

Wentworth smiled. *Gotcha now, you bastard.*

Where were the others?

Was there some kind of safe room in here?

He nosed around, didn't see them. A basement, maybe.

Well. He could collect the women and children and old preacher later. Right now, he had to finish Long.

Long moved past the dead man to the front corner of the cabin. He'd hit the man with the pistol, at least once, maybe twice, and he hadn't gone down. So he was plated under his clothes. And he had only one round left in the Smith and no more ammo. Damn.

He peered around the edge of the building. Clear. He'd heard the back door open and close, at least he thought he had over the ringing in his ears, so whoever it was must be inside.

He had to get in there. Moon and the girls were in danger.

The front seemed clear. Long scooted across the porch in a squat, ducked under the window.

Saw something shiny on the wood in front of him.

The other box must be in here somewhere, Wentworth figured. Long wouldn't have taken it with him. But if he hid it and hadn't told the woman . . .

That barrage outside had been a mistake. He could have killed Long without being certain of where the box was. Of course, he could ask *his* box and maybe it would finally stop playing games once Long was out of the picture. Maybe not.

Either way, if he could get Long to cook off his last shot, he'd have him.

How to do that?

He slipped off his jacket. He knew how.

Moon tried to keep the girls calm but she didn't feel so calm herself. All that shooting up there. Hal had told her to stay there and she didn't want to pop up and get killed, but . . . what if he was hurt?

She couldn't take this much longer, not knowing. If something didn't happen soon, she was going to have to go up.

Wentworth moved to the front door. He had his jacket closed and stuffed with a couch cushion, hooked onto the end of a broom. He unlatched the door. Opened it carefully. Took a breath and thrust the jacket on a broomstick out—

The shot knocked the jacket off the stick. Then came the *click!* of a hammer falling on an empty chamber. Nicest sound he'd ever heard.

Wentworth grinned, happier than he had been in a long time. *Too bad, Long.*

He stepped out onto the porch, Coonan held ready. Saw Long standing there, his piece dangling in one hand down by his side.

"I'm Ford Wentworth, Long. You have caused me a shitload of trouble but that's all over with now. Where is the box? Tell me, and the woman and kids stay alive."

"In the flitter," Long said.

Wentworth nodded. "Glad to see you have some class. You were good, just not good enough. You killed my best man, you have to die for that, but I'm not sadistic. A clean shot to the heart. It'll be fast."

He looked at the Smith, then back at Wentworth. "Yeah, I guess."

Long whipped his gun up and fired.

• • •

Moon couldn't stand it anymore. "Stay here!"

She shoved the trapdoor open and climbed up into the kitchen. She took the shotgun with her.

Long's bullet—the one from the cartridge he'd found on the porch—hit Wentworth's pistol right on the butt, between his fingers. Didn't even draw blood—Long was amazed he could see that—but it did knock the gun from the man's grip. Better than nothing.

Long was already moving. He threw his Smith, missed by half a meter, and barreled into Wentworth at full speed. The two of them tumbled off the porch into the snow.

Both men were trained but the fight was between two animals, snarling, wrestling, rolling around in the cold so close neither could use his best skills.

Long shot an elbow into Wentworth's nose, felt the cartilage and bone give—

Wentworth jabbed fingers at Long's eyes, missed, but dug bloody furrows in his cheek and forehead—

Long drove his knee into Wentworth's groin, but the other man twisted, blocked the strike with his own thigh—

Wentworth sank his teeth into Long's shoulder—

They managed to get to their feet somehow, dancing their martial dance. Long's foot skidded on the snow they'd just packed down as Wentworth shoved him, and Long lost his balance and fell backward. On hard ground he could have turned the fall into a roll, but in the snow, he just sank a quarter meter and stopped. He struggled to his feet.

Wentworth was already climbing onto the porch, on his hands and knees, scrambling for the damaged pistol that lay next to the wall. He grabbed the weapon as Long tried to get to him, cursing the soft snow that slowed him. Pointed the gun, fired. Wide, but it wasn't too badly damaged to shoot.

Long saw he would never make it in time. He took a deep breath and yelled, hoping to startle the other man. Saw it wouldn't work as Wentworth grinned at him. Prepared to die as best as he could in the half second left to him—

Then Wentworth's head exploded with a terrible noise.

He fell from the porch into the snow amid a spray of red and pink. His body shook, trembled, then went still.

And there stood Moon like an avenging goddess.

An avenging goddess with a twelve-gauge shotgun.

"Thank you," Long said when he found his voice.

There is something in this more than natural, if philosophy could find it out.

—William Shakespeare, *Hamlet*, II:ii

38

GREEN IDENTIFIED THE body of the man with the rifle
as Leo Sims.

"He was a Catholic priest," Green said, obviously
shaken. "He must have followed me here. Sweet Jesus.
Dear, sweet Jesus."

"A priest who was going to shoot me with a rifle," Long
said.

"He was a Jesuit," Green said, as if that explained it.

"There was another man driving the snow machine,"
Long said.

They put their plastic outrigger shoes on and trudged out
to the little vehicle. It was also dead; something on the
engine was shattered, a pool of synthoil melting the snow
next to it into a small pond of sludge.

Long had reloaded his revolver and had it out, but there
was no need. He holstered it. "There's where he jumped
off," he said, pointing at the imprint. "There are the tracks
leading away."

"Gray," Green said. "An undercover type." He shook

his head, took a couple of deep breaths. Long thought Green might throw up but he managed to avoid that.

Back at the cabin, Moon and the girls were in the kitchen. She was rattled, making a new pot of coffee.

"You okay?" Long said.

"Not really. He was going to kill you."

"You saved my life."

She poured water into the coffee maker. Her hand shook.

Green looked very tired as he sat. He rubbed at his eyes. "All this killing."

"I didn't start it," Long said. "Turn the other cheek doesn't work too well when somebody is trying to slap you with a gun."

Green just shook his head. "This is all so wrong. What are you going to do now?"

Long said, "I'm not sure. I don't think anybody else knows we're here, except your friend Gray. Wentworth didn't bring backup and my guess is that's because he wanted to keep this to himself. I think maybe we'll clean up here, dump the bodies somewhere. Least we can do for the owner of the place. After that, I don't know."

Green slapped his pocket, then did a fair imitation of a man who's suddenly discovered his wallet is missing. He patted himself frantically.

Long watched, not speaking.

"It's gone," the older man said. "The box. It was in my pocket, the flap was crowed shut, it couldn't have fallen out." He looked at Moon and the girls.

"I didn't touch it," Alyssa said.

"Me, neither," Dawn added.

Moon shook her head, kept fiddling with the coffee.

Long went into the living room, picked up the folded blanket that lay next to where the couch had been.

Under the blanket was their box, right where he'd left it. As he watched, the air shimmered and sparkled and two more boxes faded in, bracketing it.

"Come look at this," he said.

The others trooped in.

"Jesus, there's all three of them," Alyssa said.

But as they watched, the two boxes on the ends floated over and the three merged into one.

Green said, "I don't understand any of this. What are we dealing with here?"

"Reverend, if we take this thing and disappear, are you going to keep looking for us?"

"I'd have to, son. That thing says there is no Creator. It's an abomination."

"Not really," the box said.

They all stared at it.

"There is a Creator," it said. "But simply not one limited by human anthropomorphic descriptions."

Green said, "You are saying there is a God?"

"If you accept the larger definition, yes."

"But you told us we couldn't get to Him or Her—or It—from here," Moon said.

"You couldn't, then," it said. "But you passed the test.

"You can, now."

Green watched the flitter lift and depart. He pulled his com and ordered it to call home.

"Walter? You okay?"

"Yes. It's all over, hon."

"You found the other boxes?"

"Oh, yeah. And I don't think they—it—is a tool of the Devil anymore. It says there is a God—he just doesn't look like the Sunday-school pictures."

"You never really thought that He did? God is the spirit, not the flesh. Not some white-haired old white man sitting on a throne."

"I guess I didn't think about it much, but you're right. Anyway, I also don't think the box is going to cause us any more problems. These people we've been following, they don't belong to the Devil."

"That's good. When you coming home?"

Just like that, she accepted it. He wasn't so sure. Didn't know if he would ever be sure. But he wasn't going to keep hunting and being involved with killing people. Whatever God looked like when he finally got to see Him, Green didn't believe that was what He wanted. "I am on my way."

"Be careful."

He nodded. "Yes. I will."

Alyssa flew the little craft, arms rigid, face tight. "Just relax," Long told her. "You're going fine. Nothing to run into up here."

"So now what?" Moon asked.

"Well. We have a box that can tell us all kinds of things, including the winning numbers in next week's lottery. We won't starve."

"People will find out about it. This kind of thing never stays a secret."

"We have an advantage." He waved the box. "We'll be able to see them coming if they try. We passed the test, remember?" He smiled. "I think we should take a vacation. Hawaii, maybe. Somewhere warm and sunny. After that, well, we'll see. That sound okay?"

Moon nodded. "Okay."

He reached over and took her hand. "Oh, by the way: You want to get married?"

Moon stared at him. Looked at Dawn, then Alyssa.

"Go for it, Mom," Dawn said.

Alyssa nodded. "Yeah, we do."

Moon smiled. Squeezed Long's hand. "Looks like we have a consensus," she said.

"It's about time," Long said.

And, of course, it was.

Shadow Novels from
ANNE LOGSTON

Shadow is a master thief as elusive as her name. Only her dagger is as sharp as her eyes and wits. Where there's a rich merchant to rob, good food and wine to be had, or a lusty fellow to kiss...there's Shadow.

"Spiced with magic and intrigue..."–Simon R. Green
"A highly entertaining fantasy."–*Locus*

| __DAGGER'S EDGE | 0-441-00036-3/$4.99 |
| __DAGGER'S POINT | 0-441-00134-3/$4.99 |

And don't miss other Anne Logston adventures...

__GUARDIAN'S KEY   0-441-00327-3/$5.99
In Crystal Keep is an all-knowing Oracle hidden within the walls and an all-powerful Guardian who challenges those who dare to enter, even a young woman in search of her own special magic—and her own self.

__WILD BLOOD   0-441-00243-9/$4.99